THE WHALE

THE WHALE

Mark Beauregard

THE WHALE

A Love Story

VIKING

VIKING

An imprint of Penguin Random House LLC

375 Hudson Street

New York, New York 10014

penguin.com

ISBN 9780399562334 (hardcover)

ISBN 9780399562341 (ebook)

Printed in the United States of America

1 3 5 7 9 10 8 6 4 2

Set in Bulmer MT Pro

Designed by Francesca Belanger

This is a work of fiction based on actual events.

Summer 1850

Chapter 1

The Berkshires

"We'll have to cancel the picnic, Doctor. It's going to rain."

"No, it isn't."

Herman Melville sat fidgeting in a railway car next to Oliver Wendell Holmes, as their train chugged toward Stockbridge. The morning, which had started sunny and calm, was now turning melodramatic, with dark storm clouds clustering overhead like bunches of black grapes ready to spill their juice. The falling air pressure reminded Herman of Indian Ocean typhoons, where the barometer would drop and drop until the ocean seemed to suck the sky down into its depths and then spit it back out again, the exploding rain churning the watery world into chaos above and below. He gazed out the train's window, trying to find some comfort in the bilious clouds.

Herman was staying at his cousin Robert's bed-and-breakfast in the nearby town of Pittsfield, just down the road from Dr. Holmes's summer estate. He had brought his family to the Berkshires to escape the stifling, malarial heat of Manhattan (and his creditors) while he finished his latest novel, which was all but done—but he could not bring himself to write "The End." He had spent most of the last week just sitting at his cousin's desk, harpooning whales in his head the way insomniacs counted sheep. His English publisher had agreed to purchase the novel for one hundred fifty pounds upon delivery of the manuscript, and the cash would keep the Melville family afloat for another few months; but now that he had almost completed the book, he saw that it was badly conceived and poorly written. He could not imagine the genteel, middle-class ladies of America flocking to buy a novel in which frenzied sharks devoured whale gore and seagulls plucked each other's eyes out fighting for the scraps—and middle-class ladies were the only people who bought books. Even the title seemed calculated for failure: *The Whale*, as blank and prosaic as its subject, but he could think of nothing better.

On the bench across from Herman and Dr. Holmes sat Evert Duyckinck, the publisher of *Literary World* magazine, and Cornelius Mathews, the Broadway playwright, who had arrived together from Manhattan the day before, to visit Dr. Holmes. Duyckinck was long and thin and looked like an advertisement for South America, in black cotton breeches festooned with silver conchos. Mathews was a short, spherical man with robin's-egg glasses that emphasized the pudginess of his cheeks.

Duyckinck kicked Herman's foot. "Do you not like picnics, Melville? You act as if we were dragging you to a funeral."

"What?" Herman said distractedly. "No, I enjoy funerals as much as the next man."

Duyckinck gave Mathews a sidelong glance, and Mathews rolled his eyes. To pass the time, Mathews had been asking Duyckinck riddles, which Duyckinck solved immediately.

"Without a bridle or a saddle, across a thing I ride astraddle. And those I ride, by help of me, though almost blind, are made to see."

"Eyeglasses," said Duyckinck. "Next."

Dr. Holmes's lawyer, Dudley Field, and Dudley's seventeen-year-old sister, Jeanie, sat across the aisle from them. It was Dudley who had organized today's hike up Monument Mountain, as a kind of mixer for his literary clients. In Stockbridge, they would rendezvous with another of Dudley's clients—Nathaniel Hawthorne, who was riding up from Lenox to meet them. Hawthorne was by far the most famous writer among them, even more so than Holmes, owing to the sensational success of *The Scarlet Letter* earlier that year.

Mathews said, "I know a word of letters three; add two, and fewer there will be." He withdrew a flask from his waistcoat pocket, unscrewed the cap, and took a sip before offering it to Duyckinck.

"The answer is few," said Duyckinck. "Add 'er' to make 'fewer.'" He drank from the flask and offered it to Melville, who squinted at him without registering the proffered brandy.

Herman's mind always drifted far out to sea when he was working on a novel, and he could not quite make sense of the everyday world. The gray ghosts of the whales in his imagination seemed far more real than Duyckinck and his flask—massive blots of darkness adrift in the darker sea of his mind, each leviathan a horror with one giant eye on each side of its unknowing head, looking into the past and the future at once.

The Whale was a picaresque tale set aboard a Nantucket whaling vessel, an attempt to recapture the simple magic of Herman's early, popular seafaring books. In the novel, a pair of mismatched friends—a New England greenhorn named Ishmael and a Fijian harpooner named Queequeg—found adventure in the blubber and brine of the South Seas whale fishery. The story contained an unlikely quest, in which a monomaniac captain obsessively hunted a single albino whale called Moby Dick through all the wide oceans of the world. When Ahab found the whale and killed it, the adventure ended and Ishmael returned to New England.

He had intended the book to be a grand farce, full of slapstick capers and irreverent jokes; but bawdy stories of sailors cavorting with half-naked islanders, which had seemed so easy and fun to write in his first two books, held no interest for Herman anymore, and he could not make his current subject—slaughtering whales—appealing at all. The manuscript wasn't droll enough, vivid enough, outrageous enough, *anything* enough. Even the climax seemed to fall flat: all the elements of a rousing chase were there—the whaleboat seething through the vortex of water created by the harpooned monster; the line rasping and smoking through the chocks; the whale's immense blunt head surfacing in frantic throes; the waves foaming with blood; the crew, panting and exhausted, flinging themselves overboard to avoid the great beast's thrashing tail—but somehow, when Queequeg threw the final harpoon and hauled in the defeated whale, when the blood subsided and Moby Dick rolled dead in the ocean, the story died along with it.

Duyckinck kicked Herman's foot again. He waved his hand in front of Herman's face and whistled, but Melville looked right through him.

Apropos of nothing, Herman said, "Holmes, I wish you would write a poem for me, such as the one you wrote about my grandfather."

"Your grandfather's poem was a eulogy," Holmes replied. "Wouldn't you rather be dead first?"

"I am. The *Post* buried me in April."

"So we're going to a funeral after all," Duyckinck said merrily, and he and Mathews drank.

Dr. Holmes's first literary success, twenty years before, had been a poem called "The Last Leaf," which celebrated Major Thomas Melville, a leader of the Boston Tea Party. In his later years, Major Melville had often tottered back and forth through Holmes's neighborhood in Boston, wearing the tattered tricornered hat he had worn during the Revolutionary War. The poem had been reprinted widely, and Edgar Allan Poe had extolled it as an example of true American versification, bringing fame to Holmes and a last moment of notoriety to the old major.

"Perhaps we can all give it a go," Mathews said. "A poetic eulogy for the great Herman Melville, hero of the . . . what was it you were hero of, again? Well, we must work it out in the rhymes, I suppose."

Holmes sighed. "We have only ten minutes till we reach Stockbridge."

"Coleridge wrote 'Kubla Khan' in fifteen," Mathews said.

"But he had the advantage of opium," Holmes said. "And he never did finish it."

"Don't be a spoilsport, Doctor," said Duyckinck. "You won't ruin your reputation by writing one bad poem. Or one more, I should say."

Holmes sniffed.

Jeanie leaned across the aisle and said, "Shall I begin by reciting the original, Dr. Holmes, if we're going to use it as a model?"

"You know it?" said Holmes.

"Are you joking? We memorized it in school, alongside 'Yankee Doodle' and the Ten Commandments." Jeanie was a slender, gray-eyed redhead, dressed in the outfit favored by politically progressive women at the moment: a plain, knee-length dress over loose trousers gathered at the ankles. She stood, cleared her throat, and announced, "The Last Leaf."

> I saw him once before,
> As he passed by the door,
> And again
> The pavement stones resound,
> As he totters o'er the ground
> With his cane.
> They say that in his prime,
> Ere the pruning-knife of Time
> Cut him down,
> Not a better man was found
> By the Crier on his round
> Through the town.

Mathews yawned loudly. "How long is this poem, exactly?"

Holmes said, "Your recitation is admirable, Miss Field, but perhaps it would be better to skip ahead a bit."

Jeanie gave Mathews an evil look but did as Holmes requested.

> I know it is a sin
> For me to sit and grin
> At him here;
> But the old three-cornered hat,
> And the breeches, and all that,
> Are so queer!
> And if I should live to be
> The last leaf upon the tree
> In the spring,
> Let them smile, as I do now,
> At the old forsaken bough
> Where I cling.

Jeanie sat down, and Mathews applauded and huzzahed ironically; then Duyckinck joined in, clapping and hooting, until other passengers craned their necks and peered down the aisle. Jeanie said, "Pearls before swine, Doctor." Holmes shrugged. In his mind, Herman heard the hungry cries of albatrosses wheeling above dead whales shackled to ships.

"Very well," said Mathews. "Let us memorialize our favorite mariner, as he commands. Shall we each take a verse?"

Duyckinck declared that he would start. He looked off into the middle distance just beyond Herman's head for a moment to set the mood and declaimed theatrically, "I saw him in a car / with the window ajar / on a train / he asked Holmes for a verse / suitable for his hearse / thus we sang."

Mathews scoffed. "You can do better, Evert. Train does not rhyme with sang, for instance." And then he cleared his throat ostentatiously and took his turn: "His luxuriant beard / with peach marmalade smeared / from breakfast / he'll taste his peach all day / that's why he seems so fey / and jaundiced."

Duyckinck said, "Breakfast does not rhyme with jaundiced."

"Not only that, but the verse isn't true," Jeanie exclaimed.

"I had not thought truth the object," said Mathews.

"Look at Mr. Melville's fine, wavy, red beard," Jeanie went on. "It's beautiful. And anyway, even if there were jam in it, how would that make him jaundiced? He's the very picture of health." Her cheeks flushed.

"It's only a joke, Miss Field," Mathews said. "Peach marmalade sometimes has a yellow tinge."

"I have seen peach marmalade, Mr. Mathews," Jeanie said. "And I know what a joke is. But perhaps something like this would be better." Jeanie stood up again and recited directly at Herman. "Sometimes when one is strange / he's obliged to arrange / little lies / to hide his truest thought / behind some overwrought / alibis."

Mathews snorted. "Are you entirely sure you know what a joke is?"

Herman forgot about the dead whales in his head, in favor of a panic over Miss Field. He stood up, slipped between Mathews's and Duyckinck's knees and crossed the aisle to Jeanie's bench. He took Jeanie's left hand between both of his.

"What do you mean, strange?" he said.

"Why, your demeanor, of course. You seem very far away from our little group this morning." Jeanie held Herman's gaze just long enough to let him know that she had noticed something else peculiar about him, beyond his distraction. Herman's heart raced. "Consider it a compliment," she said.

"Melville has shipwrecked his brains against the rocks of his new novel," Duyckinck said.

The train slowed. A porter appeared in the car to announce the town of Stockbridge.

"Thank God," said Dudley. He stood up and said, "Will you kindly unhand my sister, Mr. Melville!"

Herman looked at him a moment before quite understanding, and then said, "Of course." He let go of Jeanie's hand and took Dudley's instead, who grudgingly shook it; but Herman continued to hold Dudley's hand in both of his and stared enigmatically into Dudley's eyes. Herman said, "Everyone is a little strange."

"Don't be so sure," Mathews said, and he broke up their hand-holding tête-à-tête before Dudley could attempt violence. Mathews slapped Herman hard on the back and led him off down the aisle. Dr. Holmes chivalrously offered Jeanie his arm, and Dudley found himself alone with his indignation when the train came to a full stop at Stockbridge.

As they walked away from the station, Holmes took a pinch of snuff from his medical bag. The doctor was a short, slight apparition of a man with a narrow peanut of a skull, and he appeared even smaller than usual strolling beside the athletic Jeanie, who was skipping and humming a little tune. Herman, still nettled by Jeanie's comments, glanced around miserably at the quaintly gabled houses and shops, hoping that pirates or brigands would suddenly charge out.

At times like this, he wished he had stayed with his friend Toby Greene, on Nuku Hiva Island, the tropical paradise where they had deserted their whaler together many years before; or that he had remained on the Navy frigate *United States* with Jack Chase, the gallant foretopman he had fallen in love with after shipping out from the Sandwich Islands in '45. Instead, he had chosen respectability, and family, and a literary career that now seemed even more fleeting than the long-ago adventures upon which it was based.

Herman's first two books, *Typee* and *Omoo*—which he had dashed off with the braggadocio of a sailor on shore leave—had become surprise sensations among the ladies' book clubs. Flush with fame, he had attempted something grander in his third book, an allegory whose scope and beauty he thought would rival Milton; but critics had viciously mocked *Mardi*, and it had failed to sell out its first printing. For his next two books, he had returned to telling more straightforward tales based on his own journeys at sea, but he had lost his easy confidence and his stories had veered into dour social commentary. *Redburn* featured graphic scenes of babies starving to death on the Liverpool docks; and *White-Jacket*, his most recent book, detailed the brutality of life in the United States Navy so vividly that it had spurred Congress to abolish shipboard flogging—but flogging victims had apparently been the only people who had bought it. Sales of *White-Jacket* had failed to cover the publisher's modest advance, which Herman now owed back to the Harper brothers.

The rain clouds bore down upon them. "We're going to get wet, and no doubt of it," Duyckinck called over his shoulder.

"No, we're not," said Holmes.

"Actually, Evert," Dudley said, adopting a lawyerly tone, "nothing is sure in the Berkshires. Those clouds may hold their rain all day, or they may drop it all in Lenox and nowhere else, possibly on a single rooftop, or the whole mountain range may be under water within the hour. In the Berkshires, as in life, one sometimes must sail with the wind and sometimes against it, but the important thing is to keep your sails full."

"With wisdom like that, Dudley," Duyckinck said sarcastically, "you could have followed your father into the pulpit."

"Look over there," Dudley said, ignoring him and pointing into the distance. "That hill is Sacrifice Mount, and beyond it you can just see our destination, Monument Mountain."

"Sacrifice Mount sounds more fitting for this crowd," said Mathews, taking a swig of brandy from his flask. "We could climb to the top and offer someone to the gods."

"Don't human sacrifices have to be virgins?" Jeanie asked. "I believe virgins are favored by the gods, are they not, Mr. Melville?"

"Yes, but only by the gods," Herman replied.

Jeanie stared unflappably back at him. He had met the young lady several times before, in New York, but he remembered her as a quiet, proper girl who wore demure, ankle-length silk skirts and said nothing even remotely provocative; now, he eyed the cuff of her trousers, which exposed the merest glimpse of bare ankles, and suspected that she had fallen in with the Young America movement, perhaps, or the suffragists.

"The sacrifice referred to is that of our *savior*," Dudley said. "Jesus Christ has relieved us of the burden of offering any sacrifices other than our souls."

"It's lucky that anyone still wants those," said Holmes. "Our souls are the least virginal things about us."

Dudley's outrage blossomed in his face; but, seeing no satisfying direction that this line of inquiry could take, he elected to change tack. "My cottage is just at the end of this lane. That's where Hawthorne and the others will meet us."

Dudley's cottage was pitched down in a little dell below the road, beside a trickling rivulet that had been dammed to form a pool. They had a view of the entire property as they approached it: the rough-hewn cottage painted a cheery daisy yellow; the little pool behind it, around which a hog and two sheep now lay; and a round yellow barn in the Shaker style, whose main door was open to reveal mounds of hay. Dudley led the party down the path from the road, and he called out to his housekeeper as he flung open the front door. "Maybelle! Do we have a loaf that six could share?"

They entered the cottage and filed through the living room, with its well-stocked bookshelves, to the kitchen, where Dudley's housekeeper was pouring out glasses of milk. They stood around the kitchen table, as if they were already at a picnic, passing a loaf of bread around, tearing off chunks and smearing them with butter, or dunking them into their milk. Dudley's housekeeper left and brought back a jar of cool water from the little stream outside.

Everyone ate ravenously, and Mathews recited the plot of the new play he was working on, which revolved around a family's festivities at Thanksgiving. The drama was a celebration of that unique American holiday, he said, because he was unaware of any theatrical work to date that dealt with the national significance of the Thanksgiving feast. "But I am having great difficulty constraining the action so as to be staged," he said. "The story keeps running out into the fields and barns. I am considering rewriting the whole work as a novel."

"Not a bad idea, Cornelius," said Herman, licking butter from his moustache. "A change of genre entirely! Perhaps that would work with my latest novel, as well." He drank off a tall glass of milk. "I wonder how I might get a whale onto a stage?"

"The same way you would haul him into a boat, I suppose," Cornelius answered.

"The trick would not be landing him," said Evert. "It would be negotiating his contract."

"One could simply suggest the whale with shadows and sounds," said Herman thoughtfully. He felt that anything would be better than the version of the story he currently had. He imagined his old whaling boat, the *Acushnet*, on a stage, cut in half lengthwise to reveal its lower holds and inner secrets to an audience. "But there would be no way of getting the truth of the whale onto the stage. The actors would have too much to explain, and the audience could not be made to taste the salt air or imagine the horrible immensity of the fish." Then he suddenly yelled, at the top of his lungs, "One cannot stage a chase across the seven seas in a cabaret!" Alarmed, Dudley's housekeeper ran out the kitchen door.

"If you want to give the truth of a subject, you take it to the lecture halls," Holmes said. The doctor's own lectures on the Lyceum Circuit had been growing in popularity, and he was constantly in demand around New England's libraries and colleges for his observations about medicine, poetry, and everyday life. "I would be happy to arrange some dates for you, Herman, in conjunction with some of my own speaking engagements. I think you would find that a lecture about such an important topic as whaling would be well received and even lucrative."

"I don't believe a whale could fit into a lecture hall any easier than it could fit into a theater. I mean the truth of the thing, not merely the facts."

"But where on earth *could* the truth of a whale fit, except the ocean?" said Jeanie. "Aren't the truth of the whale and the whale itself one and the same thing?"

"Of course not," said Duyckinck. "The truth of 'winter' is not the season of winter. Truth is a rhetorical concept and natural things just are."

"But what is the point of representing the so-called truth of any natural thing at all?" Jeanie persisted. "Thanksgiving is one matter. It's an invented ritual. It *requires* explanation. But why not let a natural thing like a whale be exactly what it is and appreciate it as such?"

"I would agree," Herman said. "Except that nothing is exactly what it appears to be."

"I suppose you would be the expert on that, Mr. Melville."

Herman could stand her insinuating banter no longer. "Have I offended you in some way, Miss Field?"

"On the contrary. I've just finished reading *Typee*, so you'll forgive me if I seem somewhat forward—your influence is entirely to blame! I'm delighted to speak with the Man Who Lived Among the Cannibals."

Herman hated this nickname, which his publishers had given him to promote his first book. It had been good for sales—they had been right about that—but its novelty had quickly worn off, and now it made him feel like a carnival exhibit. At least, he thought, it explained the young lady's alarming attentions: *Typee* had condemned the Christian missionaries in the South Seas and described the native islanders' hedonistic sexual practices with unusual frankness and sympathy—Herman had even winkingly suggested his own participation in various licentious revelries, marking him as a libertine in the public imagination.

"After all of your extraordinary experiences on the high seas," Jeanie said, blushing, "I imagine it must be difficult, sometimes, to get along in quaint old New England."

"Do you know how Melville *actually* survived the cannibals?" Mathews asked.

"Well, I've read his book," said Jeanie.

"Ask him to show you his tattoo," said Duyckinck.

Dudley's head wobbled like a slowly deflating balloon. "Surely you do not have blasphemous designs etched into your flesh, Mr. Melville? Or, at the very least, you will refrain from displaying them!"

"Say what you will about the Marquesans," Herman said. "But they are not blasphemous. They truly believe what they write on their bodies—not like Duyckinck here, who reverses everything he writes in his magazine from one week to the next."

"As you know, Melville, the advertising copy tends to leave more permanent impressions than the articles," said Duyckinck. "In any event, the next time *Literary World* issues you a check, I'll write it in invisible ink."

Holmes dunked a piece of bread into his milk. "Come to think of it, Melville, you should give lectures about cannibals. That's what people want. Something mysterious and frightening."

"What could be more mysterious and frightening than a whale?" Melville asked.

Dudley said, "If there is mystery in the world, it is the profound mystery of the Creator and the human soul. As for the truth about whales or anything else, it is all just poorly understood fact. The universe is a vast machine whose secrets the Creator will reveal to us as He sees fit."

"Are you saying that all of existence is merely mechanical but that humans beings are somehow separate?" Herman snapped. "Or that the image of God, in which we were created, is somehow too small to include both men and whales?"

"Well," said Dudley defensively. He looked around the room for help, but no one else seemed concerned by the suggestion that a whale could reflect the image of God. "Surely you will grant the mystery of the human soul, Mr. Melville—that is why we rely on God's mercy, because the soul has no explanation or salvation but Him."

"Honestly," said Jeanie, "I am much more interested in Mr. Melville's cannibal tattoo than the mysteries of the soul."

"You see, Melville," said Holmes, brushing breadcrumbs from his sleeve. "People like cannibals. They like *people*, no matter what they eat. It is difficult to make sense of a whale."

Thunder rumbled overhead, and a gust of wind whipped through the open kitchen door. "There is mystery in everything," Herman whispered, almost to himself. "And so there is poetry in everything. Even something as monstrous as a whale. But how to unlock its poetry?"

Duyckinck threw a chunk of bread that hit Herman squarely in the forehead. "If you wanted to carry on with your bombastic work, my dear Yankee, why did you leave your desk?"

"Hear, hear," said Mathews.

From outside, Maybelle yelled something indistinct just as the sounds of clopping and creaking reached their ears. "Hawthorne!" Dudley said, relieved.

They went out to see a fine covered carriage, hitched to two sleek black ponies, coming up the road. The driver was an older man wearing a red livery coat and a white wig, as if the passengers were feudal lords. The carriage stopped in front of the cottage, and the driver climbed down and opened the door.

James Fields, Hawthorne's publisher, emerged first and gave a jaunty wave: he wore a black frock coat more suitable to the opera than a picnic, and he sported a fastidiously waxed black moustache that curled at the ends. He turned and held out his hand for his child bride, Eliza, whose frilly blue dress—with white ribbons around the collar and white petticoats peeking out below the hem— made her seem like a dress-up doll. Then came Harry Sedgwick, the nephew of local novelist Catharine Sedgwick, who was the only person properly dressed for a hike, in blue dungaree trousers and a plain blue shirt, with a red kerchief tied around his neck.

Finally, Nathaniel Hawthorne poked his head out and looked up at the blackening sky. Hawthorne's features were so fine that they could have belonged to a woman: eyebrows that prettily framed his coffee brown eyes; a hawkish Roman nose; sensuous red lips, the bottom lip a wide devouring flare; and waving chestnut hair that fell in ringlets behind his ears. He stared up at the storm clouds for a very long time, as if deciding whether he would leave the carriage at all. His complete disregard of the company assembled on Dudley's porch had a mesmerizing effect on them: everyone simply waited and watched to see what he would do. At last, he put one hand on the door and the other on the driver's shoulder and launched him-self out of the carriage, landing with the awkward grace of an acrobat; and then he stood and looked at everyone as if their presence there surprised him.

Herman found this performance so strange and magnetic that he involuntarily walked directly to Hawthorne and held out his hand. Hawthorne grasped it with a look of frank bemusement.

"Forgive me," Herman said. "I am Herman Melville."

"I forgive you," said Hawthorne.

Herman could not quite explain to himself the clarity that suddenly reorganized his thoughts, a new and inarticulate idea of order that possessed him, both a spiritual awe and bodily weakness. He had never touched a man's hand as soft as Hawthorne's, as if Hawthorne had never done a day of labor in his life, and his whole self condensed into the sensation of that clasping hand and the simultaneous foreignness and familiarity of those probing brown eyes. Presently, he felt the hand squirming in his grasp, and he immediately regretted his incautious and over-ardent way of clasping it, and he flung it away.

Herman turned back to the rest of the group, blushing. Only Jeanie seemed to notice his embarrassment: her eyes twinkled inscrutably.

Since Dudley was the only person who knew everyone, he made introductions all around, absurdly trumpeting the authors' book and play titles and magazine credits in turn. Everyone exchanged hearty congratulations and vigorous handshakes, as if they were being inducted into a secret society; but Herman did not even register the illustrious credits of the other gentlemen, and he barely recognized the titles of his own novels, so fascinated had he become by the exotic Mr. Hawthorne.

"What about a toast?" said Dudley, and he asked Maybelle to open a bottle of champagne. They moved inside, poured wine and clinked glasses. In an unpremeditated show of solidarity, they all drained their champagne in one go. "And there's more where that came from," Dudley exclaimed.

"We've brought along something of a feast ourselves," Eliza said. "Some wine and a smoked beaver that I prepared last night."

"Shall we be off, then? Maybelle, did you hitch up our wagon?"

James and Eliza Fields climbed into their carriage with Sedgwick and Hawthorne, and their driver mounted the bench and snapped the reins. The group that had arrived by train clambered into Dudley's wagon, which Maybelle had supplied with picnic baskets, and they were off. Dudley sat on the bench, loosely holding the reins; and while Mathews passed his flask to Duyckinck, and Jeanie smoothed her dress over her trousers, and Holmes took another pinch of snuff from his bag, Herman sat staring fixedly forward at the small round window in the carriage in front of them, where the mysterious head of Nathaniel Hawthorne bobbed along to the rhythm of the trotting ponies.

Chapter 2

Monument Mountain

Monument Mountain awaited three miles to the east, looming like a headless sphinx on the horizon, and Mathews, as he was always wont to do, suggested they play riddle games to pass the time. Duyckinck began.

> Four wings I have, which swiftly mount on high,
> On sturdy pinions, yet I never fly;
> And though my body often moves around,
> Upon the self-same spot I'm always found,
> And, like a mother, who breaks her infant's bread,
> I chew for man before he can be fed.

"Really, Evert!" said Mathews. "We all learned that one at school. It's a windmill, of course." Then Mathews took a turn.

> Sometimes I have sense, sometimes I have none;
> Sometimes I offend, then you bid me begone;
> Sometimes I am merry, sometimes I am sad;
> Sometimes I am good, sometimes very bad;
> However, to make me, I cost many brains,
> Much labor, much thought, and a great deal of pains.

"Since you are a playwright," said Jeanie immediately, "I will guess that it's a play." Several more rounds of this game followed, each offering sometimes more and sometimes less clever and enigmatic rhymes, until they grew bored of it and fell into silence, under the spell of the gently swaying cart. Twice, a sprinkling rain began and they thought nervously of finding shelter beneath a bower of trees; and twice the rain abated and left them rolling along somewhat damp but enjoying the drama of the storm and its unknowable progress. James and Eliza Fields and Hawthorne remained concealed inside their carriage up ahead, while Sedgwick inexplicably joined their driver on his bench, out in the rain.

By the time they reached the base of Monument Mountain, a light drizzle was falling steadily, and they took a vote to determine whether they should turn back or head up the slope. The vote was unanimous to carry on with the hike, and then they again voted unanimously to open more wine. Mathews rummaged in the picnic baskets and found a bottle of Heidsieck, the new French champagne that had come into vogue that year; and as the cork flew off into the clover at the side of the road, Dudley reported that Maybelle had failed to pack cups and that they would be obliged to pass the bottle.

Feeling more ebullient and caring less and less about the rain, they guided their horses under the eaves of some nearby elms and gave them feed bags. They then secured their beasts, divvied up the picnic baskets, and set out on foot, passing the champagne as they went.

Herman charged up the hill, pointing at the humped top of the mountain and shouting, "Thar she blows." He crested the first little rise and sprinted toward a crevice between boulders. Mathews and Duyckinck and Sedgwick raced close behind, elbowing each other playfully into the bushes, and Hawthorne, loping along farther back, shouted, "There is an Indian behind that tree," and "Eyes out for convicts hiding in those rocks," and "I saw the devil's tail in that grove!" James and Eliza Fields, in their dandified city clothing and shiny leather shoes, slipped and slid on the wet grass and fell farther and farther behind, Eliza's chignon giving out in the rain and her wet hair clinging to her cheeks.

Thunder banged at their ears, and Herman leapt out onto a spit of rock and pantomimed pulling on a ship's bowline. Holmes cut a switch with a scalpel from his bag and paraded under it, as if it were a lady's parasol; and then he cut and offered more such ineffectual parasols to the others. The rain increased steadily, and by the time they were halfway up the peak, they were forced to find shelter or be soaked through. Herman bounded and gamboled like a ram, hither and yon, first to one side and then the other of the crevice they were following up the mountain, and he soon found a massive outcropping of slate just off their path—a rocky shelf that hung over a dry, gravelly space large enough to shelter the entire party. They ducked underneath this natural ceiling and shook water from their hands and puffed and whooped; James and Eliza came straggling up behind the rest of the group, their fine frockery looking much the worse for the rain, though Fields's moustache remained as sharply and attractively curled as ever.

Fields opened a bottle of brandy and passed it around, and the picnic began in earnest. The rain fell in giant drops around them and ran off the edges of the overhang in sheets. They practically had to shout to hear one another over the torrent, and as they passed around bread and salami and cheeses and peaches and smoked beaver and brandy and more champagne, they found themselves congregating naturally into little islands of two and three, the most easily to hear one another's conversation. Herman stayed close to Hawthorne; when Dudley went to search the picnic baskets for a tin of caviar, he found himself alone with the mesmeric figure, on the fringes of the party, just at the edge of the outcropping, where the splashing of water made their speech unintelligible to the others.

He leaned toward Hawthorne, wishing urgently to communicate

something of the sorceries that had bewitched him at the moment of their meeting, but he could find no words for his feelings. In fact, he imagined that no human language could ever express what he now felt, since it seemed inspired not only by Hawthorne in his person but also by some mystical new alignment in the heavens. Hawthorne seemed the living expression of an idea so well formulated in Herman's own mind that his only response could be, "Yes, true, what an elegant solution."

"This cheddar is excellent," said Hawthorne. He sliced a bite from the hunk in his hand and gave the cheese and knife to Herman, who held them out in front of himself as if they were a shield and a sword. Hawthorne stared out at the downpour.

"I have been thinking all day," Herman finally croaked out, "about the correspondence between the physical expression of a thing and the truth of the thing, and how one might infer the latter from the former."

"A thing? Any thing? Like that cheese you're holding, for instance?"

Hawthorne was fifteen years Herman's senior, but his face seemed to Herman to defy the laws of earthly decay. So noble did Hawthorne seem that Herman conjectured that some unique mechanism had gradually been transferring his inner beauty touch by touch outward toward his external features with each passing day, so that, even long into the future, when Hawthorne would be much advanced in years, his inward nobility would compensate so fully for his outward decrepitude that his face would become almost ethereal.

"Yes," said Herman. "Like this cheese."

"You mean that you have been meditating on whether or not the physical expression of this cheese might imply something even more perfectly cheesy, like its Platonic form? Or do you mean that you have been contemplating the cheese's ultimate meaning in the way that this particular block of cheese is both itself and a representative of all cheddars and also a representative of the larger class of cheese generally and of all products of man or even all material things in the universe, so that the mystery of this cheddar becomes impossible to solve, either through science or meditation; and since no starting point can be fixed for the universe, other than to propose a creator God who started everything one day on a whim, one must be content with the ambiguity of this hunk of cheddar as both concretely existing and yet having no demonstrable first cause, no matter how well known the cheese itself might be to the touch and the taste?"

"That's exactly what I meant!" Herman sliced off a hunk of the cheddar and deposited it in his mouth.

"Yes, I see your point."

"But even more than that," Herman said. "I have been considering the possibility that the facts that can be ascertained about this cheese fail to satisfy because the facts themselves mask a metaphysical truth that can be known only through the transcendent, poetic expression of the cheddar. That is, though the world itself can never truly be known, one might begin to know some truth *about* the world through a *metaphysical cheese*."

Dudley returned and stood over the two authors, who were gazing intently at the cheese in Herman's hand. "Caviar?" he said.

Hawthorne ignored Dudley and responded instead to Herman, with a passion that caught Herman off guard. "Yes! In much the same way one might propose that Jesus, while offered to us by the churches as either a physical or a moral fact, should rather be seen as the *poetry* of mankind, since the facts that can be known about Him obviously matter very little and his moral authority depends solely upon belief."

Herman said, "You're saying that Jesus came not to redeem humanity's original sin but rather to call into question the concept of sin itself through the poetry of a grand gesture? An ultimately Romantic gesture?"

"Yes, but I would not discard the idea of original sin. It's a fruitful context for meditation, even if it is merely poetical."

"But would you agree at least that the proper formulation of the problem is poetical first? And that asking the question matters more than finding the answer?"

"It sounds like you are saying," Hawthorne said, "that in the beginning was the Word, and the Word was with God, and the Word was God."

Dudley walked away with his caviar.

Herman said, "Unfortunately, there's one little thing wrong with that Scripture. It should have read, in the beginning was the Question, and the Question was with God, and the Question was God." He cut a piece of cheese. Hawthorne took and ate it, and then Herman reached for a bottle of wine near him, and he gave it to Hawthorne, and Hawthorne likewise took the wine and drank.

"The cheese that can be eaten and the wine that can be drunk are not the real cheese and the real wine," said Herman.

"Unless they are," said Hawthorne, winking.

Herman felt an acute sensation of relief, a long spiritual exhalation. Hawthorne had a magical effect on him. For the first time in as long as he could remember, a finger of light, like the first ray of dawn, shone into the dark cavern of his soul.

"It seems the end of the brandy is also the end of the storm," Mathews shouted drunkenly, and he spread his arms wide to indicate the slackening rain all around them. The sun suddenly broke through the clouds, creating a hundred tiny rainbows in the rivulets of water still splashing off the sides of the overhanging rock. Dr. Holmes held up a nearly empty bottle of brandy, from which he drank in a silent toast to the sun and the revelers, and then he passed the bottle. They managed to make the brandy last until every last member of the picnic had had a final sip. Hawthorne took the next-to-last swallow, and Herman thought that he saw Hawthorne's lips linger on the bottle just a little as his eyes met Herman's; and when he passed the bottle to Herman, its mouth was still warm with Hawthorne's slightly drunken kiss.

As the rain gave way completely to mottled sunshine, they packed up their picnic and headed back down the mountain, well lubricated and telling tales. Mathews and Duyckinck cast the rest of the party in roles for a little folderol that they made up as they tramped downhill. Mathews's alter ego was "Silver Pen" and Melville became "New Neptune"; Hawthorne was "Mr. Noble Melancholy," Jeanie "Princess Picnic," and they went on and on making up silly names and creating absurd little nursery rhymes that told of equally absurd situations.

By the time they reached their wagons at the bottom of the mountain, they were happily weary from the walk and the talk and the rhyming, and they clambered into their conveyances, to be borne back to Stockbridge. On the return trip, Jeanie rode in the Fieldses' carriage, having developed a fondness for Eliza during the picnic, and Sedgwick once again ascended to their driver's bench, this time impertinently stealing the driver's white wig for himself. Holmes rode next to Dudley on the bench of Dudley's wagon, and Herman and Hawthorne sat across from one another in the back, next to Mathews and Duyckinck.

In no time, Mathews and Duyckinck had nodded off, under the influence of the wine and the refreshingly cool air, leaving Hawthorne and Melville to stare at one another in silence. Herman shifted his leg ever so slightly toward Hawthorne's, so that the fabric of their breeches touched; and the wagon jostled them closer still. Herman felt the warmth of the older author's calf against his, and Hawthorne neither moved away nor broke Herman's gaze.

Occasionally, Mathews or Duyckinck would awaken, and Herman would peer nonchalantly over Hawthorne's shoulder, as if he were merely taking in the rain- and sun-drenched earth; but the moment their fellow passengers nodded off again, he would look back into Hawthorne's eyes, and Hawthorne continued to stare at him unabashedly, unnervingly. Herman sometimes felt that Hawthorne was laughing at him, so full of ironic humor was his gaze; but the pressure of Hawthorne's leg against his told him otherwise.

Herman forgot all about his whale manuscript, and he forgot about his debts and even about his wife and son and mother, who were, at that very moment, having tea together in Pittsfield, waiting for him to return. He forgot about himself. The only thing he knew for certain was the radiance of Nathaniel Hawthorne.

Chapter 3

Hawthorne and His Mosses

Herman climbed down from the hayloft and walked out of the barn at Broad Hall, his cousin's bed-and-breakfast. His jacket was covered in golden dust, and bits of hay stuck comically out of his auburn hair. He held the book he had been reading—*Mosses from an Old Manse*, a story collection that Hawthorne had written several years before—close to his breast.

The picnic at Monument Mountain was a few days behind him, and he had barely slept or eaten. He seemed not to need mere physical sustenance anymore, surviving instead on a spiritual alchemy of memory and desire.

The evening sky was milky with haze; toward the horizon, it became a dull ivory, the color of a tortoise egg. Herman felt as if the whiteness might crack and God himself might hatch into the landscape. The idea of God as an immense tortoise—deliberate, reptilian, silent, and hard shelled—cheered him. Bees buzzed in the meadow, and he took a full breath of the cool air and smelled the bright dusty hay on his coat and the sweet sap of clover at his feet. He felt a wave of optimism lift him up, a renewed faith that the world could deliver unanticipated wonders.

Hawthorne!

No name could be more apt to this man than Hawthorne, Herman thought: the soft ravishments of his beauty had been spun like a web of dreams from the clustered white blossoms of the intoxicatingly sweet hawthorn tree, whose flowers yet hid dangerous thorns.

Yes, Hawthorne the man, from hawthorn the tree, the wild haw, whose gossamer veins entwined its scaled and dusky bark with lobed and serrated leaves, a small wonder of symmetry cragged at the trunk and heartbreakingly delicate at the tips of its crown, shooting deep and tangling roots into the soil of Herman's soul. A whole taxonomy of Hawthorne could be written from his namesake tree, which perfectly embodied the qualities of the man.

He clutched Hawthorne's book tighter and felt the man's words bathing his soul, outlining the distinctive hue of every towering hill and far-winding vale in Herman's heart: it was as if Hawthorne, in his person and through his writing, had mapped Herman's internal geography before Herman had fully explored it himself. As if he had made an atlas of Herman's soul that traced every river of love, every freshet and cataract of wonder, every fetid pool of despair, and that, by the celestial mechanisms of this divinely inspired cartographer, the map of his soul *was* the territory.

He looked up at Broad Hall. His family would have to leave here soon—Robert reminded him daily that they had overstayed their welcome—but the thought had become intolerable! How could he return to that apartment in Manhattan, now that he knew Hawthorne awaited him here? Even Herman's mother had suggested they move to Pittsfield, as if she had been speaking for the Fates themselves. All Herman had to do was find the means to buy a house in the Berkshires . . . but his literary career seemed to have added up to nothing, just when he needed it most.

He was suddenly aware of voices. Duyckinck and Mathews strolled around the corner of Broad Hall, carrying suitcases. Duyckinck's black derby hat perched jauntily atop his head, and Mathews wore his oval spectacles on the end of his nose. They looked like a traveling minstrel act.

"Ah, Melville," Duyckinck said. "Thank you for finishing your review so quickly, but I can't possibly publish it—at least, not the way it's written right now."

When Duyckinck had seen how Melville and Hawthorne had hit it off at the picnic, he had proposed that Herman write an article for the next edition of *Literary World* magazine, comparing *The Scarlet Letter* to Thackeray's latest novel, *Pendennis*. Duyckinck believed that American readers preferred well-established English authors to relatively unknown Americans, and his new strategy for overcoming this prejudice was to compare local writers favorably to their British counterparts. However, no one had had a copy of *The Scarlet Letter* on hand, so they had decided that Herman should, instead, write a retrospective about *Mosses from an Old Manse*—which they had found on Robert's shelves. *Mosses* had been a commercial flop, but Duyckinck thought that a new review might excite new interest, especially now that Hawthorne's *Scarlet Letter* had been condemned from so many pulpits. "Remember," Duyckinck had told Melville, "mention a well-regarded English author in your review—someone respectable."

"Did Lizzie not give you the fair copy?" Herman said.

"She did." Duyckinck opened his valise and withdrew a sheaf of papers. He waved them in Herman's face. "Look, Melville, when I suggested you compare Hawthorne to a well-regarded Englishman, I meant someone like Dickens or Thackeray or Walter Scott—not Shakespeare!"

Herman brushed hay from his hair. He opened his copy of *Mosses from an Old Manse* and read aloud: "Blessed are all simple emotions, be they dark or bright! It is the lurid intermixture of the two that produces the illuminating blaze of the infernal regions." He looked up. "What do you suppose Hawthorne means by that?"

"Seems obvious," Mathews said. "Following the simplicity of pure emotion saves one from the complicated thoughts that can lead to damnation."

"But what about where he says simple emotions, *dark or bright*? If one felt a simple emotion of malice and followed it, how would that *not* lead to the infernal regions? He seems to be saying that simplicity is more valuable than morality."

"Melville," Duyckinck cried. "This is all gibberish. You simply can't compare Hawthorne to Shakespeare. And what about this?" He shuffled the pages of Herman's review until he found a passage that he read aloud. "'To what infinite height of loving wonder and admiration I may yet be borne, when, by repeatedly banqueting on these Mosses, I shall have thoroughly incorporated their whole stuff into my being—that, I cannot tell. But already I feel that this Hawthorne has dropped germinous seeds into my soul.' Really? Germinous seeds into your soul?"

"Edit that out, if you don't like it," Herman snapped. "Have you read the story called 'Rappaccini's Daughter'?"

Mathews said, "Is that the one where original sin, as represented by a birthmark on the woman's face, is the price of human existence?"

"No, that's a story called 'The Birth-Mark,'" Herman said sarcastically. "In 'Rappaccini's Daughter,' a man discovers a beautiful girl in a kind of Garden of Eden, but the girl turns out to be poisonous."

"Garden of Eden?" Mathews said. "Poisonous girl? That's original sin, too."

"Original sin is a very commercial idea," said Duyckinck. "How do you think the Bible stays in print year after year?"

"I thought Jesus sold all those copies."

Herman ignored them. "What is Hawthorne trying to say? So many of these stories seem to have hidden sexual meanings. For instance, the mark on the woman's face in 'The Birth-Mark,' which the husband, Aylmer, tries desperately to remove, seems a symbol of menstruation. Literally, a *birth* mark. After all, the mark is red, the color of blood, and Aylmer says it is 'the only defect' in his wife's perfection. And Rappaccini's poisoned garden is clearly a metaphor for women: everything in the garden is heartbreakingly beautiful but deadly poisonous, including Rappaccini's daughter, a beautiful flower that you enter through a secret gate and that destroys anything it touches. Does she have syphilis?"

Duyckinck's face soured. "For God's sake, Melville, what are you talking about? We have to catch the evening train back to New York." He put the pages back in his suitcase. "Incidentally, I had a letter from Hawthorne this morning, concerning you. Perhaps you should discuss his views on the flowering of women directly with him."

"A letter?" Herman said as casually as he could, while his heart nearly leapt out of his mouth.

"He wrote to ask me to send him some books from New York, and he wanted me to ask you if you would be willing to receive them and take them to his cottage. Apparently, the Lenox postmaster is unreliable, and he'd heard that the Pittsfield office was better. Would you mind taking some novels to him?"

"Not at all," said Herman, overjoyed. Hawthorne was engineering their next meeting covertly through Duyckinck! "I've never had any problems with the Pittsfield Post Office," he said nonchalantly.

"Good," Duyckinck said. "You know, Melville, I've known Hawthorne for ten years, and he hasn't invited me to visit him once, for *any* reason."

"That's right," Mathews added. "I never even saw Hawthorne's children until they were talking, and I've known him longer than Evert has. He's a true recluse! But he seemed almost breezy the other day at the picnic, didn't he, Evert?"

Herman beamed. "Well, send along whatever books he'd like. I'll ride them over to Lenox straightaway."

"And when are you and your family returning to Manhattan?" said Duyckinck.

The kitchen door opened, and Lizzie appeared. She was a small woman with a kindly, pale, oval face, a pudgy nose, and black hair parted down the middle; she held Malcolm on her hip. "Would you gentlemen like a morsel to eat on the train?" she said.

"Thank you, but we must be going," said Duyckinck. He strode over, shook Lizzie's hand warmly, and thanked her for translating Herman's nearly illegible review of *Mosses from an Old Manse* into a readable copy so quickly.

"It was nothing," she said.

Mathews gallantly kissed Lizzie's hand. "On the contrary, were it not for your excellent penmanship and, even more importantly, your almost occult ability to descry your husband's meanings, Herman would have no career at all." He then invited the whole Melville family to dine at his home when they returned to New York.

They waved goodbye and were off to the train station.

Chapter 4

A House in the Berkshires

Lizzie walked into Broad Hall's well-appointed kitchen and deposited the docile Malcolm in a Shaker high chair. Herman came in behind her and opened the potbellied stove, poking broken embers in the fuel box with the end of a fresh log. When the cinders glowed hellish, he tossed the log onto the grate, sending a little spray of ash and char out into the kitchen. He waited till flames licked up around the new wood and then clanked the stove door closed.

"Lizzie," said Herman, "I want to speak to you about something important."

"You don't really think that Hawthorne's book is as good as Shakespeare?" she asked. "Like you said in your review?"

"It doesn't matter what you say in a review. They're like advertisements."

"So you *don't* think Hawthorne is the American Shakespeare?" Herman waved the question away. "Well, did Mr. Duyckinck at least pay you for it?"

"Duyckinck will pay me by having Hawthorne review my next book."

"I see. You and the American Shakespeare will write advertisements for each other's work in *Literary World*. How does that pay anyone but Mr. Duyckinck? I would also remind you that the fair copy did not write itself."

"You and I will both be paid through the sales of my next book, which the good reviews in *Literary World* will generate. You know as well as I do how books are sold."

"I'm growing more familiar with how they're not sold."

She poured water from a clay jug into a pan, for Malcolm's evening porridge. The stove hissed as droplets kissed the hot steel.

Herman went into the dining room and brought back two chairs, which he set next to Malcolm's high chair. "I've been thinking about something much more important than reviews." He sat down and invited Lizzie to do the same. When they were all seated together as a family, he leaned forward, almost in a crouch at the edge of his chair. He took Lizzie's hand and stared deeply into her eyes. "I have been thinking about how much you dislike Manhattan, my dear." She had often praised her family's home in Boston over the rougher, dirtier New York. "And I've been thinking that the city is no good for Malcolm. So I think we should buy a house in the Berkshires."

Lizzie stiffened. "But how could we afford it? On what income?" Malcolm burbled and spit.

"If you're willing to borrow from your father against your inheritance, as you've said you might, then whatever house we buy will be yours."

"I've said I would borrow small sums in emergencies, to keep food on the table." Lizzie stood up and turned toward the stove. She touched her forehead and then her breastbone and spread her fingers out over her heart. "I had never thought of using it to buy a house!" She scooped dry oats and barley into the water on the stove. Malcolm stuck his left middle finger far up his right nostril. "And we are already deeply in debt to my father." Lizzie's father, Lemuel Shaw, the chief justice of the Massachusetts Supreme Court, had been subsidizing Herman's income with loans ever since his writing career had faltered.

"Those are personal loans he has made to me," said Herman. "I'm talking about the inheritance that will rightly be yours one day, no matter what."

"But how would we pay for the daily expenses of our own house, Herman? With Mr. Duyckinck's reviews? You're not writing *Typee* anymore."

"My next book will make *Typee* look like a suffragist pamphlet. You'll see! With Duyckinck's help, it will sell."

Lizzie stirred Malcolm's porridge vigorously, even though it had not yet begun to boil. Water and oats splashed out onto the stove.

"You can choose which house we buy," Herman continued. "You can do with it whatever you like, decorate it however you want. It will be *your* house. Not mine. Not my mother's. You'll make the down payment on it with your inheritance, and it will be your house—no one else's but yours—and I'll pay our expenses and upkeep with my writing. You can run the household as you see fit. And my mother will be our guest in your home."

Lizzie stopped stirring the thin gruel and sat back down. Herman's mother, Maria, was constantly nagging her to do things differently around their apartment in Manhattan, which they shared with Herman's sisters Augusta and Helen, his younger brother Allan, and Allan's wife and daughter.

"*My* home?" She looked longingly out the window, where the leaves of a maple tree fluttered in the pale evening sunshine. "But it just isn't possible, Herman. You barely earn enough now to pay half the expenses in the apartment we *share* with your brother. And there would be so many mouths to feed!" Since Herman's father and older brother had both died, Herman had become the eldest Melville and hence the head of their family; as such, he was obliged to keep his mother and his unmarried sisters under his roof. If they split up the household in Manhattan, Maria, Helen, and Augusta would almost certainly follow him to the Berkshires. "And I'll remind you that your mother is not exactly thrifty. She's downtown right now getting to know every shop in Pittsfield, and you never say a word to dissuade her. What would happen if you moved her to a house in the country and she felt restored to her 'proper station,' as she would put it?"

"A whole house here would cost less to maintain than half of that apartment in Manhattan. Look at how Holmes and Dudley Field and Hawthorne live out here, in such natural splendor and at such small expense, and their reputations grow and grow. And what better place for Malcolm to grow up? I could do it. We could do it."

"But if you're tired of Manhattan, it would be more prudent to move to Boston, near my own family."

"Boston is not the Berkshires," Herman said. "Let's make some inquiries about properties. If only to learn what the cost might be."

"Oh, Herman." Lizzie burst into tears. "I know you're frustrated with your book, but the solution is not to make the rest of your life harder."

Herman took her hand. "But this will make our lives easier! And Duyckinck and the Harper brothers will make my next book a great success. You'll see!"

The oats that had splattered onto the stove top began to burn; the acrid smell filled the kitchen. Malcolm bawled and flapped his arms.

Herman looked into Lizzie's eyes and tried to hide his shame about what he was really feeling: all he could think about was walking down the road to Hawthorne's house, imagining that, if he owned a home here, he could make that walk every single day.

How would Hawthorne feel when he learned that Herman was moving to the Berkshires? They had only just met. At the very least, he told himself, he would create the circumstances to find out how much admiration Hawthorne truly felt for him. Whatever happened in the end—however well or poorly his next book sold—Lizzie and Malcolm would still have a nice home in the Berkshires, and Judge Shaw could, in reality, afford to pay for everything. It was all fine, he told himself as he looked into his wife's eyes: it was for Lizzie's good, too, and Malcolm's.

Lizzie petted the back of her husband's head. "Do you remember why I married you, Herman? It's because you think differently from everyone else I've ever met. You have different dreams. But that doesn't mean all of your dreams are good."

"Everyone could have a private room," Herman persisted. "My mother and Augusta and Helen and even Malcolm. We could invite all of your relatives to come for the holidays. Your father will love having a Berkshire home in the family. We'll have a barn with a cow and a horse. We'll plant corn."

"Corn? What are you even saying, Herman?"

"We will write to your father about the inheritance. We'll inquire about houses. What harm can it do to propose an idea?"

Lizzie fiddled with the whalebone cameo at her neck. Herman had bought the brooch for her the previous fall, when he had gone to London to find an English publisher for *White-Jacket*: its silhouette depicted the three graces with their arms entwined.

"You are always so fanciful, Herman," Lizzie said sadly. Her tone brought tears to Herman's eyes—he could remember a time when she had said the same thing with admiration.

"But this will be *your* dream." With this lie, Herman could no longer contain himself. He slid down to his knees in front of Lizzie and wept like a child.

Herman's cousin Robert walked in and took off his hat. "What's burning?" He heard the weeping before his eyes had adjusted to the dimness of the kitchen, and he nearly tripped over the sobbing Melvilles in his haste to reach the stove.

"What goes on here?" Robert asked. He found a towel and used it to grab the hot pan. "What's wrong?"

Lizzie eased herself out of Herman's embrace and stood up. "Nothing." She snuffled. "Nothing is wrong." She smiled at Robert, who held out the ruined porridge as evidence that something was, indeed, wrong. "We have just been talking about the future."

"The future?"

Herman wiped tears from his eyes and stood up, as well. "Robert, we are moving to the Berkshires."

Robert went white. "When did you decide this?"

"Just now."

"Just now?"

"This very moment, as you were walking in. We will buy a farm somewhere near yours."

"Well, it's far from certain," said Lizzie. "It's just an idea that Herman has."

"But how can you afford it?" Robert said. "Aren't your creditors even now baying at your door in Manhattan? Isn't that why you've been staying here all month *at my expense*?"

"We just love it so much here," Herman said. "Haven't you always loved the Berkshires yourself?"

"Yes," Robert fumed. "I have always loved the Berkshires myself. But you cannot purchase a farm by loving it. Have you learned nothing from the examples of our own fathers?" Herman's and Robert's grandfathers had been prosperous businessmen and heroes of the Revolution, but that was where the success of the Melville family had ended. Herman's father had died raving mad with a fever while negotiating to avoid debtor's prison; Robert's father had died penniless on the western frontier, after a lifetime of hapless misadventures.

"What has happened, Robert?" said Lizzie. "Has something happened?"

"I have sold Broad Hall! The farm is bankrupt. I am moving my family back to Galena."

"Sold Broad Hall?" Herman asked. "Why?"

"Is there some nuance of the word 'bankrupt' that escapes you, Herman?"

"But everything seems to be going so well."

"Have you encountered a single guest at the inn since you arrived? Have you seen anyone working the fields?"

"But is it already sold then? We could not, for example, buy it ourselves?"

Robert looked at him for a moment with dumb fury before flinging the pot of burnt oatmeal at his head. Herman ducked. The pan smacked the wall and clattered across the floor, splattering gruel in its wake. Lizzie held her hands palm outward to Robert in a gesture of peace. Malcolm wailed. Robert stormed out of the kitchen and banged the front door closed behind him.

Herman lifted Malcolm out of his chair and cradled him protectively in his arms. He kissed Lizzie's head and led her up the stairs to their room. They shut the door behind them and sat together on the edge of their bed, holding Malcolm between them, shushing and comforting him, silently exchanging gentle caresses and doleful looks.

Herman began formulating an apology to Robert in his mind. He had been too preoccupied to notice his cousin's difficulties, or to notice Robert at all, really; his family always hovered just at the edge of Herman's attention—at least until a pot came flying at his head.

He thought about what Robert had said, about the example of their fathers—Herman remembered his own father's death well, because he had been with him through the delirium of his last night. Is that what I'm doing now, Herman thought, running from bad to worse like my father? But no, not all debt was the same: his father's debt had been a problem—Herman's debt would be a solution.

Half an hour passed before it seemed safe to return to the kitchen for dinner. When they did, they discovered that the oatmeal had been cleaned from the walls and floor, and the pot was once again hanging from the rack above the stove, spotless. On the table, in Robert's handwriting, they found an itemized bill for every day they had stayed at Broad Hall and every meal they had eaten.

Chapter 5

Hawthorne's Package

Herman woke early and slipped out of bed, while Lizzie snored into her pillow. They had written a letter to Lizzie's father immediately, requesting a loan against her inheritance in order to buy a house in the Berkshires, spelling out the reasons why this idea made sense; but the letter had lain on the bedside table for three days now, waiting to be posted. Lizzie was still too overwhelmed by the enormity of the idea to act on it, and Herman felt absolutely mad every time he saw Judge Shaw's name on the envelope. *Dollars*, he thought. Every time he saw Robert, he thought *dollars*. Every time he saw his hopeless manuscript on Robert's desk, he thought *dollars*. The only thought he had now that didn't immediately spiral into money was *Hawthorne*.

He splashed water on his face from a basin near the window. He was looking out at the surprisingly clear blue skies overhead when his eye wandered to the little mirror on his bedside table and, in the reflection, he saw a strange envelope lying on the floor near the bedroom door. He tiptoed over and picked it up. It was addressed to him, in handwriting he did not recognize. He opened it and unfolded a sheet of ivory-hued stationery. The penmanship seemed hasty, the letters thin and spidery in some places and blotchy and dark in others.

August 21, 1850
Lenox

My dear Melville,

*A peddler passed this way late this afternoon, selling
from his cart wreathes of laurel, diamonds, golden crowns
and various magical appurtenances, quite reasonably
priced, but I sent him away disappointed, saying that I
would trade all of his shiny baubles for a few volumes of
prose, which would be worth far more in the end.
Unfortunately, he had no items of prose and no similar
salesman freighted with novels has yet appeared in Lenox, so
I have asked Duyckinck to send me some volumes from New
York and asked him further to send them by way of Pittsfield,
in the hope that you might bring them on a visit to me, should
it not prove too much an inconvenience. I must also
compound the impertinence by requesting, moreover, if you
would not mind, that you pick up a package that is awaiting
us at the apothecary's in Pittsfield, under my name. It will
cost about $1.50, which I will repay when you come.*

*Incidentally, I wanted to tell you something, a coincidence
which I neglected to mention at the more appropriate time
when we met on Monument Mountain, but which I find too
curious not to relate; namely, that my father was a
mariner—but wait! I have not said all—and that he died of a
fever in Surinam! Perhaps this coincidence is not noteworthy
to you, since you, no doubt, are acquainted with many more
mariners than I, and succumbing to fevers in tropical climes
must be counted a hazard of the profession. But I overheard
your talk of fevers on our hike up the mountain, and how
your father and brother both died of fevers, which put me*

naturally in mind of mine own father's death, and I thought
this detail about him must interest you. I wonder how many
of our authors these days have had fathers who died of fevers?
It does not seem the most direct path to literary success, but
who can decode the secret designs of providence?

My son Julian has just advised me that the elm leaves
outside will not turn golden without our supervision, so I
must attend to Mother Nature and bid you farewell until your
visit to Lenox.

Nath. Hawthorne

P.S. Duyckinck has said that he would be sending the
books right away, and the sooner I have them in my hands,
the better. You have my thanks in advance.

Herman walked back to the window with the letter and tried to
comprehend its meanings, so rich did it seem with intimations of fate
and noble contemplations and intimacy, and even its simplest
thoughts seemed knotty with charming complications. His palms
sweated with delight. He reread it several times while Lizzie groaned
and turned in bed, twisting the covers and pillow around her to form
a cave of darkness against the morning. Should I hide it? he thought.
Was anything here suggestive or secret? Was the intimacy all in his
mind? Hawthorne's father had died of a fever. Well, what of it? Hawthorne had confirmed what Duyckinck had said, that he had asked
Duyckinck to send some books by Melville. What of that? Was it so
unusual? No, on the surface nothing here suggested untoward intimacy, and yet Herman hid the letter between the pages of his copy of
Mosses from an Old Manse and set it on the dresser behind a clock.

He recited the contents of the letter over in his head, having already memorized not only the words but also the texture of the

paper and the elegant curves of the lines across the page, the heavy
blots in the middle of f's and the tails of g's. Why had Hawthorne
begun the letter with talk of laurels and crowns and magic? Was it a
covert token of the gallantry he felt toward Herman, as Herman felt
toward him? What medicine awaited Hawthorne at the apothecary's? Was Hawthorne ill? Did he have some chronic condition,
and was this his way of confiding it to Herman? But the fever, the
fever! Yes, Hawthorne knew what it meant to lose a father to fever,
and perhaps even to madness. Why had he fixed his attention on
this talk of fathers, fever or no? Did Hawthorne himself suffer some
malady that made him fear for his sanity, and did he foresee a death
in fever and madness? Was the blackness Herman had perceived in
Mosses from an Old Manse a result of some secret that Hawthorne
was now trying to confess in this letter? But no, it was all too much!

Herman removed the letter from between the pages of Hawthorne's
book and read it again. He knew that he was becoming carried away,
interpreting secret messages where nothing but commonplace state-
ments existed. The fevers were simply biographical coincidences, and
Hawthorne was thinking less of mad fathers and more of the fact that
both Herman and Hawthorne's own father had been mariners—the
letter, in fact, said nothing deeper than that, and perhaps the apothecary was holding foot powder. No, there was nothing cryptic here or
even interesting, Herman thought. And to close the letter, Hawthorne
must have mentioned Julian because it was simply true that Julian had
interrupted him at just that moment with a childish remark about the
trees. Nothing could have been more banal. Yet Hawthorne had revealed that he had been eavesdropping on Herman's conversation
during that hike up the mountain!

Was it all a code? Oh, what did it all mean? He turned the letter
over and wished more writing would appear on the opposite side,
but the statement was complete as he had read it. He returned it to

its sacred envelope, replaced it between the pages of Hawthorne's book, and slipped the book once again behind the dresser clock, which ticked infernally.

Herman resumed washing his face. Malcolm stirred. Lizzie sat up in bed and stretched and yawned.

Herman and Lizzie descended the stairs, Lizzie bouncing Malcolm against her chest. When they reached the dining room, they found a package waiting for Herman on the table, and his heart leapt yet again. The dominoes of fate tumbled so quickly once the first had fallen. The package was addressed to the "Literary Lion of Lenox," in care of "Admiral Herman Melville" at Broad Hall, and it was rather larger than Herman had expected, a hefty cube wrapped in brown paper and twine. The twine crisscrossed the bundle in helter-skelter patterns, as if a mad spider had spent all its silk in a fit of drunken pique, and knots abounded, five times more knots than were required—butterfly knots, bowline loops, figure eights, constrictors, sheepshanks, square knots, and half hitches. The absurd configurations were Duyckinck's joke, a way of poking fun at Herman's ceaseless aggrandizements of the "ways of the sailor," and Herman fingered the loops and cinches appreciatively, all neatly and expertly tied: he admired nothing more than an elaborate and carefully executed joke. He hefted the package by the twine and it held together splendidly, even while the individual books shifted and strained against their paper wrapping.

On the table beneath the package, Herman discovered two copies of the latest *Literary World*; he set Hawthorne's books aside and flipped to his own review of *Mosses*, which he scanned for typographical errors. It was remarkably clean, considering how quickly Duyckinck had rushed it to press, and the rest of the issue was similarly of the moment—he must have assembled it on the train, Herman thought, and stayed up all that night setting it. His heart swelled with pride.

Lizzie went into the kitchen and fanned the fire in the stove. "Would you like oats or eggs, Herman?"

"I believe I'll head out to Lenox," Herman said. "I promised to deliver these books as soon as they came."

"Without breakfast?"

"I'll have a crust of bread and then saddle Lollie. Robert won't mind. I'll post our letter to your father on the way."

"I have been thinking about that letter," Lizzie said. "I don't think we ought to send it."

"But surely the next thing to do is ask your father for an advance," said Herman, panicking. "How else could we even begin to look for a house, without knowing the means available to purchase one?"

"I agree. But I think the letter is dishonest."

"Dishonest?" Herman cried.

"Maybe not dishonest, precisely. When we wrote it, I thought the idea of taking on more debt was utterly foolish, and I feel that the version we've written reflects my prejudice against the idea. I wrote it just to please you. But it is the wrong approach, because we have told him only the benefits of such a move to us and Malcolm. I believe we ought rather to explain how it might help our whole family—both of our families."

"Oh." Herman was perplexed, and pleased. "You sound more favorably disposed."

"Let me make you a cup of tea."

Herman set Duyckinck's magazine back on the table. The Sirens were singing celestial odes of Hawthorne in Herman's ears, piercingly beautiful songs beckoning him to Lenox; but he saw the possibility of crashing against the rocks, as well, and he recognized that it would be better to lash himself to the mast for the duration of a breakfast than destroy himself through foolish haste. Destroying oneself, he thought ruefully, should always be done at a deliberate pace.

"Yes, yes, of course," said Herman. "Forgive me—how foolish. Tea!" With superhuman effort, he sat down at the table and resigned himself to breakfast and an hour's delay, a most melancholy hour set against the projected joy of seeing Hawthorne's face again—but as anguished as he felt at this suspension of pleasure, he knew that the hour before him would ultimately provide richer happiness than he had ever known before, if Lizzie had decided to supplicate her father earnestly for help.

"I believe your next book could be successful—there is no reason it should not be—but we must think about something of lasting benefit that our entire family could count on, in proposing such a new expense, in the event that people do not buy your book in great quantities."

The idea offended Herman's vanity, but he saw the wisdom in it: what might Judge Shaw receive in this bargain, if Herman bankrupted himself as Robert had? "Well, if we bought a farm—"

"Yes, I know," Lizzie said. "You could plant us each a row of corn."

"What did you have in mind, then?"

"What if we offered our home as a place for my father to retire? When he's ready, he and my stepmother might come to live with us, and we could care for them in the same way we care for your mother now. Might we not find a home spacious enough for my parents to have a room of their own, just as you said each of the other family members might have?"

"Yes," he cried, with triumphant relief. How crazily his emotions whirled and pounded. "Let it be so!"

"And I could offer to bring our best heirlooms, our antiques, to the Berkshires, to furnish our home—we would have them for our practical use now, and my father could still enjoy them on visits and then when he retires."

"Indeed," Herman cried again. "Very sensible!" He pounded the table.

Lizzie said, "I thought that, after breakfast, we could rewrite the letter together, and I know my father would think much more favorably of it than the letter we wrote before."

"Wonderful, thank you, Lizzie." He stood up and kissed her cheek. "But you should not worry yourself about the prospects of my next book. It will be such a success that we'll build a whole wing on our new house for your parents."

Lizzie poured them each a cup of tea and gave him plates to set on the table. He sat down again and placed his hand on Hawthorne's package. The morning air blistered Herman's skin with happiness.

"Eggs or oats, then?"

"Eggs."

Herman's mother would soon be down, and when they told her that they were thinking of buying a house here, a predictable battle of wills would begin between Lizzie and Maria, especially when Maria learned that Judge Shaw might tip the balance of power in their household toward Lizzie—but none of that mattered now. Lizzie fried eggs and made oats for Malcolm and tried out different phrases that they might use in their letter; and Herman waxed poetic about the beauty of the Berkshires, thinking of botanicals in the woods roundabout that might especially please the judge. He ate quickly and then fed Malcolm while Lizzie wrote a new letter to her father, and in no time at all, he was out in the barn saddling Robert's horse.

At the Pittsfield Post Office, Herman pressed the letter to Judge Shaw between his hands in a gesture of prayer and then handed it reverentially to the clerk. Once it was out of his hands, he felt giddy and light. He stopped at the apothecary's and collected the small box that awaited Hawthorne there—an extraordinarily heavy white box that fit in the palm of Herman's hand—and then set off at a canter for Lenox. An occasional cool breeze relieved the oppressive swelter of summer; but the bluebottles and mosquitoes that pestered Robert's horse found Herman, as well, and he swatted and smacked his own skin, balancing Hawthorne's package precariously in front of him, a loop of its crazy twine lassoed around the saddle horn. He tried to absorb all the details of the landscape between Broad Hall and Lenox afresh, using a sailor's trick that he had learned from a Tahitian harpooner: instead of looking—actively directing his gaze to various points around him—he simply opened his eyes and saw, allowing the natural functioning of his orbs to convey images to his mind. In this manner, concentrating on removing all judgment from his impressions, he prevented himself from becoming anxious about his journey to Hawthorne and instead made a passive, moment-by-moment record of the sights and sounds of the day. This trick had always proved especially useful when, after many weeks on the high seas, out of sight of land, a ship's captain would announce that they were bound for a port yet many days away, and to check the painful impatience of anticipation, it became necessary to live entirely in the moment. Herman now blanked his mind and trotted along as if he had many leagues yet to travel.

He inhaled the sweet musky smell of his horse's sweat and observed chipmunks darting beneath logs in the shade of the woods along the road. He stopped bothering about the flies buzzing their fanatical patterns around his head, even allowing mosquitoes to land on his hands and drink their fill, a blood sacrifice of thanks to the gods. By the time he crested the hill above Lake Mahkeenac and saw Hawthorne's diminutive two-story cottage, set like a dusky ruby in the shoreside meadow, he had become as calm as Buddha staring down eternity. He clopped right up to the waist-high white picket fence and stopped, remaining mounted, taking in the scene of Hawthorne's domicile in silence.

A little dirt path, bordered by white stones, led to Hawthorne's small, charming porch, which sheltered the white-painted front door. To the left of the red cottage, a garden of tomatoes and lettuces and leafy greens grew in neatly weeded rows of black loam; to the right, a single chicken pecked about in the grass below an oak, whose canopy partially shaded the cottage; and beyond the oak, toward a thick stand of tangled woods that guarded the lake, monarch butterflies flitted and danced around a patch of wintercress with wispy yellow flowers that seemed artfully and intentionally strewn in a pattern of careless beauty. A woodpecker rapped noisily from the woods, providing off-kilter rhythm for the squeaky-wheel cries of warblers. The thick, earthwormy smell of mud wafted up from the lake.

Herman heard footsteps within the cottage, and the door opened abruptly. "Hello, it must be Mr. Melville, is it not?"

Sophia Hawthorne, the slight, brunette wife of the Literary Lion, stepped out onto the porch and walked briskly up the path. She wore her hair in the current fashion, parted severely down the middle, where gray hairs intermixed with dark brown; with each step she took, her curls bounded below her ears like springs. She wore a plain, blue cotton dress, fringed with white lace. Herman dismounted some-what awkwardly, due to the bulk of the books he had come to deliver, and Sophia gave him a frank, warm handshake.

"Mr. Duyckinck sent along these books," he said.

"Of course, of course. We've been expecting you!"

Herman had folded a copy of *Literary World* into the knotted twine and wrapping paper, and now he withdrew it and offered it to Sophia. "And I've brought along a copy of the latest *Literary World*, which has an article on your husband."

"I know, isn't it marvelous? I've only just finished reading it. Mr. Longfellow gave us a copy when he came up from New York earlier today."

Herman was disappointed that he'd been beaten to the punch,

but he nevertheless waited expectantly for Sophia to praise him for the review. They stared at one another. "Did you notice who wrote the article?" he asked.

"Yes, and isn't it the queerest byline you ever read? We have been puzzling over it all morning."

Herman fired open the magazine and found his article: indeed, the byline read not Herman Melville but rather "A Virginian Spending the Summer in Vermont." His first feeling was blind rage; but then he realized that Duyckinck must have published it anonymously in order to leave in the bits about Shakespeare and the germinous seeds. He glanced over the article again and found every one of the wildly flattering things he had said about Hawthorne, which could not properly be called literary and could conceivably bring an unpleasant backlash from readers—an idea he had not considered when writing it. Perhaps Duyckinck was simply protecting him; then so be it, he thought. It would give him the chance to surprise Hawthorne by revealing the author's true identity, in person.

Herman tied Lollie to the fence, and Sophia ushered him into the little cottage. A short entrance hall offered access to a narrow, crudely constructed staircase leading to the second floor. Below the staircase, to the right, two doors opened, one into a bedroom and the other into a tiny parlor. Sophia led him to the door on the left and into the parlor. The whole building would have fit snugly into one wing of Broad Hall, and the parlor, which apparently also served as a dining room and kitchen, was smaller than the bedroom Herman and Lizzie shared.

"Let me get you a cup of water," said Sophia. "And would you like to wash a little? I could fill a basin. Oh, I've completely forgotten myself. I should tell you that Nathaniel has taken the children for a walk along the lake. They should be back any moment. He'll be so happy to see you."

Herman reached into his pocket, withdrew the box he had received from the apothecary, and handed it to Sophia. "What weighs so much in such a small package, if you don't mind my asking, Mrs. Hawthorne?"

"Don't let's stand on formalities, Mr. Melville, please call me Sophia, it will make me so much more comfortable."

"Very well, call me Herman."

She opened the box and showed Herman a stack of charcoal gray magnets. "They're for my headaches, you see. I have the most alarming headaches from time to time, and I've tried everything to cure them and just don't know what else to do. Short of mesmerism, this is my last idea, and Nathaniel won't countenance mesmerism."

"Have you considered opium?"

"Yes, before I went to Cuba, I used opium, and laudanum, too, but they're rather expensive."

"And what took you to Cuba?"

"I was a governess there for a short time, but really my family sent me in the hope that the tropical sun would work a cure on my poor head. The doctors don't know what to do with me, I'm afraid. *Conoces Cuba?*"

"I've never been there, no, but I met some Spanish sailors from Havana on a whaler several years ago."

"Ah, yes," said Sophia, with a dreamy, faraway look. "Whaling. How violent!" She went to the dining table, which was pushed up against the far wall of the parlor, and poured Herman a cup of water from a glazed white pitcher. Then she poured some more water into a wooden bowl. She held up the magnets and said, "I'll just put these away and leave you for a moment to refresh yourself," and she went out to the entrance hall and up the stairs.

Herman set Hawthorne's package on the table, drank down the entire cup of water, and then splashed his face with cool water from the bowl. He ran his wet hand up and down the back of his sweaty neck and combed his hair with his fingers, while he examined Hawthorne's main room. Four dining chairs were pushed awkwardly under the table in the corner—he guessed that they pulled it out and rearranged the other furnishings for every meal. In the center of the north wall was a potbellied stove, and next to the stove a small cabinet contained cookware, dishes, cutlery, and serving plates. Across the room, below the generous front window, a pair of easy chairs faced each other; a table in between held an oil lamp. Low bookcases lined the walls on either side of the chairs. No portraits or decorations of any kind hung on the walls; it seemed the most humble and blank room in the world, a place where every emotion would have to be invented anew in order to be felt at all.

When he had finished washing, he unconsciously reverted to the manners of a sailor and wiped his hands on his pants. Sophia descended again with steps so light that the stairs barely registered a creak.

"So you read the review in *Literary World*, as well?" Sophia said.

"I did," said Herman. He took a moment to appraise Sophia more closely, as a rival. She was no great beauty, but her elfin ears lent her an otherworldly air, as did the oddly detached curiosity in her eyes—as if her human form were merely an instrument she had borrowed in order to convey her observations of earth to angels, spirits, and ghosts.

"I do so wonder who it is, this so-called Virginian in Vermont. Is it some kind of joke? Who on earth could possess such a rich heart and be so fine and fearless and full of such astonishing intuitions and not wish to be known? It's quite a mystery. And if I may say so without seeming too full of pride, I think this Virginian is the first person, in print, to say what I myself, in my secret mind, have often thought about Nathaniel's spiritual kinship to Shakespeare. I fear that in other ways, though, this person has misapprehended Nathaniel."

"Misapprehended how?"

Sophia took up a copy of *Literary World*, found the passage she was looking for, and unwittingly read Herman's own words aloud to him: "'Where Hawthorne is known, he seems to be deemed a pleasant writer, with a pleasant style—a sequestered, harmless man, from whom any deep and weighty thing would hardly be anticipated—a man who means no meanings.'" She looked up. "Despite the wealth of brilliance the reviewer brings to his interpretations of Nathaniel's stories, he seems never to have heard of him before or understand the fame and controversy that have followed his recent work. It seems a direct contradiction to compare Nathaniel with Shakespeare and then call him a pleasant writer who means no meanings. And if you ask for Nathaniel around Salem, you will find impressions of him there anything but harmless, after *The Scarlet Letter*."

Herman felt chagrined that he had dashed the review off so hastily, and he wondered now what he could possibly have been thinking when he wrote that sentence. He wondered if, rather than flattering Hawthorne, he might instead have found myriad ways of offending him. "I think I can clear up this misunderstanding rather easily," he said. "You see, the reviewer had simply never been acquainted with Mr. Hawthorne before; and, while he was writing this review, he asked a few acquaintances for their ideas of his early work. He was speaking of the impression one might have of Hawthorne if one had read only the surface meanings of his earlier stories."

Sophia considered this for a moment. "How can you speak with such authority about the intentions of this anonymous gentleman, Herman?"

"In fact, I'm on the most intimate terms with him." Herman had imagined confessing his secret to Nathaniel, but somehow Sophia's critique and the crack it opened in his confidence made him want to tell her first, to test the waters.

"You must tell me who it is, Herman, at once."

Herman made a low, sweeping bow and then stood back up with an embarrassed grin. "At your service."

"You? But . . . a Virginian? Vermont? I'm afraid I don't understand it."

"I think Mr. Duyckinck felt uncomfortable with some of my views regarding your husband and Shakespeare, and perhaps publishing the review anonymously allowed him to feel more at liberty to print them."

Sophia thought about this for a moment. "I'm afraid that makes no sense at all, but nevermind—what an extraordinary review, Herman! Was it all true, I mean, are these your true opinions of Nathaniel's work?"

"Very much, though I see now that I failed to do him justice regarding the particulars and may have antagonized him with many thoughtless turns of phrase. But I don't believe America has produced a finer or nobler intellect. If I may speak confidentially, however, I have not read the novel that has recently won him so much praise and fame, so I feel that I still may not have plumbed his deepest depths."

"Well, you must read it immediately. Wait here and I'll fetch you a copy!" Sophia ran upstairs, and in only a few moments she had raced back into the parlor with a copy of *The Scarlet Letter*. "I believe you will find this even better than anything that has come before, and I cannot wait to have your opinions about it. I am always so dazzled by the jewels of beauty in Nathaniel's productions that I look forward to a second reading almost as much as the first; but most of all I enjoy pondering and musing on his work with a friend. Oh, and I almost forgot to tell you—I have just espied Nathaniel and the children from the upstairs window, tramping up from the lake. They're practically upon us."

She turned and rushed out the front door, and Herman saw her through the window running down the hill toward the lake. Just at the edge of a fantastically tall screen of Buffalo grass, Sophia met Hawthorne and their two children: the steepness of the hill in that spot made Hawthorne seem to materialize out of the earth itself. Sophia gestured excitedly as she talked, and Hawthorne put his hand over his eyes to shade his view toward the cottage; and now, as Herman felt Hawthorne's gaze on the window where he stood, like a pressure against the quivering glass, the invisible winged creatures that had frolicked around Herman's head that morning reappeared and fluttered the air out of his lungs. He sipped little breaths, set *The Scarlet Letter* on the table, and walked out to greet the family, feeling as if, at any moment, he might take flight.

"So you are the Virginian," Hawthorne said by way of greeting, betraying no surprise whatsoever at this news. Despite the heat of the day, his high alabaster brow appeared cool and dry. He shook Herman's hand, holding his gaze, and Herman fell irresistibly into the depths of that vast inward sea of Hawthorne's dark eyes, where leviathans of thought and emotion swam like gods in the secret fissures at the center of the world. Sophia brought her hands together in front of her heart, as if in prayer, and Julian walked boldly up to Herman and threw his arms around his right leg. Una, their daughter, stood off at a distance, viciously swiping at the grass with a switch.

"I can shout and squeal," said Julian.

"Please don't, though, young master," Hawthorne replied.

"We are electing to be idle," Julian shouted, and then he squealed and ran into the house.

Sophia said, "That sounds like a phrase you taught him, dear."

"Yes. But, in fact, he is never idle."

Hawthorne let go of Herman's hand and took Sophia's. Herman shook inwardly with waves of joy and jealousy as Nathaniel and Sophia swung their conjoined hands and sauntered toward the cottage. He was dragged in their wake by the force of Hawthorne's spiritual weight, and Una came silently behind him. When they had all crossed the threshold, the children ran upstairs together, and Sophia paused a moment before following them up, to point out the package of books and to remind her husband that they owed Herman a dollar and a half.

"Let's see if Duyckinck found all the books I wanted," Hawthorne said with an easy smile.

Herman saw, in the older man's angelic face and blithe manner, a battlefield where anguish had once contended with beauty and—neither proving victorious—each had lain down its arms and declared peace together. He felt Hawthorne's hard-won serenity spreading into his own soul, and his abiding social discomfort evaporated like fog in the morning sun. For the first time in his life he felt perfectly at ease just standing and doing nothing; and he thought he could stay that way forever, as long as Hawthorne continued to smile at him.

Hawthorne took out a pocketknife. "Are the knots a joke on you or by you?"

"Duyckinck is the jester, in this case."

He cut a perfectly constructed butterfly knot away from the rest of the twine and placed it behind his ear for a garland; then he ripped away a section of the wrapping paper and began withdrawing volumes from the packet one by one, handing them to Herman as he read the titles aloud. "*Mardi*, excellent. *Typee. Redburn*, yes. *Omoo. White-Jacket*, tremendous." Herman found himself standing in the middle of Hawthorne's parlor holding a copy of every book he had ever written. "And finally a copy of *Pendennis*. I hope you don't mind being lumped together with Thackeray."

"You ordered every one of my books!"

Hawthorne looked commandingly at him. "I had to know what it was all about," he said.

"What *what* was all about?"

"The picnic. What kind of person had such insight about me that he could make me feel known just by talking to me!"

"But these books," Herman said, despairing. "Please do not judge me by them. They are not me. They were the best I could do at the time."

"I have read *Typee* already, of course," Hawthorne said, unconcerned. "I wrote a review of it, for the Salem *Advertiser*, when it first came out." He put his hand on Herman's shoulder. "No one knows the relative value of one's own previous work better than I do. I have not asked for these books in order to judge you by them, but in order to learn about you."

Herman's mouth had gone completely dry. He tried to formulate a thought suitable to be spoken, but even had one occurred to him, he doubted whether his brain still had any control over his tongue. Una's and Julian's light footsteps rat-a-tatted overhead, and Herman looked around, alarmed that Sophia might see them inclined toward one another so intimately.

"You know, Herman, I'm not convinced of this blackness ten times black that you see in me, that you talked about in your review. That's how you put it, isn't it?"

"Yes," he said, feeling foolish now for every word he had written in *Literary World*—for every word he had ever written. The easy philosophical banter that they had shared when they'd first met seemed a childish memory; Hawthorne had reduced him to mere reverence. He cleared his throat. "Perhaps I should have said that, in your stories, blackness competes with blackness, which would have been a better way to put it." He swallowed hard and willed his composure to come back. "Because, in your stories, you seem to understand that true dramatic moments come not when a character must choose between right and wrong but when he must choose between two wrongs."

Hawthorne looked quizzically at his younger companion and said, almost to himself, "Two wrongs. Indeed." He finally took his hand from Herman's shoulder as Sophia's footsteps pounded down the stairs. As she entered, Hawthorne asked, "What was that business about the Virginian spending July in Vermont?"

"I don't know, really."

Hawthorne took the stack of novels out of Herman's hands and set them on the table. Then he reached into his pocket and counted out a dollar and fifty cents in coins and placed them in Herman's palm. "Thank you again. Won't you have some wine and stay for lunch?" Herman looked from Nathaniel to Sophia, both of their faces eager and open.

"Yes," said Sophia. "We don't have much in the house at the moment, but I can send Una to Mrs. Tappan's for a loaf, and we'll pick some vegetables from the garden."

"I'm afraid I must be going." The words surprised Herman even as they came out of his mouth; but the moment he uttered them, he recognized their truth. He could not simultaneously remain here in this cottage and also stay in his own body: he felt as if his heart might burst out of his chest and scurry bleeding across the floor.

"Don't be ridiculous," said Hawthorne. "You've only just arrived."

Herman found that he was bathed in sweat. He felt strangely indignant, though he could find no reason to be. He seemed exotic to himself, and he wanted to be showered in sunlight and covered in dirt and have a bird's nest built in his hair, where newly hatched chicks could screech out the thoughts in his head. He certainly could not sit and make polite conversation over lunch, no matter how much wine they poured, and he knew that the moment he began talking of his review or Hawthorne's writing or God forbid Hawthorne himself, he would sacrifice himself on the altar of indiscretion and love.

Could not Sophia read, even now, his great affection for her husband, written in such large letters across his face?

"You see," Herman said, "we have just decided to move to the Berkshires, and my wife and I are looking for a house today."

"Why, how exciting," said Sophia.

Hawthorne took a great breath and exhaled it completely before offering his hand to Herman, all the while holding his gaze. They shook hands awkwardly at first, out of rhythm with one another, and they kept on shaking until their hands made a few simple oscillations together.

"It's lovely, this area, isn't it?" Nathaniel said. Now he placed his other hand over Herman's and simply held it. Herman glanced sidelong at Sophia, who smiled as if she remarked nothing at all inappropriate.

"Beyond lovely," Herman said.

"Well, thank you for taking the trouble to come all this way, then, when you are so busy," said Hawthorne. He finally let go of Herman's hand. "When you have found a place to live and settled yourself, please come back and stay for a day or two. Maybe by then I will have finished reading your books, and we'll have a great deal more to talk about."

Herman said that he would do so and started for the door. Sophia stopped him and handed him the copy of *The Scarlet Letter* that she had given him before, and Hawthorne made a show of taking the butterfly knot from behind his ear and placing it in the front of the book. The tenderness with which he made this gesture seemed absolutely shameless to Herman, but Sophia seemed barely even to notice it.

Herman was soon back upon Robert's horse and waving goodbye to Una and Julian, who watched him go from their upstairs window.

Nathaniel and Sophia stood by their white picket fence, arm in arm, and watched him go, watched him all the way up the path to the crest of the hill above the lake. As he turned and waved a last goodbye, he saw the children running out of the house to join their parents in front of the cottage, and he heard them yell three "Hip! Hip! Hoorays!" and wave at him in frantic celebration, as if he were a newly christened ship pushing out to sea.

When he was out of sight, he dismounted and sat by the roadside for a long time, light-headedly replaying every moment that had just passed at Hawthorne's cottage. How he wished he hadn't insisted on leaving. Why had he done that? How he wished he could feel the warmth of Hawthorne's smile on his face right then. Could he return now? No, there would be time yet, time to channel all of the indiscreet emotions crashing through his soul, time to become accustomed to being in Hawthorne's presence without the constant airy distress of exaltation. What a buffoon he felt. They seemed so happy together, Nathaniel and Sophia, and yet Hawthorne was probably sitting alone in his parlor at that very moment reading Melville's books. What clearer signal could Hawthorne have given him?

Herman stared up at his cousin's horse in a maelstrom of joy and confusion. Lollie flicked her mane.

Chapter 6

A Sort of Confession

Two days later, Herman and Lizzie received a letter from Judge Shaw approving their plan, along with bank drafts in the amount of three thousand dollars as an advance on Lizzie's inheritance.

Herman's first reaction was unadulterated joy: the four winds of the world sounded a melody so sublime in his ears, with harmonies so rich and sonorous, that he knew the angels themselves were singing the hosannas of his love for Hawthorne, and he heard a thousand sprites take up the tune and relay it through the woods and thickets to Lenox. He felt regal and happy. They would soon be living in the Berkshires. Lizzie waved her father's letter giddily at Malcolm, a few feet away in his crib, and Malcolm caught their enthusiasm and waved back. Herman felt acutely aware of his own mortality in a way that made him delirious with joy.

His second reaction was panic. His manuscript was no more commercial or finished than it had been before, he had no other prospects for income, and almost all of the money in his bank account had already been loaned to him by Judge Shaw. He was grateful that the judge felt favorably inclined toward the prospect of having a Berkshires manse in the family, but unless Shaw planned to retire to it in the next six months, Herman would still have to pay its keep.

Herman and Lizzie spent the next few days making inquiries into available properties, following up advertisements in the Pittsfield *Sun*, spreading the word among Robert's neighbors; and Herman kept his mother busy writing letters to the rest of the family to announce the

news of their move. Herman's brother Allan, with whom they shared
their apartment in Manhattan, was shocked. In his letters responding
to this sudden announcement, he criticized Herman for not informing him before the decision had been made, since the move so clearly
affected the entire family; and he worried that he would not be able to
afford the apartment on his own income once Herman left. Moreover,
they had no plan for dividing the household items they shared, and
Allan noted rather caustically that his wife had just had a baby and
that they had been counting on their mother's help. Why was Herman upending their family so rashly, and with no increase in his income or prospects? Allan's anger showed even in the slant of his
handwriting.

In every conversation with home sellers, lawyers, and agents,
Herman negotiated terms as if he were an ancient Persian shah with
dynastic treasures to trade. He buried his fears beneath his bluster
and made long speeches about the nobility of becoming a gentleman
farmer, and he became lighthearted with his entire family and solic-
itous toward Lizzie; only Robert remained unpersuaded by Herman's optimistic rhetoric, having just failed at exactly the enterprise
Herman now proposed for himself. Herman, as usual, failed to notice Robert's sadness and mystification.

After a week of searching, Herman and Lizzie had visited every
one of the properties that had been advertised in the most recent *Sun*
and a few others that had reached them through the grapevine, and
they had found nothing suitable. Most of the houses in their price
range were too small or too near the train depot or too decrepit, with
structural problems that were all too easy to discern. Their ideal was
Broad Hall itself, though Judge Shaw had agreed to advance them
only three thousand dollars total, which would be nothing more than
a down payment on such an estate—not to mention that they would

have to live off the money that was left over from the purchase at least until Herman finished his book, reducing their options even further. Just when they were expanding their search to nearby towns (Herman's heart thrilled when he saw a notice for a hundred-acre farm in Stockbridge, directly over the hill from Lenox), they unexpectedly discovered that the property immediately adjacent to Broad Hall was for sale.

John Brewster, a doctor whose family had lived next door to the Robert Melvilles for decades, had heard that Herman was in the market for a house. He called on them one evening, just after dinner, as a pewter half-moon was rising in the sky; and he found most of the family enjoying the evening breeze on Broad Hall's front porch.

Dr. Brewster was a wiry, gray-headed man in middle age, with seemingly too little skin for his face—it stretched tightly over his skull, like a mummy's. He wore unfashionably roomy tan riding pants and spoke with a flinty, nasal voice and clipped vowels, so that even his everyday pleasantries sounded unsympathetic. Herman remembered Brewster from his visits to Broad Hall in his youth, when Herman and Robert would skim stones on his pond and catch his chickens for sport. After greeting the Melville family and making polite inquiries about everyone's health, Brewster said, "You must come see my farm again, Herman," and he took a seat on the porch.

Brewster described the property he had come to offer for sale: the house dated from the Revolutionary War, when it had been the main tavern in Pittsfield. Brewster had commissioned its barn from the Shakers in Hancock; and its one hundred sixty acres of land included forest, streams, grazing pastures, and berry patches, in addition to farmland that produced thirty bushels of oats per acre and forty bushels of beans.

"And you have walked through my property many times, my

dear Herman, and taken a good many fish from my streams in years past, with your uncle and cousin, so you would have the advantage of already knowing the estate."

"Of course, the house is smaller than Broad Hall by a good deal," Robert said. "And Broad Hall has two hundred fifty acres."

"Yes, yes, it's smaller," Dr. Brewster cackled. "But size isn't everything, whether in houses or in whales." Brewster winked. "Dr. Holmes told me that you were writing about your whaling adventures, Herman. Well, if it interests you at all, come by tomorrow and I'll show you inside the house—we've expanded the parlor since you've seen it and added a porch—and we'll take a walk around the whole property, so I can show you its legal boundaries."

Robert said, "I had no idea you were even thinking of selling, John."

"We've been talking of moving to Boston for some time now, and I'm thinking of teaching a class at Harvard, since Dr. Holmes has recommended me for faculty." The doctor winked again at Herman and stood up. "To be honest, I wouldn't think of selling it now, Robert, if it weren't a relation of yours, and I've known Herman since he was a boy, so I could feel good about it. The hand of fate sometimes nudges us along."

"Fate," Herman said.

"Maybe if we can come to terms quickly, it will serve all of our interests. A bit of serendipity, one might say."

"Serendipity," said Herman.

"Yes, some coincidences are more than mere chance."

"Yes, chance. Coincidence!" Herman leapt to his feet. "Destiny!" He shook the doctor's hand.

"Well, come by around ten o'clock tomorrow, and we'll talk some more." He walked with a quick, purposeful gait off the porch, around the corner, and back down the road to his farm.

"Be careful, Herman," said Robert. "Dr. Brewster is a good man and a family friend, but he's shrewd, and his price often has more to do with what he wants than what things are worth. His property is mostly swamps and forest, you'll remember."

"Of course," Herman blustered, thinking, contrarily, that the doctor's estate—which he knew like a half-remembered dream from his boyhood—was so ideal that the price barely weighed into the bargain. "Swamps and forests!"

Robert said, "I sold Broad Hall for six thousand dollars, Herman— a fair price, but lower than I would have accepted under more propitious circumstances—and I want you to remember that figure, because Dr. Brewster's farm is far less desirable. Do you understand?"

"Mortgages," Herman said, "are the devil's own contracts and must be calculated in souls and not sovereigns, so I will certainly take care."

As he said this, though, Herman was estimating the number of steps from Dr. Brewster's house to Hawthorne's front porch, and he immediately launched into a rhapsody on the many advantages of Brewster's farm, beginning with the solidity of the home itself and taking in everything from the blackberry brambles to the barn to the streams he had fished as a boy. And it was already a working farm, capable of providing income from crops and animals: the estate could solve many problems at once.

Robert looked at Herman with disgust. "Do you take nothing I say to heart? Brewster sees you as an opportunity for profit! He has never talked of selling before and would not do so now if you didn't seem such an easy mark."

"Of course, Robert, of course," Herman said. "I have negotiated with cannibals in foreign tongues and Arabian sea captains and French criminals. I have bartered with demons and angels! I am not about to let a country doctor take advantage of me. But would it not be fanciful to move in next door? Is that stream that runs near the

Methodist church the same one that goes through Dr. Brewster's property?" Robert reluctantly confirmed that it was. "And do you remember that gnarled oak that we used to swing from when we were children, when your father took us hunting? Is that not the very one at the edge of Dr. Brewster's patch today?" Robert nodded. "It will be almost like being a child again."

"Need I remind you, Herman," Robert said, "that this very home, whose porch you sit on, is my *actual* childhood home, and that being like a child again is the most painful thing I can imagine right now, when I am about to leave my home forever?"

Robert jumped up from his chair and stormed across the porch, leapt over the steps, and ran down the road toward town.

Herman felt as if a pleasant dream he had been having had unexpectedly turned foul. He looked without recognition at the faces of his family, and then he looked at his own hands, which he held up to his eyes as if they were covered with blood. He got down on one knee, grabbed two fistfuls of his own beard and said, seemingly to the air, "I'm so very sorry. Please forgive me. I've been a fool. I'm sorry!" Then he leapt up and ran into the dark after his cousin.

He sprinted flat out for a quarter of a mile before he spied Robert bent at the waist, breathing heavily, in the coal-dark shadow of a stately elm. The half-moon's dim light only intensified the gloom beneath the boughs of the tree. He rushed up to his cousin and grabbed him by the shoulders, and Robert spun around with his fists up, ready to fight. They panted at each other in pugilistic stances, until Robert saw that Herman was not merely winded but also weeping.

"I'm so sorry, Robert, so so sorry. Please forgive me. I am beside myself!"

The force of Herman's regret demolished Robert's resistance; he even started to wave away the need for an apology, but Herman's speech had not ended, and Robert was much more surprised by what came next. "I have completely forgotten myself—my mind is so clouded with confusion." Herman cried harder. "I did not mean to be inconsiderate of your feelings, I never have—I am so sorry—but I have met someone who makes me think that life can be different, and I have not been able to tell a soul. And yet I have not been able to hide my joy! I have been so selfish. You must forgive me. But don't you see?"

Until that moment, even Herman had not known that he'd wanted to confide in his cousin, but, in the sudden awareness of how much pain he was causing Robert, Herman had recognized his own despair at the impossibility of his love for Hawthorne: his true motives, his true joy, had to be veiled in the wretchedness of secrecy, when all he really wanted to do was shout his love to the heavens. He suddenly thought that, if Robert only knew the truth, he would understand and forgive his thoughtlessness, and then they would both be relieved of the exaggerated and unnecessary disquiet that Herman's otherwise inexplicable emotions had created all around him. Perhaps Robert would even be happy for him.

"What do you mean, met someone?" Robert said. "Who?"

"You and I have known one another since childhood, have we not?"

"Of course."

"Then I trust you to know what I mean when I say I've found a person who makes the world seem new, who truly understands me. That person lives here in the Berkshires, and that's why I need to be here. That's why. I have the feeling that I have not yet begun to unfold the inner flower of myself, but I believe I can do so now, with the help of this special person."

"The inner flower of yourself? Are you mad?"

"No. I am completely sane for the first time in my life."

"You're having an affair!"

"No!" said Herman. In the wan moonlight, he looked deeply into Robert's eyes and saw the dark kaleidoscope of his mind combining and recombining thoughts into colorfully useless patterns.

"Who is it? Does Lizzie know?"

"I haven't been able to tell a soul until now. I thought I would open my heart to you, so you would know why I've been so thoughtless. Selfish and thoughtless! Wrapped up in my own feelings. I'm very sorry. I wanted you to know the reason." Herman's pleading face betrayed equal parts faith and fear, like a whipped dog that still hopes for love.

"And the reason is that you've met someone and you're having an affair?"

Hearing Robert's disgusted, judgmental tone, Herman realized with dismay that a confession would not do, that he had been rash even to broach the truth. No, Robert did not understand him at all. Robert could never understand him. If he confessed his love for Hawthorne, Robert might even have him arrested. "No, I'm not having an affair! I've met someone who can help me, I believe, with my new book."

"What in the name of all that's holy are you talking about?"

Herman could not hide his disappointment in Robert for not discerning his true meaning, for not letting him unburden his secret. "I've met a new editor. A mentor."

"And that's why you're moving your family to Pittsfield and taking loans you cannot possibly repay?"

"Yes," said Herman. "Please forgive me for my callousness." He felt like an unlit jack-o'-lantern.

"Well, I suppose I don't understand the importance of a mentor to a writer such as yourself."

Tears continued to roll down Herman's face. In spite of Robert's bewilderment, he gave Herman a tremendous bear hug, and Herman leaned heavily into him. Robert said, "There, there. It will be all right," and he patted his cousin on the back and made little circles between his shoulder blades.

"On a whaleship, I was beset by danger and made to suffer daily indignities, which I weathered like a stoic; now, on dry land, I brim constantly with tears."

Herman stood upright again on his own two feet. He wished he could extinguish the monotonous moon.

"Do you remember when we used to go down to the pond behind old man Cooper's farm and catch tadpoles?" Robert asked.

"Of course."

"Do you want to walk there now?"

"Yes." He wiped his nose on his sleeve. "But we should tell our wives first. I've been inconsiderate enough for one evening. For one lifetime, perhaps."

"All right."

"Thank you, Robert." They walked back toward Broad Hall, their arms around each other's shoulders. "Please don't mention this to anyone. They would laugh at me."

"Because you cried? Or because you need a mentor?"

"Because I am not made of sterner stuff."

"But tell me, Herman, why must you take such drastic action, if it brings you such heartache? Why could you not mail your manuscripts back and forth to your new mentor from New York?"

"That is not the kind of help I need."

Herman could see his cousin mentally adjudicating their long history together, deciding how he would fit this episode into Herman's many "outlandish" outbursts in the past. Will Robert ever admit to himself what he must always have known about me? Herman thought. He searched Robert's eyes for a glimmer of true sympathy but found only a resigned capitulation to life as a Melville—a family of eccentrics, outcasts, and bankrupts.

"Tell no one," said Herman. "I beg of you."

"Very well. I promise I won't."

"I truly am sorry."

Herman continued to apologize for another minute until Robert finally insisted that he stop, and then Herman apologized for continuing to apologize. As they crested a little knoll and the yellow lamplight of Broad Hall's wide porch appeared below them, Herman stopped. The whole family was still outside, enjoying the evening, his mother knitting and rocking and saying something just at the edge of hearing. He would apologize to Robert's wife, and Lizzie, and his mother; he would apologize to everyone, as he always did eventually, but he longed for a time when he could stop being sorry—when he could be understood plainly. He stared past Broad Hall, into the dark night, toward Lenox.

Chapter 7

Arrowhead

The sky thundered and billowed all morning, but its promised rain still had not fallen by nine thirty, so Lizzie, Herman, and Maria set off to meet Dr. Brewster. Herman had been telling Lizzie stories of his childhood adventures on Brewster's farm all night and morning. As they walked, she pulled Herman aside, out of earshot of his mother, and reminded him that they had only three thousand dollars, and that Robert had said the farm might be worth two thousand. She further reminded him that it would be better if they spent something like one thousand or fifteen hundred on a house, so they would have a little extra money to live on, at least until his next book was published, and that the last house they had seen in town, a very modest home behind the dry goods store that needed only a few minor repairs, cost exactly fifteen hundred and might be better suited to their needs.

"Let us keep our budget in the forefront of our minds and not be carried away by grand notions or nostalgia," Lizzie said.

"Of course, of course," said Herman.

"There is no urgency to our move," she reminded Herman. "We have plenty of time to find a new home, one that is right and that we can afford. We are just visiting today."

"You are right, my dear. You must remember, though, that my mother and I have known Dr. Brewster for many years, and I am sure he has our mutual interests at heart."

Maria said, "Herman, you'll remember that Dr. Brewster once

whipped your cousin for stealing a rooster, and the rooster turned up the next minute in his own barn."

"We all make mistakes. And he did apologize."

"Remember, too, that Robert warned you to be wary of him," said Lizzie. "And Robert has lived next door to the man for decades. You've only ever seen him on holiday."

"I only mean to say that you are right, dear Lizzie, that we should not let ourselves be carried away by anything we see today. I simply dislike the idea of erecting defenses against a man who is proposing something of benefit to us, out of regard for our family. We should at least be open and hear what he proposes."

"Why is it that even when you agree with me, it feels as if we are quarreling?" Lizzie said.

Herman kissed his wife on the cheek. "Please forgive me, my dear. You are right."

They rounded the bend in the road above Brewster's farm at just before ten o'clock. As they approached, they saw a solid, unpretentious, pleasant two-story house right on the road, with a covered workshop, a Shaker-style barn, and animal pens standing behind it, all painted bright yellow with red trim. This little cluster of buildings stood atop a hill that sloped steeply away to the north: below their feet, as they looked out over the estate, bean fields almost glowed green in the storm-tempered morning light, and beyond the beans, at the very bottom of the slope, a line of chestnuts and maple trees marked the path of a stream.

They found Dr. Brewster waiting for them on a broad front porch made of fresh blond planks, which ran the entire length of the house. By way of a greeting, he said, "In summer, we like to sit here of a morning and say hello to people passing on the road, and you have a beautiful view of October Mountain." Without letting them even say good morning, the doctor launched into a history of the house, while he shook Herman's hand and bowed to the ladies. The main house, he said, had been built in the 1780s as a pub, and he walked off the porch and around the corner of the building, still talking. They followed.

"I built that workshop last autumn," he said, "and I added the loft window up there in the barn this summer. A Shaker gentleman from Hancock built the porch out front just a few weeks ago."

"It seems that you have been industriously renovating, Doctor," Maria said. "Almost as if you'd had an idea to sell the property already."

"On the contrary, Mrs. Melville, it's better to keep one's home in good repair, wouldn't you agree? Especially if one intends to live there a long while." The doctor's flinty tone made his remark seem angry, though he delivered it with a smile. "You see that bramble patch just beyond the meadow, on the other side of the stream?" asked Brewster. Herman strained his eyes to see. "Those are blackberries, and just beyond that is a marshy bit of cattails and spike grass, where ducks breed in the spring. See there? That's the edge of the property."

Lizzie looked up at the giant oaks and elms along the north side of the house. The trees would limit the natural lighting in the lower rooms all winter. The house was much smaller than Broad Hall, but it was still large enough to need more than one fireplace—yet only one chimney pierced the roof.

Dr. Brewster followed Lizzie's gaze up. "It's a central chimney, which opens out onto fireplaces in every room, on each floor." Then he pointed across the bean fields. "Normally you see Mount Greylock more clearly in that direction, but he's hiding his head in the storm clouds today."

They followed Brewster through an enclosed back porch and into the house. It was sturdily built and spotlessly clean, a no-nonsense colonial, with, as Brewster had promised, a grand central fireplace dominating the narrow dining room into which they now walked. A bright fire was burning. "We still use this hearth for cooking," Dr. Brewster said. "Though we've been meaning to install a stove in that corner." Lizzie looked skeptically at Herman: no stove. No proper kitchen.

Brewster led them into a well-appointed parlor, where family portraits hung on every wall, and beyond that into a more spacious sitting room. He pointed out the window to a loamy herb garden with parsley, rosemary, sage, and mint, bordered by yellow and white feverfew flowers.

They ascended the steps. The large upstairs bedrooms had ceilings nearly as high as the common rooms below and featured unusually wide windows. Herman was especially enamored of the bedroom with the view to the north: a writing desk was positioned below a large window gazing out toward Mount Greylock, and the desk held a copy of Herman's own last novel, *White-Jacket*. Herman picked up the book and thumbed through it meditatively, while Maria and Lizzie exchanged incredulous looks. "I sensed that you would like this room," Dr. Brewster said. "In fact, it's my own study now and would make a capital library, where you could read and write in peace." To the left of Brewster's desk was, to Herman's mind, the most curious feature of the whole house: a long, wide closet with a round window set in the wall, like a porthole. He remarked that the closet was wide enough to put a bed in, and the round window made it seem almost like a ship's captain's quarters.

They descended the stairs and went out into the south yard, an expanse of mown grass bordered by a hedge. Near the hedge was a low, lean-to woodshed, in front of which a rabbit was lazily loping along; when it spied them, it darted into the shrubs and disappeared.

Herman strode briskly across the lawn, picked up an axe, and split a log with one mighty swing.

Dr. Brewster pointed at the flat top of a little hill, where half a dozen white ash trees had grown in a circle. "The Mohicans used to bury their chiefs atop that hill. Captain Bush's son told me so when he sold me the property, and you can't turn a shovel in this whole area without digging up arrowheads." Herman's imagination mounted up and rode out across the estate: The vanquished Mohicans? Burbling streams? Bean fields and blackberry brambles? A two-story house with a Shaker-built barn? Brewster led them around the side of the barn to the pens, where a hog, a sow, and half a dozen piglets snorfed in a muddy cavity enclosed by a slatted fence.

Heavy raindrops began to fall, and the sky belched a thunderous rumble. Dr. Brewster suggested that the ladies adjourn to the parlor for a cup of tea, while he and Herman walked the western edge of the property, down the hill in the direction of Broad Hall.

"And where are your wife and family just now, Dr. Brewster?" asked Lizzie. "Are you alone on the farm?"

"They are visiting my mother in Boston. Mrs. Brewster and I spend more and more time there, you see, as my mother grows older and needs more help."

In the parlor, Brewster hung a pot of water from a rod above the fire and shook tea from a cloth sack into a teapot. He set out porcelain cups and a glass sugar bowl on a sideboard, and he told them to make themselves at home, while he and Herman "got their britches dirty in the thickets. Please indulge your curiosity about the house. We have no secrets here." Herman could not tell by the looks on their faces whether his mother and wife would continue their usual bickering while he was gone or establish a new amity inspired by Dr. Brewster's farm, but he was already beginning to feel at home

here; and as he and Brewster walked back outside, he peeped
around the corner of the house at the pigs, and he imagined planting
corn and wheat and squash in the fields below. Not only would it be
a pleasant place to write, but he might also feed his family by the
sweat of his brow instead of the toil of his pen. He felt the raindrops
plonking refreshingly down onto his head, and he asked Brewster
what sort of income he had from the farm.

"None to speak of. We dry the beans for our own use through
the winter, and we may slaughter a pig at Christmas, but my practice
in Boston keeps me too busy to farm the place the way it deserves. I
imagine you might improve it a great deal, if you were living here all
the year round."

Brewster led Herman past the well and several hundred yards
down the road to a skinny, white dirt path edged by a tiny rivulet,
which they followed through hemlock trees and red oaks, down a
little hill and through a thicket of woody undergrowth. The doctor
occasionally related some little historical trivia as they glimpsed the
meadows through the trees; but Herman was swept up in his own
boyhood memories of wandering this land, carefree and inquisitive,
and he barely heard a word the doctor said anymore. He remembered the long family vacation he had taken at Broad Hall when his
father and older brother, Gansevoort, were both still young and sane,
unbowed by the worldly woes that would chase them into their
graves: exploring the hollows and bluffs in these very hills; hunting
and fishing with his father, the whole world as fresh and new as he
had been himself back then. He breathed deep the storm-riven air,
fragrant with the sweet, bright smell of pine, and he imagined, as he
had in his youth, that Mohicans and Iroquois lurked behind every
tree. The heavy raindrops falling now seemed like exclamation
points on the happy shouts that he heard from his childhood. He
imagined leading Hawthorne on a walk down this very trail, and the

woods became spangled with the possibilities of a new life, in which the past and future swirled together into a timeless present filled with the unwearied freshness of love. How impressed Hawthorne would be! His tiny cottage in Lenox would make little more than an outbuilding on this farm. Hawthorne might even have his own room here when he visited, Herman thought: he could stay in the north room upstairs, in the closet with the porthole window just off the study, and they could talk privately there over brandy and cigars, while gazing out at Mount Greylock.

By the time Herman and Dr. Brewster had returned to the house, Herman had agreed to terms for the purchase of the estate; and in his mind, he was already living in the tall, grand, eighteenth-century home into which he now strode confidently to meet his wife and mother. Lizzie and Maria had moved from the kitchen into the parlor and were sitting at a table, staring silently into their teacups.

"Have you had a chance to explore the house any further, ladies?"

"We would have to bring our own hutches, I believe," said Maria. "Owing to the absolute want of closets and storage space."

Herman said, "Perhaps we could devote one of the upstairs bedrooms to wardrobes."

"We cannot simply stuff all of our clothes away out of sight," Lizzie said. "As if we were aboard a ship. And we could not afford to convert an entire room to storage in any event—the house barely has enough living space for our own family, let alone your sisters, to say nothing of my parents when they retire, to say nothing of everyone's belongings. It's completely unacceptable."

The doctor said that he was sure a solution could be found to the problem of storage. "The barn, for example, is too large for the number of animals we have, and it's well insulated. It could easily be partitioned."

"The barn?" Lizzie said, aghast.

Brewster said that he would be willing to leave behind his wife's chiffoniers for their clothing, to help ease the transition. Then he said that he would ride into town that afternoon to discuss the deed with his lawyer. "After that," he said, "it will simply be a matter of signing the deed over to you when you deposit the money in my bank."

"But, Doctor," Lizzie said, "we have not yet agreed to buy the property. We haven't even learned your terms."

"The doctor and I discussed everything on our walk," said Herman. "I will tell you all about it on the way back to Broad Hall."

"What on earth do you mean? Have you agreed to buy the farm, then? Without consulting me? Have you completely forgotten our conversation this morning? Have you forgotten that you said that the house we buy would be *mine*, and it would have room for my father and stepmother, which this house clearly does not?"

Herman looked an apology at the doctor. "Of course I haven't forgotten, my dear."

"This is *my* money, Herman. This is *my* money, Dr. Brewster!"

Herman cleared his throat and refused to meet Lizzie's eyes.

Brewster said, "We had not discussed where the money for the purchase would come from, Mrs. Melville. I would not want to sell you this property without a proper discussion and understanding, of course. I am happy to discuss all the terms with everyone involved."

"Of course, of course," said Herman, eager to get his wife and mother away from Dr. Brewster in order to avoid just such a discussion. He took Lizzie's hand and practically pulled her out of her seat. She banged her knee, toppling her cup and splashing the dregs of her tea across the table. "I will tell you everything, Lizzie, everything, when we can talk by ourselves. Anything we decide must be decided as a family!" Herman pounded his fist on the table, knocking over Maria's cup, as well.

Lizzie yanked her hand out of Herman's grasp. She stalked off, flung open the door, and charged out into the rain. Herman shook Dr. Brewster's hand violently and told him they would talk in the morning; and then he grabbed his mother's elbow, lifted her to her feet, and marched her as quickly as he could out through the dining room.

"Lizzie," Herman called. He was dragging his waddling mother by the arm. "Lizzie!"

Lizzie did not turn to face them and would not even slow her enraged pace until she had descended a long hill and rounded a curve, so that Brewster's farm was well out of sight. The hem of her dress was brown with mud, and she flapped her arms against her sides, as if she were a great flightless bird trying in vain to lift off. Herman continued to call her name.

"Will you let go of me, Herman?" Maria cried. "And stop shouting and making a spectacle of us. We can talk to Lizzie when we are back at Broad Hall."

Suddenly, Lizzie stopped in the middle of the road and turned to face them. She yelled, "Why would you not discuss this with me, Herman? Have you made him any promises?"

Herman waited until they had caught up to her to say, "Fifteen hundred down and the farm is ours. With the three thousand we have against your inheritance, we can give the down payment, pay off our other debts, and have enough money to live on until my next book is published. We can move into Brewster's farm three weeks from today and have money in the bank all winter."

"Fifteen hundred down against how much?"

"He has agreed to take our note."

"For how much?"

"Six thousand five hundred."

Lizzie nearly fainted.

"No, I misspoke. The note will be only five thousand, after our down payment."

"But that is more than Broad Hall! Why would you even think of that, Herman? Why didn't you heed Robert's warning?"

"We must remember that Robert has bankrupted his farm," Herman said. "His judgment is not sound. Truth be told, *we* have taken advantage of Brewster! His property is far better and worth far more than Broad Hall and has many superior advantages in terms of location and water and arable land, which Robert does not really understand."

Lizzie staggered to the ditch at the edge of the road and sat down on a large stone, with her shoes in a rivulet of muddy water. She put her elbows on her knees and held her head firmly in both hands. "How will we pay such a mortgage? It isn't possible. Tell me you haven't agreed to this." She looked down at the dirty hem of her dress. Herman said nothing. She struggled to her feet and continued walking, now in a desultory trudge.

Herman and his mother adopted Lizzie's gloomy pace; and despite Lizzie's wrath and Maria's silent but unmistakable censure, Herman's thoughts became more and more sanguine as they put the dreadful scene in Dr. Brewster's parlor further and further behind them. Lizzie would come around, he thought, as she always did—when they were all living in the Berkshires, they would not remember or care how it had happened or what it had cost. They would all get something they wanted from their new home. He pictured little Malcolm tottering through a field of clover behind the barn. Lizzie would settle in, happily, he imagined, to manage her own house. His mother would live in a country house again, instead of the cramped apartment that she had always detested. And his books would be successful again. Everything would come out well.

Herman thought how beautiful the Berkshires were in the rain, and how they would all take walks in the forest and have picnics down by the blackberry brambles. He heard birdsong through the splattering raindrops, and finally his thoughts turned once again to their true object: in his imagination, not only Hawthorne's namesake trees but every flowering and growing thing in view became a natural emblem of Hawthorne the man; every goldenrod flower and pickerel weed by the side of the road, every grouse and cardinal and chickadee they startled from the branches overhead became a sign of the inevitability of his present course, a course that ultimately led down this road to Lenox. Down this very road, he thought—a road that began in the mists of his childhood and ended in a little red cottage with a white picket fence.

"Herman," his mother said, spoiling his reverie.

"What is it, mother?"

"You should remember that your father-in-law is a judge, and that even *our* church makes provisions for divorce."

Herman stopped and met his mother's disapproving eyes, and then he let her walk down the road ahead of him. He began mentally crafting the letter of explanation that he would write to Judge Shaw the moment they got back to Broad Hall.

Chapter 8

Letters

My dear Melville,

I have read your works with a progressive appreciation of the quality of your writing and also of the author himself. No writer ever put the reality of poverty and isolation before the reader more unflinchingly than you do in Redburn, *and* White-Jacket *offers an impressively imagined and sympathetic view of the common navy sailor that I'm sure my own father would have approved.* Mardi *is a rich book, with depths here and there that compel a man to swim for his life—it is so good that I am willing to pardon you for not having brooded over it longer so as to make it a good deal better.* Typee *and* Omoo *seem much of a piece—as I mentioned to you previously, I wrote a favorable review of* Typee *when it first came out, for the Salem* Advertiser, *so I had vagabonded about these islands with you before, somewhat unwittingly. These books are lightly but charmingly and vigorously written, and I am acquainted with no other works that give freer or more effective pictures of barbarian life, in that unadulterated state of which so few specimens now remain. Your view especially of the Edenic beauty of the island men and women is voluptuously colored yet not more so than the exigencies of the subject appear to require, and you have a freedom of view—in some, it might even be called laxity of principles, my dear man!—which renders you tolerant of codes of morals that may be little in accordance with our own; an attitude that I would welcome exploring with you in more depth. I sense in these books, however, a development toward something which has not yet appeared from your pen, which is hinted at most in* Mardi *or perhaps in a combination of the approaches of* Mardi *and* Redburn, *I don't know; but I am loath to offer advice where none is asked. How near completion is this whaling romance you are working on now? Duyckinck says you have it almost finished. I would be most interested in having a peek at it, as you prepare it for the printers, since I am currently in thrall of the Melville way with words and I have run through all of his available books.*

yours,
Nath. Hawthorne

August 30, 1850
Pittsfield

My dear Hawthorne,

Farmers know that there are goodly harvests which ripen late, especially when the grain is strong; thus, my hope for my own writing. One might say that my corn has

*tasseled but not yet silked, and I feel that my latest
work, which I am calling* The Whale, *will not bring my
full maturity as a novelist any closer to harvest. It is too
like my earlier works, too whimsical, too realistic, too . . .
too . . . everything that I have said before and yet
something that I cannot name. And while I am most
appreciative of your flattering portrayal of my earlier
work, I do indeed ask for your advice about this new one,
which I hope you will give to me freely and frankly—for I,
too, feel that I am developing toward something more but
must find the mechanism to release it. I have enclosed a fair
copy of my whale manuscript, which my publisher tasks me
for even now and which I could call done, if I were not so
damnably sure that it merely repeats earlier books of mine
with less success.*

*I have bought a grand old house in Pittsfield,
Hawthorne! It is formerly a public house, built just
after the War for Independence, and I intend to make it
something of a public house again, where eminent
philosophers such as yourself may come and clink cups and
speak the language of the gods! When my new home is
rightfully and truly mine, you must inaugurate it—you
will be my first guest, a position which, once held, may
never be usurped!*

*your
Melville*

September 18, 1850
Lenox

My dear Melville,

I have been inspired by the prodigality of your literary
production. I am sitting down this very day to begin work on
a new romance, a fanciful story based upon the legend of a
curse and some entanglements that go along with it. But since
you have asked for my opinion of your own new romance The
Whale, I must tell you my recommendation before I wholly
lose myself in my own work.

I believe that you have here, in this version, a vision of
existence potentially much deeper than your story actually
satisfies in execution. Or, let me be more plain: you have the
opportunity in this work to swim in very deep, unknown, and
dangerous waters but have chosen to navigate instead along
the safe and well-known trade routes. Your story of the
friendship of Ishmael and Queequeg is pleasant and
amusing, but I believe that their story merely fulfills a wish of
your own for the society that you have previously found
aboard a whaleship; and though their friendship is truly and
realistically portrayed, the drama of your romance lies
properly not in their relationship (in my opinion) but in the
conflict between your monomaniac captain and his vast fishy
prey. Ahab as he stands now is a figure used to deliver
irreverent barbs against Quakers—but, in my fancy, he
might be much more. If you will allow me a vision of
allegorical grandeur, I see Ahab in his flashes of anger as
potentially a Lear figure (as long as you are going to compare
me in public to Shakespeare, my good man, you must indulge
me in comparing one of your characters to one of the Bard's);

and this white whale of yours, while menacing, is frankly unconvincing as a figure representing reality—no matter that he may in fact be based upon a real and fearsome fish. He offers every opportunity to become symbolic, and a mighty symbol he could be, as vast metaphorically as a sperm whale is in reality (symbolic of what, precisely? you must decide for yourself, of course). I do not believe the real story here is of the two friends on a grand adventure, which, as you say, you have already written before; I believe the story you have here, if rightly told, would be the confrontation of an heroic personage against a single object which overpowers reason. But I am always inclined to seek the Soul inside the Machinery and the heart in the steel, as it were, so I naturally think in terms of allegory and symbol. However, that is where my insight stops: what this white whale may mean to your captain must come from somewhere inside your own soul, which I know is large and generous enough to provide a true meaning; and what role your two bosom friends Ishmael and Queequeg might play also escapes me; but I do believe that you have something ethereal in your story, beyond all the harpoons and ropes, and that is the thing you must bring out. The jokes are all very well; but it does not seem to me that you are writing a comedy but rather the story of a true quest, which you might rig out in mythic dimensions the way your whaler is rigged out in hawsers and planks. The reality of your whaleship quite amazes me; but I believe that you are capable of rendering the whole enterprise of whaling as something more than "really" real, and that reality is meager compared to the story you want to tell in your heart. I believe that this whale may swim beyond reality if only you should let it.

*Now I am off to conjure up that new romance of my own,
one which I hope will be more than merely a realistic story itself.*

*I look forward to the day, very soon now, when you and I
shall truly be neighbors and may have more leisure to indulge
in such conversations in person.*

yours,

Nath. Hawthorne

*P.S. Sophia asks me to tell you that our children find you
very gentle and entertaining and agreeable, and that she
believes you are a man with a true warm heart and soul and
intellect, and reverent, though not in a way many people are
accustomed to. As for this last, I must say that I agree that not
many would find you reverent.*

September 19, 1850

Pittsfield

My dear Hawthorne,

*Please pass along my compliments to your wife: about the
Hawthornes, at least, let it be said that I am the most
reverent shaman in the New World; about other matters
spiritual and divine, let others be the judge!*

*How it pains me to leave the Berkshires, even for a
moment, knowing that it contains my current joy and the
prospect of my future joy, but indeed leave it I must, in order
to come back again for well and for good. Soon the true
literature of this sleepy nation will shine out from the starry
constellations of the Berkshires.*

Thank you for your skillful harpooning of my Whale*!
Indeed, I had felt that the present version, while dealing with
the novelty of the whale fishery and therefore somewhat fresh
as an adventure, still lacked vitality. After reading your
comments, I see that, truly, I have underexploited the whale
itself and must aim my dart at its very life and stab deep,
until the oceans seethe with its blood! Have you read Owen
Chase's excellent true tale of desperation called* Narrative of
the Most Extraordinary and Distressing Shipwreck of the
Whale-Ship Essex? *It is the story of a boat stove by a whale
and the consequences of that wreck, upon which my adventure
is somewhat remotely based. I read Chase's book on the open
seas during a gam with a ship on which his son was serving,
very near the same latitude where the* Essex *was sunk; and it
was this very son who loaned me a copy of his father's book. I
must tell you the tale sometime, a tale whose horror cannot
lightly be condensed!*

    *My dear Hawthorne, I would sleep my life away if, by
doing so, I could dream myself into an endless conversation
with you; and though I am off to New York now, we will soon
lift the eternal chalice of dreams to each other's lips and drink
deeply.*

                    your
                    Melville

September 20, 1850
Lenox

My dear Melville,

When you have settled into your new manse, come visit us again in Lenox, and we will take a stroll around the lake behind our cottage. There is a matter of some urgency I wish to discuss with you.

yours,
Nath. Hawthorne

Chapter 9

Scarlet Letters

Hawthorne was walking several paces ahead of Herman, slowly and deliberately hacking a path through the tangled undergrowth along Lake Mahkeenac, half a mile or so from his cottage. Here, the buckthorns and hemlock trees grew right down to the water's edge, and, in their shade, mountain laurels and azaleas created a dense, prickly thicket; on such an unbearably warm, late summer day, the canopy of leaves overhead provided shelter from the sun but no respite from the heat, which lacquered the men's shirts to their bodies.

"You know how it is, Melville, when you create a dramatic story out of historical events that everyone thinks they already understand. People are likely to mistake fancy for fact in your story, and fact for fancy, if facts can be discerned at all anymore. The truth, in a fictional work based upon real incidents, speaks as much to the heart as to the head."

As they progressed around the lake, they walked more and more in the shallows of the water, their pantlegs rolled up to let the gentle waves baptize their knees. Herman felt like a young man again, watching the sun sparkle off the ripples across the water, while ducks dived for fish and herons circled the pine-choked island in the distance. Hawthorne had spotted a distant beaver freighting twigs across the lake, though Herman could not confirm the sighting with his aching eyes, which were strained past the dazzling point by his all-night rereading of *The Scarlet Letter*, which they were now discussing.

"While it's true," Nathaniel continued, "that my own great-great-great-grandfather, William Hathorne, appears often in the court records of old Salem—even personally whipping a woman named Hester, for adultery, in 1668—these facts are not the most important real-life analogs to my tale. They have little relevance to the emotions or truth of *The Scarlet Letter*. Yes, my family was personally involved in the fornication trials during the early settlement of Salem, but what of it? I was not writing history, and the historical truth of William Hathorne did not interest me foremost."

"Are you saying 'Hathorne'? Pronounced like 'math,' instead of like 'awe'?"

"I added the 'w' later, to distance the pronunciation of my own name from that of my ancestors."

"That is a curious coincidence," Herman said. "I added the final 'e' to my name, because I thought it looked better when written. My ancestors, and most of my living relations, are Melvill, without the silent 'e.' Strange what a difference a single letter may make."

"Especially when that letter is scarlet," said Hawthorne, with a wry glance. "It can also make a tremendous difference which of the letters turns out to be scarlet, if you follow my meaning."

Herman thought of the 'w' in Hawthorne's name and his own silent 'e,' turning each scarlet with various potential sins; but he could think of no great crime against God or man that began with either letter. "Your own scarlet A in the book stands for adultery, of course," Herman said. "Though I could not help noticing that you never actually name that sin in the pages of your romance."

Herman saw a patch of wild strawberries among the underbrush, plucked an especially ripe one, and popped it into his mouth, stem and all; then he found a juicy-looking one for Hawthorne. He picked it and then caught up to the older author, tapped him on the shoulder, and handed it to him; and he watched with great relish as Hawthorne also ate the entire strawberry, in one bite.

"Many sexual sins were committed in the early days of New England," Hawthorne said. "All of them were well enough known to be shortened to their initials. The letter A was the most popular, or sometimes the magistrates sewed AD onto the clothes of sinners. They distinguished between adultery and fornication, though they did not use the letter F. A scarlet F would have been too close to another F word that also means fornication—that old Anglo-Saxon word that the Puritans could not even suggest without imperiling their souls. They also found a fair number of occasions to use R, I, and S."

"An alphabet of sin!" Herman exclaimed. He leafed through his moral encyclopedia and quickly located "incest" for the letter I and "rape" for R. He was stumped for the moment about S. "Did you find, in your researches, that Puritans were concerned with sexual sins primarily?"

"No, but I would say that the Puritans punished sexual sins most viciously because sins of the flesh demonstrate the animal nature in man. They wished to behave as if they were angelic spirits who merely had the misfortune of inhabiting the earth, temporarily: taking the Lord's name in vain is rather an easy sin for an angel to resist, even if he's trapped in human form, and the punishment was correspondingly light; but having relations with your neighbor's lonely wife meant that you were more body than angel, and the body could not be admitted into the community of angels."

They emerged from the woods onto a pebbly beach free of vegetation, and Hawthorne indicated a log at the edge of the water, where they sat down. They pushed their rolled-up trousers all the way above their knees and lolled their feet in the cool water.

This excursion was their first meeting since Herman had moved to Arrowhead. He had packed the things from his family's Manhattan apartment and shipped them to Pittsfield and then had immediately written to Hawthorne to arrange a visit; his family's belongings were still in crates in his new home, and even now, while he lazed by this lake with Hawthorne, Lizzie and Maria, and Herman's sisters Helen and Augusta, and two servant girls were hard at work at their new estate unpacking trunks. Herman had barely even been inside his new home yet, so eager had he been to see Hawthorne again.

Herman felt that, though he and Hawthorne had not openly declared any deeper sentiment, they had certainly offered each other tokens of admiration unmistakable in their meaning; and though even their warmest embraces might have passed as the affectionate touches of friends, Hawthorne could not fail to interpret Herman's move to Pittsfield as anything but an act of devotion. And now Hawthorne had invited him out here to the lake, alone, in order to discuss "a matter of some urgency," as Hawthorne had put it in his note.

As Herman stared at Hawthorne's lush, silken brown hair—like a Renaissance Apollo's, crowned with highlights of sun-burnished gold—a laurel leaf fluttered down from on high and caught just above his right ear. Herman reached out to pluck the leaf away but found himself instead combing Hawthorne's hair with his fingers; and then, when the leaf had dropped to the ground, he continued to run his fingers through Hawthorne's hair, first somewhat timidly and then, when Hawthorne did not stop him, with more urgency, petting his temple with the knuckle of his index finger, gently caressing some long, loose strands into place behind his ear. He felt the dampness of his beloved's perspiration, and he let his fingertips linger for a moment on Hawthorne's neck, where he felt his pulse quicken against his fingers. He looked into Hawthorne's eyes, which revealed a helplessness so deeply sad and wild that Herman caught his breath and drew his hand away.

Hawthorne took Herman's hand and guided it back to Melville's own knee, and patted it, as he might a child's; then he took a slow, deep breath and turned away, picked up a flat stone, and skipped it across the water. It skidded three times before sinking below the surface, and when he looked back at Herman again, he seemed more composed.

"The most serious problem with sexual sins," Hawthorne said, "is not the fornication but the betrayal of trust that those sins represent. For instance, adultery is only incidentally sexual. It is betrayal *through* a sexual act."

"Perhaps," said Herman. "But the point seems moot, since one cannot commit adultery without sex. Or at least some act of physical intimacy."

"I'm not convinced that's true," Hawthorne said. "Adultery occurs whenever a spouse develops an admiration for someone else, and attraction exists, and the admirer and the object of admiration become intimates. It is an emotional sin. Adultery might occur in the heart alone."

"I find it difficult to believe that the Puritans would brand people, or lash them with whips, or put them in stockades, or exile them altogether merely for having feelings. How could a society that punishes every potentially sinful thought even function, and how would such thoughts and feelings come to light, except through actions?"

A pair of quacking ducks spied them and swam near. Upon ascertaining that the two authors had no morsels for them, they quacked off again toward the center of the lake. Herman ran his fingertips lightly along the edge of Hawthorne's shoulder blade, a reserved caress that Hawthorne shrugged away. It finally occurred to Herman that the Puritans' scarlet S stood for sodomy.

He said, "If I were a Puritan and I desired—merely desired, say, as a passing fancy or an unbidden dream—to have intimate relations with a man, would I deserve an S? Would the Puritan fathers hand out scarlet A's to all the women who combed each other's hair and took a small measure of secret comfort from doing so?" Hawthorne would no longer meet his eyes, so Herman stared at the surface of the lake, as if it were a magic looking glass that might show him the darkest depths of Hawthorne's soul. "I think your standard of purity might confound even a Puritan."

"I am trying to tell you something serious, Melville!" He lifted his legs and kicked both heels into the lake, splashing water over both of them. "The truth of *The Scarlet Letter* is my own truth—it is closely entwined with the historical facts of my ancestors, yes, and their interpretations of sin, but it touches me personally in ways that are difficult to explain, and that are not obvious, that are not *factual*, and I am trying to make you understand—but I am not talking about Puritans."

"Then let us stop speaking of them. Tell me plainly what you mean."

"I am talking about you and me. I am saying that, right now, sitting by this lake together, we both would earn our scarlet A's. And deserve them."

"But we're both men."

Hawthorne smiled mirthlessly. "That is not lost on me."

"Adultery is a crime against *marriage*, the union of a man and a woman. How could one man's admiration of another threaten a marriage?"

"That is a dangerous and decadent attitude, Melville. And I cannot believe that even you subscribe to the opinion you've just stated."

"We are not speaking of the vote, Nathaniel! We are talking about intimate relations, where men and women most certainly are different."

Herman tried to understand how they had arrived at this impasse. Hawthorne had just said that he considered them to be having an adulterous affair! And yet, they had barely shared even a

single intimate caress. Even if relations between men and men were
to be judged by the same moral standards as those between men and
women, nothing improper had happened whatsoever.

"How could anyone consider us adulterers, Nathaniel? What
have we done but exchange a few letters?"

Hawthorne blushed. "That is not all that we have done." He
seemed to be weighing something imponderable in his mind, and
Herman flushed with the pounding of his own heart.

"*What* have we done?"

Hawthorne turned to study Herman's face, and he felt as if Hawthorne were trying to judge the effect of some revelation, a secret
that he cherished but feared sullying through its confession. Tell me
you love me, Herman thought. Is that what we have done—fallen in
love? Just say it plainly.

"I want to tell you something about my wife," said Hawthorne.

"Your wife?" Herman let his head fall back. He stared up at the
streaky clouds spoiling the heavens. "Your wife." He stood up and
walked several steps into the lake, cupped his hand in the water,
and splashed his face and beard and neck. He then shook his head
like a golden retriever, spraying droplets of water out in every direction. "Very well," he said. "Your wife."

"There's no need for theatrics, Melville. I am trying to be serious."

The feeling of youthful optimism that had invigorated Herman
on their walk out to the lake vanished, and he suddenly felt as old as
the stones beneath his feet. Hawthorne was about to end their
friendship: he could feel it coming as clearly as a shipboard rat pre-
dicts a typhoon.

Hawthorne said, "Years ago, when I first began to write stories
for the magazines, a woman named Elizabeth Peabody noticed my
work and began writing me letters. She found something enigmatic
in my stories, and she encouraged me to develop certain themes. I

often found her suggestions quite brilliant. I began responding to her letters, and she drew me out into a larger conversation about life and literature.

"I was quite reclusive then, Herman. I know that I have the reputation of a recluse still, but I am a veritable Ottoman sultan compared to how I used to live. My mother and two sisters and I lived together in the same house, and we survived quite poorly on a meager income from my mother's Manning relations—so I was not obliged to work, but we had no money for diversions. Except for long walks with my sister Ebe, I simply remained in the house, reading books and writing stories all day; and my mother devoted herself eternally to her grief over my father's death. It was a somber household.

"It came to pass one day that Elizabeth Peabody invited me to her house for tea. We lived a very short distance from one another, so it would have been most convenient, on any one of my walks, simply to stop in and say hello, but I was, as I say, practically a hermit, and after many refusals and invented excuses not to go, Elizabeth finally asked my sister to tea instead, and Ebe persuaded me to go along with her. That is how I met Sophia—Elizabeth Peabody's sister. Sophia was an invalid at the time. That is why I'm telling you this story."

"Yes," said Herman gloomily. "She told me about her headaches."

"Headaches were the least of it. Many days she could not even get out of bed; but after we met, she wrote to me, often, sometimes twice a day, and she sent me little drawings and paintings by her own hand—she is quite a fine artist, and I was charmed by the strange concoction of innocence and sophistication in her drawings, and in her letters, and in herself. It soon became apparent that she was truly the hallowed heart of the Peabody house, revered by all who knew her, and I returned there again and again. And as I returned and sat with her, her health improved."

Herman thought of the fetid depths of the lake, the dismal shadows beneath the brilliant surface. Far underneath, below the bullfrogs hiding in the roots of the swaying brown cattails; below the fish suspended in the murky water, devouring one another in an endless cycle of savage death; below the deepest dives of the ducks and herons; below the grubby floor where snails laid eggs, and poisonous snakes cruised among slimy rocks; in those depths, his body might provide a few final meals for the sightless worms churning life through their tiny ravenous gullets. As many close encounters with watery death as he had had in his career as a lowly whaleman on the high seas, he had never before thought of willfully drowning himself—an ironic thought, to drown within easy reach of so much homely land—but now he thought how easy it might be to tie some blocks to his feet and walk slowly down to the gates of Neptune's palace. He had just mortgaged his entire future so that he could spend afternoons like these with Hawthorne, and Hawthorne was talking about scarlet A's and his wife.

Hawthorne continued, "When I met Sophia, she and her entire family thought she would remain bedridden forever, unable to marry or bear children, unable to experience love; and I, too, when I met her, was unable to experience the joy of companionship, living in the miasmic thrall of my mother's grief—a grief from which she never truly recovered—living in the grip of my sister's iron-fisted control of our daily lives. We changed each other, Sophia and I: we each owe the other a great debt.

"This was many years ago, Herman, and the changes I am describing occurred slowly, over time, and with enormous effort and dedication—but Sophia is vigorous now, despite her occasional setbacks, and she enjoys her life and our children, and it is through Sophia's love and support that I have become a true romancer. She believed in me so much that I became the man you see before you, for whatever he is worth. So you may say that what men do privately among themselves does not affect marital relations, but if Sophia ever found out what is between you and me, her belief in me might be destroyed, and that would in turn destroy me and devastate her. To say nothing of Una and Julian."

"But what is between you and me but the utmost regard and admiration?"

"You should not be coy, Herman."

"But how could such great admiration be wrong? How could it be a sin to wander the halls of each other's imaginations together, discovering and building new rooms there? Could you not enjoy my praise and respect?"

Hawthorne stood up and turned away. "I don't know which you intend, Herman—to deceive me or yourself—but I know that you attempt to deceive me in vain. You may call it admiration or respect, but I know what letter the Puritans would assign your friendship."

"What do Puritans and their ancient mad letters have to do with a regard as rare and noble as ours?"

Hawthorne turned back and looked at him with something like hatred. "You think you are the only one who feels!"

The venom in his voice paralyzed Herman. "But why do you not acknowledge the truth of your feelings then? Why must you deny them with ancient codes?"

"I do not deny them. That is why I must deny *you*." He momentarily assumed a fighter's stance, and Herman turned his palms outward in peace.

Hawthorne continued, "Sophia is my salvation, and I am hers. Do you know how rare salvation is? So rare that the sacrifice of a single person for the cause of salvation can build a whole religion, a civilization! And I must honor my own salvation by maintaining my place as Sophia's husband, which has saved us both from a lifetime of suffering—I cannot deny her that. And for that I will sacrifice your bosom friendship." He started walking back toward the path they had cleared through the underbrush.

Herman chased him and grabbed him by the elbow. "May I say nothing else?"

"Please understand! You are a rare and remarkable friend, but I cannot wear the A that comes with your friendship. Now let me go. I want to walk back to my cottage in peace."

"But—did you bring me here just to leave me?"

"You know that I'm right."

"I do not."

"Nevertheless, I *am* right. Let me go."

He rapidly retraced their steps. Herman stood amazed, watching the tall grasses and laurel branches swallow up Hawthorne's figure. He listened to the receding footsteps and the slapping and swishing of branches, which continued long after Hawthorne had disappeared from sight.

He could not quite arrange the puzzle pieces of what had just happened into a picture. All Herman knew for certain was that Hawthorne had just ended their "affair" before it had even started. After a while, even the echoes of Hawthorne's departure faded, and he was left alone with the quiet lapping of water against the stones along the shore.

Autumn 1850–
Winter 1851

Chapter 10

A Covert Message

Beautifully dying, dusky yellow oak leaves spun in the gentle breeze, catching the soft afternoon sunlight. As Jeanie Field's buggy approached Arrowhead, the gaudy rubies of sumac trees beckoned her gaze up toward the blond and crimson crowns of maples and ashes and finally to the tips of the fading yellow oaks, which glowed in the full light far above. The whole landscape fluttered and changed with every breath of air, as if the Berkshires were nothing more than Jeanie's own giant kaleidoscope of brilliantly lit autumn colors.

The cool breeze caressed her neck and cheeks. Her mare strained up the last hill out of Pittsfield, and she guided the horse off the road and onto the cart track that led into the Melvilles' farm.

As her buggy came to a stop at the house, the front door swung open, and Jeanie heard loud female grunting from inside, and then the heavy scuffling of feet. She sat for a moment, waiting for someone to appear and greet her, but no one did, and the doorway remained dark. She grabbed her handbag and stepped down out of the buggy.

A woman in a maid's uniform emerged, walking backward out of the house onto the porch, stooped and struggling with a heavy load. Jeanie soon saw that the woman was carrying one end of an immense, rolled Persian rug; on the other end, another woman, dressed more for luncheon than labor, struggled with its weight. The middle of the rug dragged against the ground. Jeanie ran across the lawn, leapt onto the porch, and cradled her arms under the sagging carpet, and the three together trundled it out to the edge of the porch and dropped it with a thump.

The maid stood with her chest heaving and sweat beading on her forehead. "Thank you very much," she said. She spoke with a thick Irish brogue. "Where did you come from, miss, and I'm glad you did."

"From heaven." Jeanie smiled kindly.

"I'm not sure I take your meaning, miss."

"I'm your angel of mercy."

The other woman frowned and said sternly, "Angels don't drive buggies, Miss . . . ?"

"Jeanie Field." She held out her hand. "I'm Dudley Field's sister. Perhaps Mr. Melville has mentioned us? From Stockbridge. I've come to give Mr. Melville a book." She opened her handbag and produced a slender, leather-bound volume.

"I'm Mr. Melville's sister Augusta, and this is Mary, our maid. You'll have to excuse us, Miss Field, my sister Helen and I have only just moved into the house, and we are still somewhat in disarray."

"God created the earth as a formless void and then arranged the furnishings later, so we can hardly be blamed for following His example."

Augusta folded her arms and took a good, hard look at Jeanie, who was wearing a dark cherry-red cotton dress with a décolletage that was rather more revealing than the current fashion and decorative black cordwork down the front. Her red hair swirled up into a bird's nest, wildly chaotic compared with the severely combed hair that every other girl in New England favored that autumn. She looked vaguely piratical.

"Your brother lets you drive a buggy by yourself and pay social calls unaccompanied?" Augusta asked.

"Well, what am I to do, if I have a book to give a friend and no males wish to take a buggy ride with me? Must we submit eternally to male tyranny?"

"My brother insists on driving all the ladies of our household wherever they wish to go," said Augusta. "We think of it as consideration rather than tyranny. But do come in. Mary, would you let the others know that we have a guest and then put on the kettle for tea?"

Mary hurried toward the dining room, and Augusta ushered Jeanie into the parlor, where they sat down in high-backed chairs near the fireplace. A great oaken sideboard held china cups and crystal glasses, and an étagère in the corner displayed porcelain figurines. A dozen family portraits adorned the walls—severe, patrician faces surveying each other with a frostiness that chilled the air.

"My brother is writing at the moment. We usually summon him for lunch at two."

"But it's almost four."

"If his writing is going well, he will remain in his study."

"Until when?"

They heard footsteps simultaneously on the stairs and from the next room, and Lizzie and Maria appeared in the parlor at the same time, from opposite directions. Jeanie stood up and introduced herself.

"Miss Field," Lizzie said. "What a surprise. Is your brother not coming in?"

"I've come alone."

Lizzie's eyes narrowed. "I see. Have you met my mother-in-law?" Jeanie made a perfunctory curtsy and then shook Maria's hand. They all took chairs and sat for a moment in awkward silence.

Jeanie said, "Your home is lovely, and it's a pleasure meeting you all, but I don't wish to interrupt your afternoon. Really, I just brought a book for Mr. Melville."

· "Welcoming guests is never an interruption," said Maria, in a throaty rattle of indignation. "The more established Dutch families here often pay us visits—though, of course, they notify us in advance—but it makes us feel most at home. Perhaps you already know that my family is Dutch, and my father, Peter Gansevoort, figured prominently in the Revolution?"

"I didn't know, but it's good that our families share that in common," Jeanie said.

"Your family is Dutch, Miss Field?"

"No, I meant that my family also had a prominent role in the Revolution. My grandfather powdered General Washington's wigs."

The Melville ladies squinted quizzically at Jeanie. In the next room, Mary clattered teacups.

"Miss Augusta says that Mr. Melville is hard at work writing," Jeanie said to Lizzie. "And that it's possible he'll ignore us."

"I don't believe 'ignore' is the right word. Sometimes he becomes so involved in his work that he forgets himself. It is perfectly understandable in an artist of his stature."

"Is he a-whaling, then?" said Jeanie.

Lizzie glanced at Augusta in alarm. "Did Mr. Melville tell you about his book?"

"Hasn't he told everyone? It sounds quite grand and unpleasant, a romance about slaughtering monstrous fish far out at sea. Have you read it?"

Augusta said, "Lizzie and my sister Helen and I collaborate on the fair copies—we copy out everything he writes, by hand, so of course we read it."

"Why do you do that?"

"Because penmanship matters more to the publisher than it does to my brother."

"I see. He writes in hieroglyphs, and you three have the Rosetta stone."

Maria said, "Penmanship is no laughing matter, Miss Field."

"No, I suppose not." Jeanie sighed. She detested small talk. "And how do you like Herman's new romance?"

Lizzie gasped and sat rigidly upright in her seat.

"Pardon me!" said Jeanie. "I mean, *Mr. Melville's* new romance. His descriptions made it sound quite ghastly and wonderful."

"Indeed," Augusta sniffed.

Mary reappeared, carrying a tray of shortbread and tea settings.

"Mrs. Melville, Miss Melville, Mrs. Melville," said Jeanie, addressing each of the ladies in turn. "I appreciate your kindness, but I do see that I have come at an unpropitious moment. If you could call Mr. Melville, I will give him the book I've brought and be on my way; or, if he can't be disturbed, I will leave it with you. It is a matter of no great importance."

Augusta told Mary to go up to Mr. Melville's study and announce their visitor. Mary set her tray down on the sideboard, and Augusta began pouring out cups of tea. Jeanie and Lizzie and Maria sat and stared at one another, while they listened to Mary climb the stairs and knock. After a brief silence, she knocked again, waited, and then knocked a third time. Finally, she yelled the news of Jeanie's arrival, and they heard Herman's voice shout indistinctly in response. The maid marched back downstairs and into the parlor.

"Mr. Melville would like to see Miss Field in his study," said Mary. "He asked me to send her up alone."

The Melville women's mouths all dropped open at the same time. Without hesitating, Jeanie stood up and strode out of the room. She held up her book, said, "I'll only be a moment," and practically ran up the stairs.

She found Herman waiting in the doorway of his study—the room Dr. Brewster had used for his own study, with the window facing Mount Greylock. He looked dazed, his hair standing straight out from his head in all directions. He was sweating generously, his collar soaked through despite the chill in the room, and he clutched his quill pen with white knuckles. He took Jeanie's hand and bowed, then stood aside so that she could enter. In a final affront to etiquette, he closed the door behind her, and they were alone.

The walls were completely bare except for a harpoon hanging on iron hooks above the fireplace. A large oaken desk sat in the middle of the room, facing the window. Manuscript pages were strewn across the desk, and Jeanie lingered for a moment over one. A single bookcase, stuffed full of leather-bound volumes, completed the room's furnishings.

"You brought me a book," Herman said quietly, from the distance of a faraway thought.

"I believe you'll find it of incidental interest compared with the person who sent it. Nathaniel Hawthorne."

Herman's heart skipped. He had neither seen nor heard from the man for more than a month, since their confrontation by Lake Mahkeenac, and he had tormented himself nearly every waking second of that time, repeating their conversation word by word in his mind, rereading Hawthorne's letters, fretting about how he might approach him again. Now, Hawthorne had come to him! Jeanie held the book up so that he could read the gold-embossed title: Samuel Taylor Coleridge's *The Friend*. He put down his pen and accepted it.

"My brother and I visited his family in Lenox last week, and Mr. Hawthorne took me aside and charged me with this special errand."

Herman opened *The Friend* as if Hawthorne's own voice might speak from its pages. "And is there a message?"

"No."

Herman read the table of contents and then flipped quickly through the pages. He held the book by its spine and butterflied it open, shaking it to encourage any letter that might be stuck between its pages to flutter out; but none did.

"Do you know why I accepted this errand, Herman?" She stepped closer to him. "May I call you Herman?"

"Of course," he said distractedly.

Jeanie smelled the sperm-oil pomade in Herman's beard. "I came because it is hardly a secret that you and Mr. Hawthorne have become close since you arrived in the Berkshires, and I'm concerned for you."

"What on earth are you talking about?"

"Mr. and Mrs. Tappan have noticed you coming and going at Hawthorne's cottage." The Tappans owned the little cottage and lived in a house nearby. "I had lunch with Mrs. Tappan recently, and she told me that her husband does not think very highly of you and disapproves of your visits to their property."

"I have not been there in more than a month, and I have barely said two words to Tappan."

"He thinks you are unchristian and dangerous—I think on account of *Typee*. Fortunately for you, most people fail to understand completely what you wrote in *Typee*, because they don't want to know or can't recognize it, but the Tappans have eyes to see that those dissolute escapades you describe with naked women—and men—must have included the author."

"Why should this concern you?"

"Because I have eyes to see, as well, and if you continue to carry on so brazenly, others will be forced out of their blindness. You will end up tarred and feathered, or worse."

Melville was taken aback. "How have I behaved brazenly?"

"Everyone has learned that you are the Virginian so fond of Hawthorne—could you have declared yourself any more boldly? And in print, for all the world to see! And my friend Eliza Fields told me that her husband—Hawthorne's publisher—told her that Hawthorne himself has confessed that you have beguiled him." Herman's heart raced in earnest now. "And here is this secret message from Hawthorne that I've just delivered. It's obvious that you two admire one another rather ardently."

"A book is not a secret message."

"Some books are."

"But I've not even seen Hawthorne for weeks. And who in his right mind would construe a few innocent visits and a book review in a magazine as ardent? What conclusions could you possibly draw from such scant evidence?"

"I *know* what's going on, Herman."

"There is nothing to know!" Herman said. He flung *The Friend* violently onto his desk. It bounced once, scattering papers in a great flurry, and smacked into the wainscoting near Jeanie's feet. She looked at the book in surprise, as Herman's manuscript pages fluttered to the floor; and then she looked at Herman with fear in her eyes. She picked the book up and set it gently on his desk, and made a great show of gathering up the scattered papers, shuffling them into a neat stack and handing them to him.

"I did not mean to throw the book," he said. "I would not have hit you with it. I apologize." He realized that he was ravenously hungry, and that the emptiness in his stomach had burbled up to his mind. He tossed the manuscript pages carelessly onto his desk and sat down, feeling dazed and defeated; but he considered the Coleridge book, now crumpled somewhat at the top of its spine, and a little thrill of hope surfaced in the otherwise unpleasant stew of confusion and irritation he felt.

Jeanie slid between Herman and his desk and half sat on the desktop, facing him; her petticoats brushed his pantlegs. She placed her hand on top of his. "I have been telling everyone that you and I are smitten with one another."

"What? Why?"

"Because I love you, Herman. I want to protect you."

"By destroying my marriage *and* my reputation?"

"By keeping suspicion away from you and Mr. Hawthorne. I know how you feel. I see who you are!"

"You certainly do not. And spreading rumors about you and me will in no way protect me—quite the opposite!"

"You cannot shake me with fatuous dismissals. Don't you see? You don't have to hide from me."

"Who thinks this? Who has heard about your supposed affair with me?"

"I've told anyone who's suggested anything inappropriate between you and Mr. Hawthorne."

"But who has done such a thing?" Herman groaned. "Miss Field, I have seen you even less than I have seen Hawthorne. No one will believe that you and I are lovers."

"Really? What will your wife think, now that you have invited me into your study?"

"Don't be ridiculous. No man would flaunt such a dalliance in front of his wife and family."

"Do you not understand your own culture, Herman, or do you think you're exempt from it?"

Herman considered: despite his assertion to the contrary, he became aware that inviting Jeanie up alone had been an incredibly careless breach of propriety—especially in light of the rumors she was spreading—and she had now spent far too long in his study. Her ambush was complete. "Could you please say plainly what you mean and go?"

"You cannot have an affair with Mr. Hawthorne," Jeanie said, with sudden heat. Herman leapt up and clapped his hand over Jeanie's mouth. She bit his finger, and he snatched it away. "You do not know the effect you have on people, Herman." She grabbed two handfuls of Herman's beard and pulled his lips to hers in a hard, dry kiss. Her lids parted to offer Herman a naked view of the whites of her eyes. By the time he finally managed to extricate himself from her lips, they were both breathless. Herman rubbed his smarting cheeks.

"What if your wife had come in just now and caught us kissing? What would she have thought?"

"Obviously—"

"And if she saw you and Mr. Hawthorne doing the same thing? What then? You'd be ruined."

"I'd be ruined either way."

"Not in the same way."

"But I have not been kissing Hawthorne!"

Herman pulled himself up straight and nearly tumbled backward over his chair. While he righted himself, Jeanie straightened her bodice and patted her hair.

"Do you know about the Fourierist phalanx in New Lebanon, just down the road?" she asked.

"I know that every commune based on Fourier's ideas collapses."

"Brook Farm is not every Fourierist commune, and the New Lebanon community is thriving precisely because of Fourier's ideas. We believe in openness and equality. We believe in abolition. We believe that monogamous marriage is untrue to the human heart and that individuals may share deep admiration and affection with more than one person at a time, with men or women or both."

Herman began to wonder how he might manage Jeanie's departure: if he simply threw her out of his study, what might she say to Lizzie? Would he be obliged to escort her into the parlor and make polite conversation with his whole family?

Jeanie placed her hand on Herman's chest and said, "You do not belong in this place, Herman."

"My own home?"

"And your admiration for Hawthorne will come to nothing. Hawthorne is a Puritan at heart. You need a real friend."

Herman touched *The Friend*. "I must escort you out now." He walked to the door. "Thank you for bringing the book. Please pretend that Dudley sent it to me, if anyone asks. I will invite you and your brother to dine with us as you leave, in front of my wife. Please accept. I'll ask the Morewoods, as well—they've just moved into Broad Hall— and we'll see if Dr. Holmes and his wife are in town. You and I will smooth over this debacle by being appropriately sociable, in public, in front of all the neighbors and my family, for everyone to see. I will kiss my wife and you will shake her hand."

"That's fine, Herman, but come visit me in New Lebanon, as well." She walked over to him, put her hand on his chest again, and kissed him lightly on the lips. "Let me be your island girl in the Berkshires."

Herman wondered if he could buy back every copy of *Typee* and burn them all at once. For years, devout Christians had condemned the book for its corrupt morals, but now he saw that it was not the Christian moralists he had to defend himself against—it was the libertines. He opened his study door and escorted Jeanie into the hallway.

They found a woman in a dowdy blue frock at the far end of the hall, holding Malcolm. The moment Herman appeared, Malcolm burst into tears.

"Miss Jeanie Field," Herman said. "May I present my sister Helen Melville." Jeanie made a deep curtsy, and the two ladies exchanged how-do-you-dos. "How is Malcolm?" said Herman.

"A little lame in his limbs still, but at least he has been eating again."

"Malcolm has been sick ever since we moved from New York," Herman explained. "Babies are sensitive to everything that happens around them."

"Then he may never get better," said Jeanie.

Herman took Malcolm from Helen and propped him against his shoulder, like a little sack of flour, and his crying calmed into a dull leaking of fluids. Herman accompanied Jeanie downstairs, where they met Lizzie in the entryway, dusting a table that was already absolutely spotless. Jeanie nodded demurely to her. Augusta appeared at the parlor door, her face more worried than sour but sour nevertheless, and Maria hovered behind her. Helen followed them downstairs, so that the entire Melville clan now crowded into the hallway around Jeanie. Herman made a great show of bouncing Malcolm a few times.

"Thank you all for letting me intrude," said Jeanie. "You have a delightful house."

"We enjoy having visitors," said Lizzie coldly. "Next time, we will expect the pleasure of meeting your brother, as well."

"Yes," Herman said. "Why don't you bring him for dinner next Thursday evening? We'll invite some of our neighbors and make it a housewarming."

"Herman," Lizzie said, "you know that we could not possibly receive guests next week. I'm sorry, Miss Field, my husband does not comprehend domestic matters. But we will be delighted to write to your brother when we are ready to welcome company."

"Thank you, Mrs. Melville," Jeanie said. "My brother and I would be delighted to come, any time you would be so gracious as to invite us." Herman opened the front door, and Jeanie stepped out onto the porch.

"And please tell your brother how pleased I am with the book," Herman said, looking helplessly at Jeanie.

"I will. Good afternoon."

"Good afternoon!" the choir of Melvilles answered dismissively.

Jeanie walked deliberately to her buggy, without looking back, climbed in, and sat down. The buggy was facing the wrong way, so she would have to drive further into the Melville farm, beyond the house to the open area near the barn, in order to turn around; she would have to pass the family twice. She looked up at them now, all the Melvilles plus their maid in a little cluster on the front porch, Herman standing farthest out, holding Malcolm up over his head with his arms outstretched. Jeanie snapped the reins and guided her mare toward the barn, made a wide semicircle, and headed back up the track. She waved at them all as she passed: they stood in precisely the same tableau the second time around, and even Malcolm seemed not to have moved a muscle.

The sun was shining low through the trees. The evening chill caused her horse to snort and trot more briskly. Jeanie turned in her seat and looked one last time at the Melvilles and almost laughed: it seemed possible that they might never move again.

Chapter 11

A Lonely Thanksgiving

Herman read *The Friend* in a state of agitation, scrutinizing every sentence for secret connotations, searching for the code that would unlock the meaning of Hawthorne's silent communication; but nothing emerged. The book itself was disappointing: a collection of two years' worth of essays that Coleridge had published and circulated himself as a weekly periodical called *The Friend*. In the essays, the author mused about politics, ethics, current events, ancient literature, human relationships, and virtually everything else under the sun—it was a miscellany, much like the essays that Oliver Wendell Holmes was writing for the popular magazines, sometimes erudite, often obscure—but nothing in *The Friend* bore any direct relation that Herman could discover to his relationship with Hawthorne. The word "friend" in the title seemed to be the primary message, but did this mean that Hawthorne consented to be on terms of polite amity, or to occasionally read a missive that Herman might send, or to resume a more normal development of the sociability they had already begun, only now in a more reserved manner? Had Hawthorne experienced a change of heart about which letters in his alphabet of sin he might assign to Herman, or was he making all of the letters silent?

He sat down at his desk to write a thank-you note, to communicate to Hawthorne that he wished to accept the proffered friendship, whatever it might be; and yet, he knew that this letter must walk a tightrope over Niagara Falls. He must make it clear that he understood that the friendship Hawthorne now offered would be different from the one they had discussed so fervently by Lake Mahkeenac, even if he could not know exactly how it would be different.

Yet Herman had seen Hawthorne's love shining unmistakably in his eyes. He had heard it quiver in his voice. He thought, what else could Hawthorne's declarations by the lake have meant but love; what else would cause such violent emotions and denunciations? To Herman's mind, Hawthorne had all but confessed his love and he was, in a way, confessing it again by sending this book: it was clear to him that, no matter how much Hawthorne wished the situation were different, he simply could not stay away from Herman. And what of Jeanie's report—that Hawthorne had confessed his beguilement to James and Eliza Fields? The ennobling feeling of loving Hawthorne swept Herman away again: it made life seem grander than he had ever imagined it could be, and he felt certain that Hawthorne felt the same way.

He took pen in hand. His note could not be filled with tragic yearning, nor could it be cold and distant: it had to be merely but genuinely friendly and leave further possibilities open, without naming them. Herman was entering a labyrinth filled with emotional Minotaurs sent by Hawthorne to destroy him, and yet, there, in the center of that maze, Hawthorne himself awaited.

He stood up and paced his study. How he hated the contorted logic that he now applied to their love, as if the human heart were a courtroom. How he hated the tortured carefulness that Hawthorne forced upon him.

November 12, 1850
Arrowhead, Pittsfield

My dear Hawthorne,

I have just dined on a savory dish that I believe you will find delicious, and I am writing to commend it to you. I am calling it Hope. Oh! my friend, hearken to me! For it is the most delectable chowder one may imagine—made of small juicy titbits of Wishes, scarcely bigger than hazelnuts, mixed with pounded Disappointments, and salted with Setbacks cut up into little flakes! The whole is enriched with Faith, and plentifully seasoned with Conviction. When your appetite is sharpened by persistent Failure and frosty Despair, a warm bowl of Hope is just the thing to set your mind and spirit right. And where does one find such surpassingly excellent chowder? Most inns won't serve it, to be sure, and most country houses would ban its aroma from their kitchens—it smells too distinctly of Ambition and Pride, for who but the arrogant would hope for any dish other than the one that God Himself has set down before him? What is this Hope for something else, and what right do we have to it? But you may sometimes detect its savory steam in the most downhearted boarding-houses, in Negro churches, in the stewpots of South American shanties, where the beggars pause their weeping and gnashing just long enough for a spoonful!

And where did I taste this invigorating chowder? I found it in a volume of Coleridge: no! not in the words of the book nor even creased between its pages, but wafting heartily from between the lines. While plying my spiritual spoon in this great bowl of Hope, I thought to myself: I wonder now if this chowder has had an effect on my head? Hope can make chowder-heads of us all! So I mixed in a dash of Skepticism and stirred it all with the bones of a fish called Uncertainty, and garnished it with Acceptance, and drank the bowl right down and had another besides, and my head never felt less chowdery. For Hope, when simmered in Reality, is just the stew that keeps Death away from your doorstep. I would send you back Coleridge's recipe, which you so kindly sent to me, but better to cook a pot for you and serve it up at my table, where we can season it each to our own tastes and enjoy it together.

What say you, Hawthorne? You sent me the recipe, now come taste the chowder! Come have a bowl of Hope with me, and we'll break the bread of Friendship and crumble it into the broth. Dine with me, and soon, and we shall talk of Coleridge and the cure for blight and the Whigs and many airy things!

Your

Melville

Herman put down his pen and read the letter. It was ridiculous. Hope. Chowder. He had been reduced to clowning about the most important thing in his life—as usual. He folded the note into an envelope, sealed it, and addressed it. He could do no better: he would have to rely on Hawthorne's compassion. He left his study, descended the stairs, walked outside, and strode purposefully down the road toward the Pittsfield Post Office. He felt like harpooning himself.

"We have been invited to Boston for Thanksgiving," Lizzie announced the next evening at dinner. Lizzie had invited her Boston family members to the Berkshires, but her father had declined and insisted on his own traditional Thanksgiving in Boston instead. The Shaws, like most New England families, made Thanksgiving the high point of their year and celebrated it lavishly, with half a week of feasting and dancing and roasting chestnuts on hearth fires. Lizzie had written letters almost begging her family to come, so that her heavily mortgaged house might feel more like a home; but their polite refusals showed that they had failed to grasp the urgency of her requests.

"Who has been invited, exactly?" Maria asked.

Lizzie's face hardened. "I thought that Herman and Malcolm and I could go, as we do every year. Your sister's family are in Albany for the holiday, are they not? You could go there or to New York."

Maria took an accusatory bite of roast beef and spoke with her mouth full. "I was hoping we might have all the New York Melvilles here."

"At Arrowhead?" Lizzie looked around the tiny dining room, which also served as the kitchen. It was the only room with a fireplace large enough to cook in and a dining area big enough to seat the six current residents. "But we don't even have a stove. How would you prepare a Thanksgiving meal?"

"We've celebrated Thanksgiving in this family far longer than we've had stoves, Lizzie."

"But where would you *dine*? There's barely room for us now."

Herman was sitting quietly at the head of the table, staring into the fire, his mind far out to sea. His days had become an exhausting blur of fictional whales, farming chores, and a constant, needling longing for Hawthorne, made worse by Hawthorne's continuing refusal to answer his letter. Every day, Herman woke in the morning before dawn to chop wood and carry fresh water into the house; then he spent a few long, affectionate moments cutting pumpkins for his cow and watching her eat. He slopped the pigs, scattered seeds for the chickens, and gave his horse oats; and then he climbed the stairs to his study with a cup of tea and sat scribbling madly about the open seas for six or eight hours in a row, trying to keep the different versions of his story straight in his head. He was writing his whaling adventure *at*

Hawthorne now, channeling all of his frustrations and affections, which he could express to no one in real life, into the operatic desires of his fishy allegory. The adventure story he had written as a first draft seemed paltry to him now, a mincing piece of beggary; in revision, he was letting *The Whale* become the wildest storm of desperation he could imagine, a grand allegory that he hoped would out-Hawthorne Hawthorne, a revelation of masculine beauty that Hawthorne could not help but recognize as an act of love. But he was also having trouble keeping the revision anchored to the details of the story in his first draft—characters slipped in and out of scenes from the original to the revision without much rhyme or reason; a whole coterie of swarthy devils had appeared in Ahab's cabin during rewriting, and Herman could not seem to get rid of them. He was attempting now an encyclo-pedic poetry of whale fat, but the more he attempted to describe the reality of whaling, in all its utterly concrete specificity, the more easily his tale wriggled out of his grasp, and it seemed to swim farther and farther from the story he had originally written. In short, it was becom-ing a frightful mess, but he was loath to start over from scratch—not with his publisher still waiting impatiently for the finished manuscript, and not with his debts mounting at an accelerating rate.

He knew that it was difficult for Lizzie and the rest of his family to understand the violence that he experienced every day locked in his study, since he seemed only to be sitting and writing, with his cup of tea; and as he withdrew further into the savage quest for eternity in his imagination, he found it harder to comprehend the concerns of the women around him. Only women lived in his house, except for his in-fant son: Helen and Augusta and his mother and Lizzie, and the maid, Mary, and the new cook they had just hired, another Irishwoman also named Mary—six women at Arrowhead, two draining the coffers di-rectly. Herman found the fact that Lizzie had hired the two Marys unconscionable—but it was not a battle he was willing to fight. If that was how Lizzie wanted to go to the almshouse, so be it. It was her inheritance, he thought; but Herman felt the full weight of his debt crushing him anew at the mere thought of providing a Thanksgiving feast for a dozen people or more at Arrowhead.

"We could always set up a dining table in the parlor," said Augusta.

"Or we could turn Herman's study into a dining hall for one day," Maria said. "That room would be large enough to accommodate—"

"I cannot go to Boston for Thanksgiving, Lizzie," Herman finally said, interrupting his mother. "I must stay and work on my book."

"But you surely won't write on Thanksgiving Day?" said Lizzie, genuinely shocked. "What possible difference could a day or two make in the writing of a book that has already taken close to a year?"

Now, it was Herman's turn to be surprised. "What difference could a day or two make in the writing of a novel?" Herman said. "Are you joking?"

"No," Lizzie said. "Are you?"

Herman stared across the abyss of incomprehension that had suddenly opened between him and his wife. "Perhaps we could go to Boston for a day," he conceded in a low growl.

"We can't go to Boston for only one day," Lizzie shouted. "It's Thanksgiving." She threw her napkin down on the table and stood up. "Well, I am going *home* for Thanksgiving, for the whole week, if not more, and I'm taking Malcolm with me, and anyone who wants to come for a real holiday is welcome to join us." It was a rare statement of pure revolt, and to emphasize it, she picked Malcolm up out of his high chair and stormed out of the room with him. They all listened to her footsteps pounding up the stairs.

Maria said, "She is right, of course, Herman. No civilized family would think of celebrating Thanksgiving in a single day."

"You once told me that even whaleships on the high seas set

aside time for Thanksgiving," said Augusta. Helen excused herself and followed Lizzie upstairs.

Herman pushed his chair back slowly and stood up from the table; then he walked out to the enclosed back porch, where Mary the maid and Mary the cook were quietly eating their own dinners. He opened the porch door and walked into the night.

The mild air still preserved some of the balm of Indian summer, and he breathed deeply the fragrant smoke of his own kitchen fire, which wafted down to him from the great central chimney. He looked up and saw the light of an oil lamp flickering through his bedroom window. He withdrew his pipe from his pocket and struck a match against the side of his house, and the bitter aroma of anise from his tobacco blotted out the welcoming, homey smoke of the hearth fire inside.

Silhouetted against their bedroom window upstairs, Lizzie held Malcolm to her breast, and Helen stood beside them, her hand on Lizzie's shoulder. Herman felt as if he were a shade of the dark shadows of night, his blackness within turned out; at every puff of his pipe, the burning tobacco made a tiny brimstone glow, a momentary consolation against the darkness.

His marriage to Lizzie had been as close to an arranged marriage as could be. The Melvilles and Shaws had been family friends for generations, and Lizzie had been close to Herman's sister Helen since their childhood. Lizzie's father, Lemuel, had served as the executor of the estate of Major Thomas Melville, the hero of the Boston Tea Party memorialized by Dr. Holmes, and Lemuel had even been engaged to marry Herman's aunt Nancy, until her untimely death had prevented their union. As a result of this attachment, and in spite of its tragic end, Lemuel had shown an avuncular interest in Herman from the time of his childhood.

When Herman had returned from nearly four years of whaling and vagabonding in the South Pacific, he had stopped to see the

Shaws in Boston even before visiting his own family, and Lizzie had been there to welcome him. She had sat in rapt attention, along with the rest of her family, as he had regaled them with strange tales of the high seas. It was, in part, because of the Shaw family's fascination with Herman's stories that he had been persuaded to write them down, and he had dedicated *Typee* to Judge Shaw.

After Herman's first two books became sensations, his marriage to Lizzie had been almost a fait accompli, since it satisfied so many desires: Judge Shaw's desire to formalize the alliance between the Melvilles and Shaws, Maria's to shore up the Melville fortunes, Lizzie's to become something like a real sister to Helen, and Herman's to be accepted by society. The desires it hadn't satisfied were the ones Herman and Lizzie experienced every evening at their dinner table, every night in their bed, and every day when Herman set sail across the lonely oceans of his mind, chasing unheeding phantoms across an endless horizon of empty white pages.

Herman thought constantly of the silly thank-you note he had sent Hawthorne. He recited its contents over and over again in his mind, cringing. Still, no answer came. He became so consumed with Hawthorne's silence that he barely noticed when Lizzie and Malcolm left for Boston.

He walked in the woods at night, accompanied by the ghostly shushing of Hawthorne's sighs; he fed his cow in the morning, and it was Hawthorne who peered at him through her moony bovine eyes; the babbling cascade of the brook beyond his barn murmured Hawthorne's unintelligible secrets. Every evening, an oriole in the tree outside Herman's study, late departing on her migration south, warbled Hawthorne's laughter in twittering song; and though Herman felt Hawthorne's spirit with him everywhere and always, the real Hawthorne would not speak a word. Day after day dissolved into loneliness, and still no letter came.

No more riddling books as gifts. Hawthorne himself refused to appear striding up the hill toward Arrowhead. How much richer would a single ordinary word from Hawthorne's own lips have been than all the glories of love in Herman's imagination!

As the days passed without a sign from Hawthorne, the older author became a nightmare as much as a fantasy, so completely did he confound Herman's hours. Herman began to hoard tiny daily memories, in order to offer them to Hawthorne later: the setting sun glinting orange on the handle of a silver spoon; the drum-tightness of his cheeks in the frosty predawn air; the way the midnight stars crowned the bare branches of the elm tree down the road. Fleeting impressions and passing fancies became the currency of Herman's lonely kingdom, and he stored them like a miser, in case the dream of sharing them with Hawthorne became the only treasure that life ever offered him again.

By Thanksgiving Day, Herman had still heard nothing in response to his note. Hawthorne was there, a short ride away, in his little red cottage, where he was no doubt chopping wood and reading to Sophia and bouncing little Julian on his knee; and surely Hawthorne found time during the course of his days to write letters to his sister and his publisher and that goat Longfellow and perhaps even to Dr. Holmes, who was spending the holidays just over the next hill from Herman's house. Yet he would not spare a single word for Herman.

November 28, 1850
Arrowhead, Pittsfield

My dear Hawthorne,

I write still in the last flush of Thanksgiving glory to send you a report on that sanctified holiday from Pittsfield. I hope that your first Thanksgiving in Lenox was more than

*satisfactory and am sorry only that we did not quaff a few
tureens of gravy together—but even your own little clan may
not have fit at Arrowhead this year: the entire Melville tribe
came whooping around Pittsfield. How the Berkshires have
made country devils of us all!*

*Thanksgiving dawned stormy (as it always seems to be in
this country), and a warm rain fell throughout the morning.
My Aunt Mary made the bone-jolting ride over the hills from
Albany with all of our Lansingburgh relations piled into a
bed of straw in the back of a great lumber wagon. They
arrived completely hidden from sight beneath piles of cloaks
and buffalo robes and umbrellas. They attacked our home
like sailors just arrived in harbor ransacking a public house,
and there was such a shaking out of dresses and rubbing of
backs and puffing by the fire as you can scarcely imagine.
Aunt Mary led the way—the tribe of Melville following one by
one, up the stairs to my study, which was the only room large
enough and empty enough to accommodate the whole party.
The room looked beautiful, though at the cost of displacing all
of my work, since we laid my desk end to end with a dining
table from downstairs (there are gravy stains on my desk
still). We numbered a dozen all told, plus the two serving
girls, who sat with us at dinner as guests. My wife, Lizzie,
and son, Malcolm, were the only ones missing from the
Melville festivities, having taken their accustomed
Thanksgiving journey to Boston. Everything was beautifully
cooked, the skin of the turkey a golden crispy brown, and how
you would have admired the squash soup. We ate with
happiness, and after several glasses of champagne, my sister
Augusta pranced about the room serving everyone, carving
and ladling and dishing. After dinner, we passed the evening*

looking at the French Portfolio through the glass and having our fortunes told by Augusta with cards that I acquired from a Portuguese sailor in Peru. We handed around tea at seven o'clock and egg nog at nine, the appetites of the company so fully satisfied that they begged not to be asked to partake of anything more, even if it were Thanksgiving! At this, I forced each person to take an extra sip of brandy.

At ten—just an hour ago, now—they rumbled off in their cumbrous vehicle, and we have left the cleaning up for tomorrow—all except my desk, that is, which I immediately cleared and set right, so that I could write you this missive and begin running out my whale again first thing tomorrow.

And now that Thanksgiving has passed, I will take a moonlight ramble through the woods—yes, the city has its culture and cafes, and the sea has its drama, but for now give me the fallen leaves and rolling hills and the smell of the earth after a rain! Give me that over all the operas on earth, so long as I can harpoon whales with my pen!

Hawthorne, my family has returned whence they came, and Lizzie and Malcolm will remain in Boston for a week or more: there is a room awaiting you now at Arrowhead, if, after your own feasts and festivities, you would like to walk up the road and have a friendly discussion about Coleridge or anything else. As you see, I have put away my chowder-headed metaphors and send you only this straightforward greeting from a Berkshire Thanksgiving turkey—namely, yours truly,

Melville

Chapter 12

Merry Christmas, Nathaniel

After Thanksgiving, Lizzie wrote to say that she would be staying indefinitely in Boston. She delivered the decision offhandedly—it was a single line in a long paragraph about a new armoire that her father had purchased. Even when Augusta wrote to Lizzie to include her in the plans they were making for Christmas at Arrowhead, Lizzie wrote back instead of the Shaws' planned celebrations and her accustomed role in them, making it clear that she might not return to the Berkshires for Yuletide, either.

In Lizzie's and Malcolm's absence, Herman settled into a stable pattern of work, which nevertheless failed to bring him peace of mind, as he spent nearly every waking moment pining for Hawthorne. And beyond the tension of Lizzie's indefinite sojourn in Boston, which felt more like a standoff every day, and beyond his obsession with Hawthorne, the wider world continued to aggravate Herman's emotions, as well: he ordered several books on whaling from Harper and Brothers—his own publisher—in New York, and they declined to fulfill the order, informing him that they could not extend him even a paltry credit of $8.43: sales of his recent novels still had not recuperated the advances they had paid, so not only did they refuse his book order, but they also sent him a bill for $695.86.

This state of affairs, and Hawthorne's maddening silence, continued all the way through the winter solstice, which brought the first real snowstorm of the season. It started when the lightest wisp of a snowflake fell against the window of Herman's study, and he traced its watery expiration down the pane with his finger.

Here, he thought, is the mystery of all life, in the transformations of water, the vast roaring swells of the ocean ascending drop by drop and moment by moment as vapors floating like angels into clouds, gliding far away from the mothering sea, floating inland over the solid earth, and then fluttering in crystalline loneliness down from the heavens—and how could this single drop of frozen water falling from the clouds, this lonely container for all of heaven and earth, return to the great unknowing ocean from which it had ascended? All of creation and all of human longing trickled down Herman's windowpane before him, every secret of the universe locked in drops of water. Oh, Nathaniel, we humans are but droplets of the essence of God, lost on the fertile earth, all separate but remembering the same vast ocean from which we came. Oh, Nathaniel, I know that you felt the pull of this tide of love in your heart—we are split from the same original impulse, and together we create not just love but creation itself, the God of love waiting to arise from each of us. Herman pressed his sweating forehead against the cold glass and felt as if he were on fire. This fever of longing is not love, he thought, it is the opposite of love. It is the separation from love that burns like the fires of hell.

More and more snowflakes fell, lonely souls blown by the fates and the winter winds, each separate and unique, each falling blindly, hoping against hope to land in the original ocean of love and finding instead only more lonely souls collecting on the ground. The snow transformed the landscape, at first pleasantly erasing the grass and the dirt and the sharp edges and corners of the house and barn; but then, as the flakes became heavier and bigger and fell faster and faster, the air itself turned white, a blank wall against which Herman's longing was just another ghost.

Herman's cow stepped out of the barn into the newly whitened world, and the steam of her breath circled her head like a nun's wimple; she retreated again to the warmth of her hay. Normally Herman could at least produce a few new manuscript pages every day, but on this day he could not bring himself even to step away from his window: peering out on the blizzard, on the mantle of new snow collecting rapidly through the afternoon, he imagined that the whole earth was being swallowed by the all-consuming albino whale in his mind, that it had breached the pages of his book and devoured the landscape and he gazed out now on the great beast's gullet—that this vast cosmic whale was as white inside as out. At last, he thought, he knew how Jonah had felt. But as desolate as the landscape seemed, Herman still saw that the whiteness paradoxically enhanced the beauty of every object it touched: the rotting roof of the lean-to over the woodpile, now hidden by an un-broken plaster of snow; the newly statuesque solemnity of the old out-house, redeemed into politeness by its alabaster coat; and the spindly bare branches of maple trees, rising like the marbled fingers of Bernini sculptures from the blank white pedestal of earth below. This is how beauty must be, he thought, not pretty and safe but unbearable and blank and fierce with the horror of isolation. The whiteness provided a visual uniformity from which Herman's ideas could emerge, a canvas of terrifying emptiness; and the sudden winter death of the world, merci-fully, made Hawthorne's silence tolerable, for the whole earth now be-came silent with an icy calm. Herman occasionally opened his study window, to let the freezing air in, to numb his body if not his mind to the emptiness of Hawthorne's absence, and as his fingers turned stiff and red, he thought, I am freezing inside, and my heart will harden into an icicle of longing, but, oh, Nathaniel, you could thaw me with a word, a glance!

On the morning after the blizzard, in the midst of this wintry captiva-tion, Herman's imagination suddenly loosened and broke free, like a calving glacier exploding into the sea. His ideas came with such urgency that he found himself cursing both his quill pen and his metal nib, as he blotted line after line struggling to match the speed of his mind with the pace of his hand. He was so enthralled that, at first, he paid no attention to the heavy pounding on the front door, but simply kept writing as fast as his fingers would allow; but soon he heard squeaking hinges downstairs and the voice of Mary the maid, and then a man's voice, and then another, and he could not help wondering what errand would bring someone to Arrowhead through such formidable conditions. He opened his study door a crack to see Oliver Wendell Holmes and James Fields stepping inside.

Fields was wearing a striking knee-length green coat with fluffy fur lapels and a massive fur collar. Twenty beavers must have died to make it. Fields handed his walking stick to Holmes and then elaborately removed the coat, to extraordinary effect: he swooped it off like a matador flashing a cape, and then he whipped it around his head in an elegant parabola, dashingly and improbably missing the heads of Holmes and Mary and only grazing the paintings on the wall. The coat's white silk lining was speckled with cherry polka dots, which had a hypnotic effect. Fields then tossed the coat into the air, nonchalantly took his walking stick back from Holmes, and neatly caught the coat over his shoulder with it, as if the heavy fur weighed nothing. Beneath his coat, Fields wore a sleek suit of lemon yellow, with a cinnamon-colored tie. It was dandyism elevated to theater, and Herman thought he might try to reproduce it himself sometime. Holmes, by comparison, seemed like a man who had dressed conscientiously for a funeral and then been run over by a milk wagon.

Herman smoothed his hair and stepped out onto the landing.

"What's the meaning of this, Melville?" Holmes said, when he caught sight of the disheveled author above him.

"The meaning of what?"

"We must speak to you confidentially," said Fields.

Herman shrugged. "Very well. In honor of your tropical appearance, Fields, I will offer you a sunny beverage against the chill. What do you say to a brandy?" Herman descended the stairs.

Fields replied, "My doctor has advised me never to drink brandy without also smoking a cigar."

"I'm your doctor," Holmes said, "and I never said any such thing."

"Brandy and cigars, then!" Herman announced.

"But it's only eleven o'clock in the morning," said Holmes.

Herman scoffed. "Why must you object to *everything*?" He led the way into the parlor, where he threw two new logs onto the embers in the fireplace and blew the blaze noisily to life. He excused himself and returned with a bottle of brandy, three snifters, and three cigars. When he had poured everyone a glass and they had puffed their Havanas ablaze, Fields asked, "May we close the doors, Melville? We have something rather confidential to discuss."

"The ladies will spend the next week railing against the evils of cigar smoke, but as you wish." He closed both doors to the parlor and sat back down, and the smoke immediately began accumulating above them. Herman thought of the smoking cauldron of the three witches from *Macbeth*, and he thought of Shadrach, Meshach, and Abednego, smoking bodily in the Babylonian furnace; and his mind seethed with historical and mythical groups of threes: the Wise Men from the New Testament, the Roman Triumverates, the Great Schism of the Catholic Church and the Avignon popes, the Three Fates, the Christian Trinity, Buddhism's Three Jewels. He realized that he had left his writing desk too quickly, and that his brain was laboring to make the three of them sitting there by his fire mean something, connect to something, symbolize something, and he suddenly saw the enterprise of literature as essentially mad. Here were two gentlemen in his parlor on a social visit, and he was thinking of ancient kings and popes. He became aware that Holmes and Fields were staring at him, and he suddenly wondered how long he had been lost in his own thoughts.

Holmes pulled his chair closer to Herman and puffed his cigar at him. "There's no point hemming and hawing," he said. "Dudley is hopping mad and demands that you discontinue your ridiculous affair with his sister. He sent us to tell you, so that he wouldn't have to come himself and challenge you."

"Challenge?" Herman was still thinking about the Avignon popes.

"To a duel."

Fields cleared his throat. "Everyone knows that your wife has left you, and you're throwing your life away on Jeanie. It's unseemly. She's pretty and smart, yes, but this is no way for a family man to behave. Not to mention that you're the son-in-law of the most prominent jurist in Massachusetts. Truly, we have your best interests at heart. We have come to save you from yourself and spare you further embarrassment. Stop this nonsense!"

It took Herman a few seconds to comprehend completely what they were saying. When he finally did, he nearly laughed, but Fields and Holmes were so solemn that all of his incredulity got stuck in a sideways grin: Herman suddenly looked like an extra in an opera buffa. Try as he might, he could not wipe the smile from his face. He drew on his cigar and took a long drink of brandy: fire and brimstone, he thought, strong drink and the burning of leaves and the thick smoke that catches in your throat. He spied a piece of gray lint on Holmes's white collar, and the texture of it seemed hideous. Everything was too real, all of a sudden. He could not bring his mind down from its writing frenzy, and he vowed never to let himself be interrupted in the middle of writing a sentence again. He felt sweat seeping from his scalp and oozing in slow drops around his hair follicles like worms slithering out from the inside of his head.

"Do you have nothing to say, Melville?"

The two gentlemen were looking at him with both concern and moral censure. So this was the literary community of the Berkshires, Herman thought, outwardly sophisticated and broad-minded but privately priggish and reactionary.

"I'm sorry to disappoint such a well-intentioned social call, but Lizzie hasn't left me, and I'm not having an affair with Jeanie Field."

"Come, come, Melville," said Holmes. "Everyone knows that Mrs. Melville has gone to live with her parents."

"My wife is spending the holidays in Boston, as she always does, while I remain here to finish my novel. I am working against deadline, Holmes, an idea you might be familiar with, and Jeanie Field has made exactly one visit to our house, while my wife and mother were both here. I have not even laid eyes on the girl in more than a month now."

"Don't obscure the issue, Melville," said Fields. "Even Hawthorne says you're having an affair, and Hawthorne is no gossip!"

"Hawthorne?" Herman's heart raced. "What has Hawthorne got to do with it?"

"Well, nothing," said Fields. "But we were there yesterday, and it happened to come up. If even Hawthorne mentions a rumor, it's probably true."

Herman puzzled over this new bit of innuendo. Why would Hawthorne profess to believe a scandalous rumor about him and Jeanie, when Hawthorne himself had trusted Jeanie to privately convey a message to him?

"Stop being obstinate, Melville," said Holmes. "We are doing you a favor, and you sit there grinning like a jackanapes."

Herman had stopped listening. Was it possible that Hawthorne genuinely thought he was having an affair with Jeanie, and *that* was why he hadn't responded to Herman's letters? Could Hawthorne be not merely aloof and protective of his own wife's honor but also jealous? Herman knew that he had to see him immediately—a potentially catastrophic misunderstanding had happened, and he had to set things right!

"Are you going to give up the affair or not?" Fields said.

"Of course not!" Herman answered. "Since there is no affair to give up." He could no longer even talk to these two gentlemen, so fully was his mind consumed with Hawthorne and the untoward possibility that rumormongers were interfering with the *actual* affair he wanted to have. Hawthorne must know the truth—that he and he alone held the key to Herman's heart. He drained off his brandy and stood up. "If you'll excuse me, I'll thank you for coming and bid you good day. I have rather pressing business to attend to."

Fields and Holmes looked at one another. Holmes said, "Don't you remember what happened with Poe's affair and all of that nonsense in New York? And Dudley is a frightfully good shot. You don't want a duel with him."

"I certainly will not fight a duel over a fictional matter of fictional honor. I should challenge *you* to a duel for besmirching *my* honor, Holmes. Really, to be taken in by scurrilous gossip."

"I am merely trying to keep the peace, Melville. As your neighbor, I have an interest in seeing that you don't stain my fields with your blood."

"Please smoke your cigars on the walk back to your own estates. Good day!"

They stood up. Herman showed them to the front door. Fields remantled himself with flare, and Herman practically shoved them out the door.

During their brief conference in the parlor, a new blizzard had swirled to life outside, and now heavy snowflakes were falling fast, filling the frigid air with thick blots of fluffy whiteness. Herman watched Fields and Holmes walk all the way to the main road, where the snow swallowed them up, and then he turned back inside to get his coat. He had to go to Lenox immediately. It was one thing for Hawthorne to be reticent about Herman's love, but it was another matter entirely if their relationship had been derailed by unfounded and ridiculous rumors of an affair with Jeanie Field. Perhaps Hawthorne loved him but felt betrayed by how inconstant and unsubstantial Herman's affections might seem.

For some reason, he thought again of Shadrach, Meshach, and Abednego, and the three popes, and the Three Fates. His mind was stuck in a novel, but the novel had become his life. He had the unsettling thought that nothing in his head was real, that nothing he thought or felt or remembered was real, and for a moment, he wondered if he himself were real. What is this love that I feel, Hawthorne? And he realized with a shock that he needed to see Hawthorne not to dispel the rumors of Jeanie Field and not to confirm his most ardently felt emotions: he needed to see Hawthorne because only Hawthorne could make him real.

Herman put a salami and a loaf of bread in a canvas bag, along with a bottle of brandy and a pair of cigars; then he put on his coat and went out to hitch his cart to his horse. The snow was falling in great, downy flakes that clung to Herman's hair and beard and coat. Seemingly insubstantial objects bobbed eerily on the white surface of the world—shrubs and posts, the ghostly outline of a bench—all pure white forms, dreamed into being by God in a vacant, unconscious reverie at the beginning of time, surrounding the invisible souls of the living with meaningless matter. What was matter but the dream life of God, and what was time but the dream itself, and how could one govern oneself according to the illogical rules of a sleeping deity's dreamworld? The only thing that was real was that thing that seemed least substantial to the senses: love. That was the grandeur of humankind—that one could willingly throw off the hard-won developments of logic and science and philosophy and religion and history and everything that had made human beings exceptional in the world—throw off everything in order to return to the dreamy insensibility of love, the one thing that could not be defined in material terms and therefore escaped the relentless negative calculus of entropy. Love and love alone was eternal.

Herman stared up at the falling snow and thought about how his father had caught his death, traveling through a winter storm similar to this one. Creditors had been pursuing him in Manhattan, so he had taken the entire Melville family and all of their belongings in secret to Albany; when he had returned to negotiate a settlement of the claims against him, his steamboat had become stranded in ice on the Hudson. In a state of irrational agitation and urgency, he had decided that he could not afford to wait for the ice to clear, so he'd arranged passage by land in an open wagon, for which he was not properly dressed. During the trip, he became ill with a fever, from which he never recovered. He had died raving mad, leaving Herman and his family destitute.

Was a trip to Lenox through the frosty snow worth the risk of death, Herman asked himself. Yes, because a trip to Lenox through the snow expressed something greater than death, greater than life, and to transcend life and death, one had to be willing to sacrifice everything. That was the home truth of all religions, he thought—that life itself was insufficient. He threw his own canvas bag and a bag of oats for the horse into his buggy, hopped in, and snapped the reins.

Despite the heavy snow of the previous night, a narrow path had been cleared down the center of the road, and the current snow had only just begun to cover it. He wondered who could have been so industrious on the morning after such a blizzard, even while snow was still falling; the romantic futility of such work appealed to him deeply. He soon encountered an older gentleman driving the oppo-site way in a barouche, and after much negotiating of horses and wagons so that they could pass one another, Melville asked the stranger who might be responsible for the excellent state of the road.

"Melville, you cad," the older man said. "It's the Berkshire Agri-cultural Society, which you would know if you ever came to the meet-ings." The gentleman turned out to be none other than the society's president, who accepted a drink from Herman's brandy bottle and then upbraided him for not socializing with the other farmers. "Did you not receive our housewarming gifts?"

"Possibly," Herman conceded.

"Why did you invite none of us to your home, then? Have you no manners?"

"No, I'm sorry, I don't."

They parted amicably, and Herman promised to drag the road down to the Housatonic with a wedge plow after the current storm. He did not mention that he had no wedge plow and was not sure where to get one or how to use it once he had it.

Herman snapped the reins hard, and his horse trotted on. Along the way, he saw sledding children, children throwing snowballs, chil-dren flopped on the ground making snow angels, and even a group of adults sitting on logs around a roaring fire, out in the middle of a field—they cheered heartily and raised a bottle to him as he passed—but all of this merry activity left him even more desolate than before. He could not imagine himself and Hawthorne making such jolly fun in the snow—everything suddenly seemed hopeless. People all around him were enjoying the winter, enjoying their families in this holiday season, while he was driving miles and miles away from his own family to de-clare himself to a man who wanted no such declaration, in front of the man's wife and children. He took a long swig of brandy.

The farther outside of Pittsfield he drove, the fewer people he saw and the worse the state of the road became, until eventually he stopped seeing people altogether; and a little more than halfway to Lenox, the plowed path ended at a farmhouse. The road beyond became indistinguishable from the fields around it. He dismounted his wagon and knocked on the door of the house, but no one answered. He stared up at the sky, now nothing more than a vague grayness behind the falling blotches of white. The silence was so encompassing that he could hear snowflakes landing around him.

Herman unhitched his horse and installed him in the barn with his bag of oats. He took another drink of brandy to fortify himself; then he set off on foot across the fields.

His body quickly warmed with the exertion. By the time he came to the woods, sweat was streaming down his face, and he unbuttoned his coat and loosened his scarf. His ankles felt elastic as his boots crunched through the snow to the invisible ground below, and he took great strides with his rolling seaman's gait. He realized that sitting at his desk for weeks on end had made him morbid, and the simple act of putting one foot in front of another across this crunchy white landscape made him feel joyful. Even after he had entered the bracken-filled undergrowth of the woods and the low-hanging branches were scratching at his face, he felt relieved and happy.

Herman became more and more sweaty and uncomfortable as he trudged on, until he opened his shirt and walked along with nothing but his flannels between him and the falling snow. In a moment of fantasy, he thought of taking all of his clothes off and walking to Lenox naked. He thought back to the lovely naked brown limbs and breasts of the island women he had known; and then he thought of Jeanie, his "island girl of the Berkshires"; then suddenly and unwontedly he imagined Hawthorne out walking behind his cottage, disrobed: he could not quite conjure the whole of Hawthorne nude in the snow, but he saw him stripped to the waist, chopping wood, sweating; saw the steam from his breath wreathe his face and neck, his chest and arms taut as he swung a massive red axe. The image acquired its own life, Hawthorne chopping and chopping, chips of wood flying up around him, sweat-soaked strands of his wavy hair flopping about his face with each swing of the axe, clinging to his dirty neck. Hawthorne looked up at him, took a long, slow breath, and leaned on the axe, and the image aroused Herman physically.

This trek was now altogether different from the journey he had originally set out on: instead of riding up to Hawthorne's front door in his wagon on a casually adventurous holiday jaunt through dreamy virginal snow, he would now be trudging up, sweating through his clothes, his pants soaking wet with snow, his face red and his mind burning with naked images of Nathaniel. He was walking through a blizzard to pay a casual social call, after weeks and weeks of silence. It was ridiculous.

By the time he stood atop the hill overlooking Hawthorne's home, he felt quite exhausted from his slogging walk and self-devouring emotions. He took a moment to button up his shirt and coat, and then he ate a handful of snow and placed another handful on the back of his neck. He could see sled tracks and a confusion of footprints immediately in front of him—Hawthorne and his children had been sleighing—and as he tromped down the hill toward the idyllically snow-encrusted red cottage, he began to hear voices. Una first, and then Julian, and then the mellifluous tenor of Hawthorne. They were outside somewhere now, playing.

"He will catch cold without a scarf," Hawthorne said.

"But he's a snowman," Una giggled. "He's already frozen."

"Why don't you use your own scarf, Papa?" said Julian.

They seemed to be on the other side of the cottage from Herman, toward the lake, because he heard them clearly but saw no one. As he drew level with the picket fence in front, he saw a tiny black-clad arm swing up at the corner of the house, and then Una ran into view, with her back to Herman, utterly unaware of his presence; then she ran back around the corner of the house again, out of sight. When Herman rounded the corner himself, he came upon a cheery Christmas scene: a congregation of three snowmen, with a sort of clerical snowman at their head, who was wearing a black collar and a derby hat, apparently preaching to them with an upraised stick-arm and a shouting "O" of a mouth (made of little coal nuggets): leave it to Hawthorne, Herman thought, to turn his children's snow scene into a morality play.

Julian was the first to see Herman, and his mouth and eyes became as round as the snow minister's. A thin, high-pitched whistle, like a boiling kettle, steamed out of his mouth, and he ran as fast as his little legs could carry him through the deep snow right up to Melville, where he threw his arms around both of Herman's legs. Hawthorne watched, at first amazed at Herman's unexpected appearance and then, as Julian clung to Herman and continued screaming, increasingly amused; until suddenly Una shouted, as well, almost a seal's bark, which Melville found somewhat bizarre issuing from the little girl, and she also began running, but toward the house, where she dashed inside and slammed the door shut, barking all the while. He thought, Hawthorne is raising a brood of heathen.

Herman was still breathing hard from his walk, so the fact that he began nearly hyperventilating with anxiety now that he was in Hawthorne's presence passed unnoticed. "Does young Master Julian always fling his arms around your visitors' legs," Herman panted, "or have I been granted special privilege?"

Hawthorne smiled, betraying no sign of displeasure or alarm. "It is a habit we've been trying to break."

He wore a red shirt unbuttoned to the sternum and no coat, and he had worked up a healthy lather helping his children engineer their snowmen. Perspiration ran down his chest and, just as in Herman's fantasy, strands of his chestnut hair clung to his neck. His only concessions to the cold were his knee-high black boots and a black scarf that he had tied around his waist, but which now he unwound and wrapped dashingly around his neck—mostly but not completely covering the bare flesh of his exposed chest. He did it so self-consciously that Herman suspected for a moment that he might be flaunting himself: he was even more beautiful and sexual than Herman's wood-chopping fantasy had been. He strode up and shook Herman's hand warmly, as if they were simply old friends meeting at a lively public house. After the many weeks of silence, his aplomb shocked Herman.

"Don't tell me you've walked all the way from Pittsfield?"

"My horse did most of the walking, in fact, but the road was blocked outside of Lenox, and I couldn't allow the prospect of a little Eskimo stroll to scare me back to my hovel."

"Always the adventurer, eh?"

Julian's maniacal whistling shout had wound down into a barely audible rasp, and now Hawthorne took Julian's head in both hands and forcibly shut his mouth. He peeled his son off Herman's legs and told him to go inside and get dry, and the boy whirled and ran into the house.

"What have you brought?" Hawthorne pointed at the sack in Melville's white-knuckled fist. "Yule gifts?"

"You might say." Herman was beginning to catch his breath, but he felt somewhat light-headed and continued to pant with stress, like a frightened dog. How could Hawthorne be so casual? Had his obstinate silence these many weeks meant nothing? Herman withdrew the bottle of brandy and cigars from the bag. "Since you cannot be bothered to jot a simple note to a friend, I thought I would play Saint Nicholas and come to you."

Hawthorne laughed a holiday ho-ho-ho. "Sophia may not consider brandy and cigars an appropriately Christian sort of Christmas gift, but she might receive them more kindly if you say they're in celebration of the baby. It's even traditional, cigars and babies!" He turned and motioned Herman toward the house. "Come in, in any event."

"Baby?" Herman asked. "Whatever do you mean?"

"I'm sorry. I had thought you might have heard the news from Holmes by now. She's expecting our third child, my dear Melville." He opened the cottage door and stood aside so that Herman could enter, and he clapped Herman hard on the back when he did. The feeling of Nathaniel's palm remained stingingly imprinted between his shoulder blades. "She's not feeling her best just now," Hawthorne continued, "but perhaps we could induce her to sit up in bed and say hello."

Herman was flabbergasted: Sophia pregnant? He felt astonished that Hawthorne could still be having marital relations with his wife, and then he felt embarrassed and ashamed at his own surprise. Of course Hawthorne was having relations with his wife! Had Hawthorne not declared that he wished to preserve the sanctity of his marriage? Herman had not realized until this very moment that he had unconsciously developed the belief that he and Hawthorne were playing out a lovers' contest of wills, in total isolation from everyone else around them; he thought only and always of Hawthorne and somehow, in this obsession, he had discounted the reality of Sophia as a flesh and blood woman, and of Hawthorne as a husband. My God, he thought! The idea was so appalling to Herman that he felt as if he had surprised them in the act. He almost reached out to touch Hawthorne's arm—to comfort him even, for having to copulate with his own wife—and then he felt supremely ridiculous. Hawthorne's silence all these weeks, and his easy composure now, became not just diabolical but deeply insulting to the core of Herman's being. Hawthorne had not been thinking of him at all! How could I have been so wrong, Herman thought. How could I be making such a fool of myself? Not for the first time, nor the last, he heard Jeanie Field's voice in his head: "Hawthorne is a Puritan."

"Mine ownest dear," Hawthorne called up the stairs. Herman thought he might be sick. Is this how the profound Nathaniel Hawthorne, possessed of a soul ten times black, addressed his wife? Was this the man so tormented by his past, so beholden to duty that he had been forced to cast Melville cruelly aside—so that he could blandish his sick wife with grammatical lollipops? *Ownest dear?* Sophia answered unintelligibly from upstairs. Hawthorne again called up to her: "Mr. Omoo has trekked across the frozen tundra to pay us a visit." *Mr. Omoo,* Herman thought, *is that what he thinks of me?*

No answer came from Sophia now. Hawthorne asked Herman to wait while he went up and ascertained his wife's state of being.

Herman walked into the parlor. A mostly exhausted fire shimmered through the iron slats in the door of the potbellied stove. The warmth in the room stung his ears. The dining table had been pulled out into the center of the room, and manuscript pages were strewn across it. He picked up a page and started to read: a confrontation between a Judge Pyncheon and a Hepzibah. He thumbed the whole sheaf of written pages and then realized that little stacks of tidy manuscript piles lay all around the room—on the table, on nearly all of the chairs, on the low bookcase. He read a page here and there from different stacks: they all concerned Hepzibah, and a character named Phoebe, and the Pyncheon family, and it became clear that Hawthorne was well into the writing of a new novel. So that's it, Herman thought: all this while, I've been worrying what Hawthorne thinks of me, and he's been writing a novel and impregnating his wife.

Presently, Hawthorne descended the stairs and said, "Unfortunately, Mrs. Hawthorne has asked me to give you her regards and say that she will try to trundle herself downstairs to say hello, but she makes no promises." He lowered his voice and said, with a twinkle in his eye, "That leaves us to enjoy the brandy and cigars somewhat more liberally." A wave of confusion washed violently over the bowsprit of Herman's mind. "Ah, I see you've found my new novel." Herman held up some pages. "You seem well into it."

"I'm almost finished, my dear Melville—most of the fair copy is already with the publisher—and I blame you. You've been on my mind constantly this autumn."

Herman blanched. He had been on Hawthorne's mind constantly? Yet he couldn't be bothered to write even a polite note, choosing instead to let Melville hang in an agony of silence, like a criminal's corpse gibbeted on the edge of town?

"How have I been on your mind?"

"It can be no secret how much more productive you are than I," Hawthorne said. "Why, you're writing novels faster than I can write epigrams. So I set myself the task to develop habits a bit more like yours, to write roguishly and with abandon, and see! I've nearly finished a novel in just a few weeks, where previously it had taken me twice as long to write even a short story."

Hawthorne took the bottle of brandy and poured two glasses. They heard Una and Julian upstairs running from one room to another, shouting happily to their mother. Hawthorne handed Herman a glass and clinked it.

"Really, Melville, I have you to thank for this productivity, and I don't think the narrative is half bad, either. My publisher told me that I should carry on following your example—in every particular!"

Herman sipped the brandy. What did Hawthorne mean by "every particular"? What could he have said about Herman to James Fields that would have inspired such a comment, when Fields himself had just come to Herman's house to censure him? "Did you not receive my letters?" Herman asked.

"I did, thank you." Again, he lowered his voice confidentially. "Considering how we had parted, I was not sure what to say to your invitations. It all seems silly, now, of course, seeing you here. I had nothing to worry about, clearly; but between the imagining and the doing, sometimes a great chasm opens in one's heart, and the blackness in between seems to threaten life itself. I did not know how to cross that chasm to you. Do you understand?" Hawthorne drank off his brandy and turned to the stove, where he opened the door, placed a new log in its belly, and blew on it till it caught.

"Of course," Herman said. "I tried to be as friendly as possible in the letters, as you seemed to want."

"Yes, I see. Well, it was not a very good book I sent you, Melville, I apologize for that. Coleridge is such a pedant; but between you and me, I often do not have much to say and prefer to say nothing at all, and the situation was confounding. I sent the book more as an impulse, since I thought I had to say something, after all. It seemed ridiculous that we should not be friends."

Herman was astonished at Hawthorne's confessional tone and gregariousness. It seemed that he had been waiting all this time just for Herman to visit so that he could say to him in person what he had not been able to say in a letter. "But you believe we should be friends, then?" Herman asked. "Real friends, who speak to one another and occasionally write each other notes?"

"I said we should be friends before, if you'll recall, when we parted by the lake." Hawthorne shrugged. "All the same, difficulties remain, of course."

Herman wondered what difficulties exactly Hawthorne had in mind—he could not help hearing this as an admission that Hawthorne felt more for him than friendship—but he did not wish to ruin the moment by asking. He turned back to the manuscript. "Won't you tell me about your new novel, then, since it owes so much to my influence?" He had intended the comment to be a light joke, but it caught hoarsely in the back of his throat and came out ironic. He looked directly into Nathaniel's eyes and felt more confused and vulnerable than ever. Hawthorne smiled and took the pages from him.

"I'm superstitious. I'll let you read it when it's published."

Herman could hardly believe his ears: while he had been hunting his whale for months without so much as darting a line into it, Hawthorne had already sailed around the world and was coming into port with his hold full of oil. Herman drank off his brandy and waved for Hawthorne to refill it. He topped up both their glasses.

"I will tell you that it's the romance I wrote to you about," said Hawthorne merrily, "the legend of a curse that besets a family. It's a story that has been haunting me for some years and has now come pouring out like a lake that suddenly bursts its dam. It's called *The House of the Seven Gables*. Quite fanciful, I think, and I feel more optimistic than ever because of it—it has rather a sunny ending, even. And now Sophia is with child again, and all seems right with the world. Really, Melville, I've rarely felt so sanguine. Shall we smoke?" He motioned toward the front door. "And thank you, incidentally, for these cordial gifts, and for coming all this way. If you had left it up to me, we might never have seen one another again, but I feel quite glad that you're here and quite foolish that I made so much of it."

Herman followed him out to the front porch, where the cold air now seemed shocking and unpleasant. He immediately bundled and buttoned himself back into his clothes and smelled the clamminess of his sweat turning sour. Somehow, Herman felt, he and Hawthorne had changed positions: now Herman was the sullen, quiet, slow-moving observer, and Hawthorne had become the zealous bon vivant, full of light and life.

"May I ask you a rather indelicate question?" Herman cleared his throat and stared sheepishly at his boots. "I have just had a visit from Holmes and Fields—they say there is a rumor that Jeanie Field and I are having an affair, and that you told them so. Is that true?"

"No. Holmes said that Dudley had told him about the rumor, and I said that I had heard the same—but I meant only that Dudley had expressed concern about his sister's deportment to me, as well. I thought nothing of it—Jeanie has been fomenting revolution at New Lebanon, and Dudley is trying to return us all to the witch trials, and they are waging their family battles in public."

The paroxysms of anxiety Herman had experienced all the while he had been driving and walking to Lenox seemed to have been completely beside the point. Indeed, most of his misgivings about Hawthorne these many weeks seemed to have missed the mark. How could two such diametrically opposed beings live simultaneously in the same Hawthorne—this casual, congenial soul standing before Herman speaking frankly about his friends and optimistically about the future; and the tortured, inward-gazing seer of doom, obsessed with his own sins and the sins of his forefathers? They bit the ends off their cigars, lit them and puffed in silence for a while, watching the smoke and the steam from their breath mingle with the still-falling snowflakes. Herman was afraid to say anything now, for fear that that other Hawthorne, the careful, morbidly fastidious family man who had condemned their affections, might return and send him on his way back into the snow, forever. Herman puffed and waited, but he didn't have to wait long before Hawthorne was talking offhandedly again, this time about finally accepting Melville's invitation to dine with him at Arrowhead, when *Seven Gables* was finished and the weather had cleared.

"Yes," Herman said cautiously. "Come any time. You are always welcome."

"Of course, I may be indisposed for a period, taking care of Sophia. These things are never easy for her."

"Of course."

"But I should very much like to see the new home that you're so proud of. I promise I will visit."

They heard a skittering-scurrying on the stairs inside and then Julian burst through the door outside. "Come quick, come quick!"

"What is it?"

"Mother slipped trying to get out of bed."

Hawthorne threw his cigar into the snow and bolted up the stairs. Herman followed, lingering at the bottom of the stairwell out of propriety but ready to vault up if needed. It quickly become apparent from their voices that Mrs. Hawthorne was not seriously injured, and so Herman relaxed; but it was quite a few minutes before anyone said anything that he could make out clearly, so he closed the front door and added another log to the stove in the parlor. When a few more minutes passed and he could hear only silence from upstairs, Herman poured himself another brandy and drank it down. He stared at the manuscript pages and longed to read through them—he suddenly felt insanely competitive and wished he were sitting at his own writing desk, so he could get down to the business of bettering Hawthorne's new effort. A quarter of an hour passed before Hawthorne came back downstairs, now wearing a heavy, blue woolen sweater.

"Sorry, Melville." He jerked his head toward the front door. "You understand?" It was clear that Hawthorne was not only entreating Herman's understanding but also requesting his departure.

Herman looked out the window. The snow had stopped, and the sun was dipping toward the horizon. There would not be much light left by the time he returned to his horse. He nodded yes, he understood, but suddenly he felt a crushing heaviness at the thought of leaving Hawthorne so suddenly after such a short time with him, when things seemed to have been going so well—at least, in one manner of speaking. Would it always be like this, he wondered.

Were they never again to sit in the sun and talk for hours and experience the true celestial kinship of brothers and bosom friends? Would Hawthorne continue to toy with his love thoughtlessly, as if it meant nothing to him? And yet, he thought, I have inspired Hawthorne in the writing of this new novel. Herman was confusion itself, and he wished he could throw his arms around Hawthorne and receive some comfort, some real understanding from him.

"Is she well, then?"

"Just a scare, and the pain of the headaches again. It's hard for her, because she so wants to have a normal life."

Hawthorne seemed to bethink himself of an idea, and he strode to the bookcase beneath the picture window. He found a two-volume set of books, bound in matching green cloth, which he took to his table; and he opened each volume in turn and wrote something in the frontispieces and then handed them to Herman. His own *Twice-Told Tales*. "To keep you company until we meet again," Hawthorne said warmly, and Herman was so befuddled by this outpouring of seemingly genuine warmth that he simply could stand no more, and he burst into tears.

After a moment in which Hawthorne let him stand helplessly in front of him, weeping, he embraced Herman, who sobbed all the more and went limp in Hawthorne's arms. He did the best he could to quickly snuffle back his tears and regain his composure, while Hawthorne continued rubbing his back. When he had finally stopped crying, Herman felt himself becoming aroused, and he gasped and backed out of Nathaniel's arms.

They heard little footsteps on the landing above. "Daddy," Una called. "Mama wants you to bring her some water."

"Thank you," said Herman, clutching Hawthorne's books to his chest. "I will read them straightaway." They walked together to the front door. "Please give my best wishes to Sophia, and congratulations on the newest Hawthorne on the way."

Hawthorne opened the door, and Herman stepped outside. "Thank you again, Melville, and Merry Christmas."

"Yes," Herman agreed. "Merry Christmas."

Hawthorne closed the door. Once again, Herman stood alone in the snow. He looked up at the second level of the cottage, where the pregnant Sophia Hawthorne lay infirm. Nathaniel was finishing books and making children and doting on his wife, while the only thing Herman had been doing all autumn was alienating his own wife and family and fruitlessly churning at his own novel, which was long overdue and still far from its end. He wiped the tears from his eyes and started the long, cold trek home.

Chapter 13

The One True Prophet: Ahab

Fierce blizzards continued through New Year's Day and beyond, trapping Lizzie and Malcolm in Boston, so that they could not have come home even if they had wanted to; and the snow effectively imprisoned the rest of the Melvilles at Arrowhead. By the end of the first week of January, with the weather so bad that they dared not even go into Pittsfield, and the stores in Pittsfield likely empty anyway, they had consumed all of the food in Arrowhead's larder but some salted beef and jars of preserves. Except for the few eggs that Herman's pampered chickens continued to lay, their meals reminded Herman of the fare aboard a whaler. The ladies began desperately to miss Lizzie and Malcolm at table, since their presence provided a buttress against Herman's baleful, disparaging silence and his nameless gloom about *The Whale*; and every negative feeling seemed magnified by the fact that they could not move about freely because of the incessant snow.

Now that Herman knew that Hawthorne had industriously started and finished an entire novel in the time that Herman had wasted, he felt a pressure so great that he could barely breathe when he was not sitting at his desk: pressure to write a *better* novel than Hawthorne had written, to earn enough money to pay back his debts, to impress Hawthorne and communicate his love for him in a way that Hawthorne would understand. And now came an entirely new feeling: as he poured all of his longing for Hawthorne into

Captain Ahab's mad quest for Moby Dick, he found himself gripped by an obsession even grander and crazier than Ahab's—to turn his novel into an epic that revealed the truth of God himself, to give shape to the impossible and therefore reveal its possibilities. Hawthorne was always writing allegories of good and evil, observing the evil closely in order to reaffirm the good; and so Herman now conceived an answer to Hawthorne's work and to the whole Christian tradition that had caused Hawthorne to deny his love for Melville—he would write an allegory to show that God was, in reality, on the side of evil. He saw clearly, through Ahab's eyes, that the vengeful and capricious God of the Israelites was a deep Cosmic Shadow that had created light only in order to see its own darkness. He began to feel his love for Hawthorne as a hatred of God, because that supposedly loving God had made Herman capable of an all-consuming love that was forbidden and reviled, a love whose very nature condemned him to hell.

Dwelling on Hawthorne's indecipherable intentions became as infuriating to Herman as dwelling on the whereabouts of Moby Dick proved to Ahab. He worked tirelessly, producing page after page of increasingly livid and abstract prose—even simple digressions into the plain facts of whaling, such as the average amount of hard cheese stocked in Dutch whalers, took on mythic and philosophical dimensions—and all the while, with every word he wrote, he imagined Hawthorne reading the book and feeling the immensity of Herman's love. He grew weary of his yearning, yet his only response, as Ahab's, was to sail the watery globe of his mind, always just skimming the surface of meaning but with eyes peeled toward the depths.

Herman's mind became paradoxical to itself: on the one hand filled with boundless love, through which he felt a sublime benevolence toward the whole world and everything in it; and on the other hand consumed by the violence of loneliness and longing.

When the snowstorms finally subsided long enough for crews to clear the roads, Lizzie and Malcolm returned, and Melville's sisters threw an impromptu party, splurging at Farley's Dry Goods on enough sugar to make a massive gingerbread cake. Even Maria was relieved to have Lizzie back, to break the spell of Herman's increasingly blustery private misery; and the ladies passed Malcolm happily from bosom to bosom all day long. Herman surprised himself by melting into Lizzie's loving embrace when she arrived—he was genuinely happy to see her after such a long absence—and he cried sentimentally when Malcolm called him Papa and yanked his beard; but this unexpected wave of happiness crashed almost immediately into Ahab's monomania, and Herman went back to his desk. On the very evening they arrived, the snow returned heavier than ever before—almost as soon as Lizzie had set down her trunk—trapping everyone in their cramped rooms once again.

The harpoon that hung on iron hooks over the fireplace in his study now became a black magic talisman for calling forth devils: Herman paced back and forth, using the harpoon for a walking stick, so that, with every other step, he made a jarring thud into the ceiling of the parlor below, exactly as if he were walking on a peg leg. He recited improvised soliloquies in a bombastic manner; and, for the rest of the household, traversing the landing outside the study became like passing the stage door of a theater, complete with leaps, groans, and growls from inside. Herman shouted things like "tempered in blood and tempered in lightning" and "avast, I say, with your hand-spikes" and much longer though less comprehensible mutterings in a strange diction, punctuated by the thump of the harpoon; and then silence reigned again for hours. Occasionally, he emerged with great urgency and said things like, "What is the Minotaur's riddle," upon which he would disappear into his study again and pace—tock-thump-tock-thump-tock-thump-pivot and then back across the study again, and again, and again, polka-dotting divots into the center of the room. His baritone would sometimes fill the house with whaling songs, "Ho the fair wind / ho-ye, cheerly, men!" and his harpoony pacing would briefly take on the rhythm of the shanty, followed by more hours of silence.

Herman worried that he might be flattening the round earth of his imagination and sailing right off the edge.

The heavy snows made it impossible for Helen, Augusta, and Lizzie to make neighborly house calls or walk into Pittsfield, and no one called at Arrowhead, either; so they began gathering around the dining table in the afternoons to make fair copies for the printer. It was irksome drudgery, made worse by the fact that Herman insisted on inserting the final punctuation marks himself, meaning they had to guess exactly where to leave spaces in his often long, convoluted sentences.

Herman's cramped writing was all but illegible at the best of times, and now, in his haste, he often smudged and streaked the indigo ink, and his ideas became ever more obscure little cryptograms, all the more puzzling because of his book's bizarre vocabulary. No one relished asking the gloomy, agitated mariner for clarifications of spelling or meaning, so they passed around the most perplexing passages and made guesses.

Helen held up a page and pointed to a tiny footnote jotted below a long, blotchy line. "Wooden pigeon?"

"Piggin," said Augusta. "The clue is bailer." She pointed to the word "bailer" in the next clause of Melville's sentence and silently read the rest of the footnote. "Yes, he's talking about bailing water.

Remember grandmother used to say piggin for pail? Bigger than a noggin but smaller than a pitcher. It's an old Dutch word, I think."

"Scottish," Lizzie said. "My grandmother called a milk pail a piggin."

They continued working in silence. Mary the maid passed from the parlor through the kitchen and out the back door, and a frigid wind ruffled their papers.

Lizzie said, "Did you know that Herman turned down a commission to write an article for *Holden's Dollar Magazine*? The Duyckinck brothers are taking it over in the spring, and they were going to print a daguerreotype of his face above the article."

"I don't think he cares for such innovations," said Helen. "Or for the magazines themselves, if truth be told."

"It would have paid actual money," said Lizzie.

"I sometimes think he doesn't care for that, either."

Augusta held up the page she was working on. "Gambage?"

Helen squinted and mumbled the passage aloud. She shook her head no. Lizzie took the page and held it first toward the window and the pale afternoon sunlight and then toward the bright, warm flames of the fire in the hearth.

"G-a-m-b-o-g-e, I think," said Lizzie. She handed the page to Helen.

"Gamboge ghost of a Fedallah," Helen read aloud, raised her eyebrows and shrugged. She glanced over the rest of the page, and read again: "Doesn't the devil live for ever; who ever heard that the devil was dead? Did you ever see any parson a-wearing mourning clothes for the devil? And if the devil has a latch-key to get into the admiral's cabin, don't you suppose he can crawl into a port-hole?" Her eyes met Augusta's and Lizzie's in turn. "Herman is so determined to be profound that I think he outsmarts himself." She handed the page back to Augusta. "What is a Fedallah?"

"The question is, who is Fedallah?"

They heard a series of loud thumps and bangs from Herman's study. His footsteps stomped back and forth across the room, rattling cups on the mantel shelf above the kitchen hearth; then all was silent.

"It might be more peaceful to live with a gamboge ghost," said Augusta.

"Perhaps a gamboge ghost is a kind of poltergeist," Helen said mirthlessly. "Shall we look it up?"

They stared at one another for a long moment, and then Helen turned toward the dictionary on its stand in the corner but did not get up. Augusta sighed. Each went back to copying her separate pages. The crackling of the fire and the scratching of their quills against parchment lent a pleasant, percussive rhythm to their work.

Half an hour passed before Augusta said, "Do you think anyone will read this book?"

"That is blasphemy," said Lizzie. "I fervently hope so."

"We have been copying out his novels longer than you have, Lizzie," Helen said. "You have the zeal of a convert. We have the doubts of the clergy."

"If this book doesn't sell, we shall all wear the rags of supplicants."

They heard banging once again from Herman's study, and then a long, violent clattering, as if a hailstorm had erupted upstairs and marbles of ice were pelting the floors. In the parlor, Malcolm, who had been sleeping soundly, stirred and started to cry; and as the inexplicable pelting faded away, they heard Herman racing down the stairs.

He rushed past Malcolm and into the kitchen, his red face drenched in sweat, his shirt soaked and disheveled. The frightened look in Herman's wild eyes, the cascading tangles of hair clinging to his forehead, and his shortness of breath spoke of a tropical fever.

"Who has the *Rose-bud*?" Herman said.

"The what?"

"The *Pequod* meets the *Rose-bud*. Two ships!"

The three women leafed through their stacks of pages, while Herman danced in place and shook his hands with impatience. Herman's mother appeared in the doorway behind him, cradling Malcolm in her arms. Finally, Augusta said, "Here," and held up a sheaf.

Herman rushed to her side and pawed the pages until he had found the ones he wanted. He turned to run back upstairs and ran smack into his mother, leaving them both momentarily stunned and Malcolm the worse for the collision. Malcolm cried harder. Maria shushed him.

"Easy now," said Maria. "Easy." She gave Herman the evil eye. "Both of you—easy!"

"I have no time, Mother!"

"There is nothing but time, Herman," said Maria.

Herman came up short and considered this earnestly. Nothing but time? After a long moment of puffing, in which his breathing finally grew calmer, he said, "There is space."

"Herman," Helen said. "What is a Fedallah?"

He turned to face her. He now seemed confused rather than panicked. "It means favored by God. He's a Parsee."

"A what?"

"A Zoroastrian."

"What does that mean?"

"A Manichean sort of prophet."

"I don't know what that means."

"A gnostic. Persian." Herman took a sharp breath in and came out of his trance. He looked at the pages in his hands. "It doesn't matter." He shoved past his mother and nearly sprinted through the parlor.

"Your papa doesn't mean it," Maria said to Malcolm. They heard Herman take the steps up to his study two at a time. Lizzie got up and took her inconsolable infant from her mother-in-law and sat back down at the table. Helen and Augusta exchanged dark, rankled looks.

Helen said, "I wish I could get a proper job."

"As what?" Augusta asked.

Helen thought about it for a moment. "I see your point."

The kitchen door swung open, and Mary came in with an armful of firewood. Both Mary and the wood were wet with melting snow, and Mary's hands were bright red with cold. She set the wood in a basket next to the hearth and looked quizzically at the screaming baby.

"Everything all right?" she asked.

From upstairs, they heard tock-thump-tock-thump-tock-thump. Lizzie felt as if she should write to her father, ask for the rest of her inheritance, and throw it directly into the fire.

Chapter 14

Shipwrecks, Fires, Famines, and Other Calamities

At the end of January, Sophia Hawthorne wrote Herman a brief letter saying that Nathaniel had finished *The House of the Seven Gables* but was too busy shepherding it through the press to visit Arrowhead, as he had promised to do. Herman wrote to Hawthorne immediately demanding the visit anyway, in a plain letter without rhetorical flourishes; and, much to Herman's surprise, this unadorned, bold, simple note was answered with a confirmation that Hawthorne would, indeed, come soon. Melville had to laugh at himself: he had spent so much energy in the past divining exactly what he should write to Hawthorne, crafting ridiculous prose and devising stratagems, none of which had coaxed so much as a hello; and now, the simplest of notes in the simplest language, jotted off in haste, had proven effective. Taking this success as a cue, Herman formed a habit of writing some simple thing to Hawthorne every few days, whenever the weather allowed mail—observations about his cow or the grandfather clock or something that had happened in the village, largely unembellished; and he saved all of his flights of fancy for *The Whale*. Herman's progress on his novel accelerated still more; and, in place of the silence that had reigned between them for the entire autumn, Hawthorne responded to Herman's pettifogging notes with dry little everyday communications of his own, so that it began to seem very natural that they were friends again. With each successful exchange, Herman's mood lightened, and everyone at Arrowhead became encouraged at the prospect of his finishing the book and earning some money again.

At the beginning of March, a sudden thaw melted so much snow that the black earth reappeared from beneath its wintry blanket and Pittsfield awoke, a Sleeping Beauty kissed back to life by the sun. Carts began to pass regularly on the road in front of Arrowhead, and the Melville ladies joined the daily promenade into town. Herman dashed off a five-word message to Hawthorne, "Come now if you can," and Hawthorne replied the next day that he would soon be on his way with his daughter, Una, by his side, that they would leave young Julian to stay at home and care for any needs Sophia might have while they were gone, and that Melville should look for him in a day or two. The detail of this response seemed warm and chatty to Herman, disarmingly congenial, and he was filled with an affection that felt fraternal and almost, he thought, appropriate.

Perhaps, Herman reasoned, my obsession with Hawthorne has been governed entirely by my need for an obsession—any obsession—to feed the creation of my monomaniac captain; perhaps, with *The Whale* nearly done and our communications quite normal and easy now, Hawthorne and I can actually become friends, real friends, and I can leave all of this torment behind. In preparation for the visit, he went to town and stocked up on brandy and cigars and bought a case of Heidsieck champagne on credit.

He was feeling quite calm, even optimistic—until he answered a knock at his front door and found Hawthorne himself on the porch. As usual, he was dressed simply, in a red shirt, red-and-black checkered scarf, and a black overcoat. The simplicity of his attire accentuated the ethereal beauty of his face and the magnificence of his high forehead, and his luxurious chestnut hair swept over his collar. Herman's knees jellified with panic and desire.

Hawthorne set his leather satchel down and stepped aside, revealing Una, who stepped forward and curtsied. "Thank you for inviting us to your home, Mr. Melville." She looked up at her father, who nodded his approval.

"It is my pleasure. Thank you for coming. Shall we tend to your horse, Miss Una, or would you like some refreshments first, after your journey?" He looked over Hawthorne's shoulder for the carriage that had brought them.

"As you'll no doubt conclude," Hawthorne said, with a sweep of his arm toward the road, "we have no horse, so we cannot tend to him. I suppose we could 'pretend' to him, but that would be a horse of a different color." Hawthorne smiled warmly.

For a moment, Herman struggled with the desire to kiss him. He even leaned forward a little but caught himself and said, with a blush, "Did you take the train?"

"I dislike trains. They make you look at everything from unnaturally straight lines. From a train, the whole countryside seems like the wrong side of a tapestry."

"Has Una walked the entire way from Lenox, then?"

"We hitched a few miles here and there in the back of a wagon," said Hawthorne. "But Una has the fortitude of a soldier, and marching alongside her in the mud was rather pleasant, after all the snow we've had." Hawthorne wiped his shoes on the porch and picked up his satchel again. "What about those refreshments?"

Una ran in and gave Mary the cook an unsolicited report about her adventures on the road from Lenox. Herman introduced Mary, then knelt down in front of Una and said, "We have water for your thirst, and milk and shortbread for your soul, and birch candy for your dreams. Which would you like first?"

"Birch candy!"

"Dreams first, then. A wise choice." Herman patted her on the head.

"Mary has gone to let the others know that your guests have arrived," said Mary.

"I thought *your* name was Mary," Hawthorne said.

"The housemaid is also named Mary," said Mary.

Hawthorne pulled Herman aside and whispered, "Do you mean to tell me, in all seriousness, that you retain a housekeeper *and* a cook and both are named Mary?"

"I would not say anything in *all* seriousness, but it's true. They're both Irish, as well—it isn't so unusual."

Overhearing this, Una said, "Mary Mary Mary Mary Mary Mary. Now I'm a Mary, too."

"We can all be Marys," said Herman with a wink. "In our own ways."

They heard steps on the landing, and soon Mary the maid appeared with Maria, Helen, and Augusta from upstairs, and Lizzie came through the back door with Malcolm, so that the entire company of Melvilles and their servants suddenly stood crowded around Hawthorne and Una in the kitchen. As everyone was being introduced, Malcolm—resting on Lizzie's hip—swiped at Hawthorne's hair but missed and ejected a trail of snot down his mouth and chin and onto the floor.

They drained three bottles of champagne by way of a reception and became so jolly that they even served the Marys a glass each, as well. Una gorged herself on shortbread. Malcolm covered several large rocks of birch candy with slobber before flinging them across the room. Herman then gave Hawthorne a tour of the estate, while Una helped entertain Malcolm.

Nathaniel complimented the design of Arrowhead—"a stately hive compassing a brooding hearth," as he put it—and Herman welcomed him with great ceremoniousness into his study, where the other members of the household were almost never allowed. He showed Hawthorne the tiny closet of a room that opened off the study, explaining that that was where he slept when his back pain was too bad to allow him to rest peacefully next to Lizzie (he failed to mention that it was also the bed where his fantasies of Hawthorne turned most frequently from his mind to his body), and he proposed stationing Hawthorne and Una there during their visit. Hawthorne said he would be honored to sleep wherever Herman would suffer him to lay his head, a comment Herman found excruciating.

By the time they had returned to the parlor, Una was engaged in a game of checkers with Helen, while the rest of the Melville women stood around them and quizzed Una about her life, which Una enjoyed as if she were a princess holding forth in her own court. Hawthorne smiled broadly and mussed her hair, while she declared, apropos of nothing, "Massachusetts became a state on February 6, 1788."

"She's like her mother in that way," Hawthorne said. "Answering questions that no one has posed."

Herman led Hawthorne back into the dining area, where Mary the cook was encouraging the hearth fire with a bellows. He took a bottle of brandy and two glasses from the shelf and motioned for Hawthorne to follow him out the back door. The air was bracingly cold, and the setting sun seemed watery and weak, as if it were shining through beveled glass.

"My barn is the most pleasant spot on the property," Herman said. "I'll introduce you to Zenobia."

"Zenobia?"

"My cow."

"An excellent name."

"I borrowed it from the queen of Palmyra."

"I must remember that. Have you used it in a book yet?"

"No, it's yours," Herman said. "With my blessings."

Melville and Hawthorne entered the barn through its huge yellow double doors, and then Herman shut them in. It was quite dim, the loft window letting in only a tiny square of wan daylight. Chickens clucked from their pen in the far corner, and a pig, invisible in the deep darkness, grunted deliberately three times, as if ordering from a menu. They patted Herman's horse and petted Zenobia, who nuzzled them both affectionately. The sweet smell of hay and the rankness of drying manure mixed pleasantly in the back of their throats. Herman found an oil lamp on a bench and lit it, then produced two cigars from a wooden box.

"Do you often smoke with the animals?" Hawthorne asked.

"Only Zenobia smokes, but the pig likes his liquor."

They lit their cigars and poured some brandy and drank. Herman directed Hawthorne to a bale of hay, where they sat down; and Herman spread a horse blanket across their legs. A mild but persistent draft produced a constant precipitation of hay dust that mingled with their cigar smoke, creating halos over their heads in the lamplight.

To Herman, the house seemed a thousand miles away, and his body seemed airy and full of light, so happy did he feel to be sitting once again beside this man of such ennobling beauty, who was in such good humor. Hawthorne was the most beautiful creature Herman had ever seen, perhaps the most beautiful creature that had ever existed. He felt like Icarus flying defiantly toward the sun.

"To sunny journeys through stormy lands," Herman toasted.

Hawthorne clinked his glass. "And vice versa." He reclined against the bale behind him, and little stalks of hay nestled into his hair, like strands of spun gold in a fairy tale. It required all of Herman's will not to brush it gently from Hawthorne's hair. "I have been reading a great deal of Balzac."

"Balzac?" Herman exclaimed. "Beef and gravy!"

"He does enjoy his own descriptions, doesn't he? Sometimes, though, I want a good story more than I want a proper moral, and he tells good stories."

"Good stories are sometimes enough," said Herman. "Sometimes."

"I like writers who write very unlike I do," said Hawthorne. Herman thought he detected a significant look in Hawthorne's eye, as if he might have been talking about Herman himself. "I enjoy books that I could not possibly have written. Would it not be a relief to give up one's normal preoccupations with morals and sins?"

"You mean, wouldn't it be a relief to know all the answers, so as not to have to write stories about the questions?" Herman drained off his brandy and poured himself another.

"Perhaps. But I believe that one inherits one's preoccupations as much as invents or discovers them. I have a yen for exploring the past, for instance, not because I am fascinated by historical reality, but because I believe the past governs us, in the present, in ways that are subtle, and insidious—one might almost say that the past is a supernatural power. I believe our impulses are handed down to us, even more than our morals."

"Even the impulse to love another?"

"How can one decide, with the mind, whom to love? And if the lover hasn't decided love, then it must be inspired by some other agency. Call it Divine Providence, or the collective weight of history, or the supernatural—call it what you will. We individually make choices in reaction to the whole weight of history, which has been cre-ated collectively through the power of traditions we never fully under-stand. That is the true supernatural—the ungovernable complexity of history, stretching infinitely back in time." Hawthorne gazed past their lamp into the shadow, at the cud-chewing Zenobia.

"I cannot tell if you are an atheist or a true believer," said Herman.

"I am often unsure myself. But I have just been meditating anew on the influence of the past in *The House of the Seven Gables*. It concerns the reactions of people who find themselves influenced by secret histories that they feel in their hearts more than they understand with their minds, and how incomprehensible longings may still compel decent people to act immorally."

Herman topped up Hawthorne's brandy and scooted closer to him. He felt the warmth of Nathaniel's thigh radiating under the blanket.

Hawthorne smiled ruefully. "To be honest with you, Melville, I sometimes don't have the faintest idea what I'm trying to say with my damned allegories. I feel as if I'm writing with invisible ink."

Something profound happened to Herman as Hawthorne said this, as if Hawthorne had turned a mystical key and the tumblers of Herman's soul had aligned. The feeling delighted him; yet, in contemplating what Hawthorne had said, he discerned nothing extraordinarily profound or witty: he simply felt that, in some subtle but critical way beyond the reach of the rest of the world, Hawthorne thought as he thought. It was a divine sympathy. Herman puffed up a great volume of cigar smoke.

"When will your seven-gabled house be erected for us to see?"

"It will be published next month. Fields, my publisher, assures me that it will be a great success. But what else can a publisher say?"

"I'm sure everyone will flock to read it, but you should not give a damn what the public thinks. Even if the world passes it by, you shall have at least one avid reader who will enjoy it immensely. And I am a special reader, you must remember: I can read between the lines on the page and I see invisible ink, as well. Nothing escapes me!"

Hawthorne looked at Herman with something like fear. "Yes, my wife believes you have special powers of discernment." He took a healthy drink of brandy. "I suppose I do, too." He looked away and blushed. "But I hope the world does not pass it by, since I have a new baby on the way. You may read the invisible ink and tell me what I meant, after all, but let ten thousand others read the words that appear plainly in black, and pay to do so."

Herman again raised his glass in a toast. "To the black *and* the invisible."

Dimly, at the edge of Herman's understanding, he heard a woman's voice yelling. She seemed to be calling the same words over and over. Finally, he tore his attention away from Hawthorne's beautiful, manly face and understood the words, "Mr. Melville, Mr. Hawthorne, supper." It was Mary the cook. Herman was mortified that she might start banging a pan with a spoon.

They cast off their blanket and stood, and Herman looked around him and flinched. He and Hawthorne had both finished their cigars, and the window above the loft showed that it was completely dark outside. They had been suspended in time: their conversation seemed to have lasted only a few moments, yet when they emerged from the barn and saw the lights in the house all ablaze, Herman realized that they must have been talking for more than an hour. A few wispy snowflakes were falling as they followed Mary inside.

What is this dream, Herman thought, in which an hour with Hawthorne feels like only an instant and every second away from him feels like an eternity? If the universe were just, it would be the other way around.

At dinner, Una proved outgoing and entertaining and seemed right in her element. Unlike the skitterish and shy child Herman knew from his visits to Lenox, she lit up with enthusiasm at the Melville ladies' questions. Herman had never seen a family that flipped so dramatically from one tendency to its opposite so quickly or so often as the Hawthornes did: Sophia with her glib bantering on the one hand and morbid confinement on the other; Una with her shyness at home that turned to carnival barking on a visit; Hawthorne himself, who seemed to flip from dark to light as rapidly as a coin spinning through moonlit air. Only Julian seemed fixed in his character, since he was mindlessly rambunctious at all times and appeared to have no secrets at all.

After they had eaten, they retired to the parlor and pulled their chairs up close around the fireplace. Pleasantly exhausted from her encyclopedic chattering at the table, Una curled up on a pillow at her father's feet and quickly fell asleep.

Hawthorne said, "Have you heard that the Harper brothers are soliciting stories for their new magazine?"

Herman nodded. "They asked me for something about the South Seas, but they are paying only in prestige."

Lizzie chimed in. "Has that currency lost its value? I thought if you earned enough of it, you could trade it for dollars."

"You can," said Hawthorne. "But the exchange rate is rather poor."

"A good name is better than great riches," Lizzie said ironically, quoting one of Herman's favorite Bible verses directly at him.

"I suppose we should be glad their magazine is a success," said Herman, ignoring her. "But they have printed six issues now containing almost nothing but pirated English material. Great swaths of Dickens and Trollope."

"Next to advertisements for vanishing creams and corsets," said Hawthorne.

"And must everything they produce be called Harper's?" said Herman. "The only name they can think of is their own." He made an elaborate presentation of serving port. Hawthorne toasted their health and then turned solicitously to Lizzie.

"I'm afraid, Mrs. Melville, that the Harpers and Duyckincks truly believe they can make Americans fall in love with American authors by printing them alongside English writers that everyone already knows. But I would be more convinced if the strategy did not require outright theft from our English counterparts and virtual theft from us."

"But how should we fight against it?" said Herman. "We can hardly print and sell books ourselves, and the Harper brothers will never have incentive to pay American authors for their work when they can print Dickens for free. Who will enforce an English copyright on American soil, and if their copyrights cannot be enforced, what value will ours have?"

"The problem, in my opinion, is not the copyright question," said Lizzie. "The problem lies between the covers of the books. Readers don't really know or care who earns the money from a book—if an author writes something that people want to read, they will buy it. People buy Thackeray and Dickens because they like the stories they write, not because of some abstract considerations concerning the nationality of the writers or the legal standing of their copyrights. People also buy the novels of Catharine Sedgwick and George Lippard— American authors who sell many thousands of books—because they enjoy their work. If there were enough American authors writing the kinds of stories Americans want to read, the publishers would pay them what they deserve, because the sales would justify the advances. Our own writers could then earn a living, and the courts would sort out the copyright question in due time."

Herman felt stung by her comments. "Surely you are not saying that all American authors should write in the insipid style of Catharine Sedgwick?"

"Of course not." Lizzie put her hands together in a gesture of prayer and looked to Hawthorne for help. "I am not speaking of the quality of books as literature. I am talking about sales, which is what *you* were talking about."

"I must agree with Mrs. Melville and even take her point a step further," said Hawthorne. "The problem, when you look at it honestly, is not that publishers will always seek the most profit possible but rather that the sheer number and variety of English authors far outstrips the number of our own writers. Even if every American writer were paid top dollar for every story and novel, our own publishers would still print English novels and still profit by them. We are a tiny militia fighting a great army, and we have not yet recruited enough soldiers to win the war—but we defeated the British once, and we shall do it again." He lifted his glass to Lizzie.

Herman was unwilling to countenance this allegiance of Hawthorne and his wife against him. "But every American author is *not* paid top dollar for every novel and story, as you well know, and the copyright issue cuts both ways. Has *The Scarlet Letter* not been pirated in England? I have lost untold sales in England through unauthorized British reprints, and surely this has nothing to do with the number and variety of English authors available to the public—it is immoral moneygrubbing by the publishers, plain and simple, at the expense of individual authors on both sides of the Atlantic, who have no recourse in the courts."

Herman suddenly realized that he had been shouting. Hawthorne glanced an apology at Lizzie and Augusta, and Herman felt foolish.

"It is a difficult subject," said Hawthorne, "as you all know too well."

Augusta said, "Would it not be better to talk more of the great poetry and beauty of books than their sales? Especially since we have such an accomplished writer as our special guest?"

Augusta asked Hawthorne to read from his own *Twice-Told Tales*, and Hawthorne surprised them by giving a dramatic reading of "The May-Pole of Merry Mount," performing the voices of each character convincingly and somehow enlivening the dour Puritan tale into a kind of ghost story; and he followed it with the midnight meditation of "The Haunted Mind." Herman sat in a rocking chair so close to Hawthorne that, when he rocked forward, he occasionally felt the brush of the older man's sleeve against his hand. He closed his eyes and forgot about the marketplace and his own embarrassing outburst and let Nathaniel's words bathe his mind and heart and soul.

When they awoke the next morning, a crusty new glaze of snow covered the ground, and the roads had again become impassable. With the exception of Maria, who stayed inside to look after Malcolm, all of the Melville women joined Una outside, building snowmen and throwing snowballs. Helen, Augusta, and especially Lizzie were thrilled to have an excuse to release some pent-up energy in the fresh air.

Herman was delighted, as well—as long as the snow continued, Hawthorne would be his hostage. He had imagined taking long walks alone with Nathaniel during his visit, but instead, after breakfast, they found themselves returning to the barn for another chat, which was even better than Herman's fantasies; it was so cozy to sit among the animals nestled into the warmth of the hay that Herman could compare his joy only to the happiness that the swaddled infant Jesus must have inspired around Him, in that manger so far away. It pleased Herman that the analogies he could find for his love for Hawthorne so often seemed religious, since the feeling was as encompassing and mystical as sacred devotion.

Hawthorne carried with him this morning a book wrapped in brown paper and twine; and when they had established themselves on the bale of hay in the barn—again with cigars but this time with steaming tankards of tea—he handed the book to Herman. "A gift," he said. "Which I hope will prove most useful in the writing of your whale story."

Herman unwrapped the book greedily and discovered a well-worn and roughly used copy of Archibald Duncan's *The Mariner's Chronicle; Being a Collection of the Most Interesting Narratives of Shipwrecks, Fires, Famines, and Other Calamities Incident to a Life of Maritime Enterprise*. His eyes welled, and he leaned over to embrace Hawthorne, an impulse he checked immediately with an embarrassed, jerky movement; but Nathaniel put his arm around Herman and gave him a warm squeeze anyway, and then left his arm around Herman's shoulder. Herman leaned into him and opened the book. It was autographed by Richard Manning, dated 1812, and then again by Hawthorne himself, dated 1832.

Hawthorne said, "Richard Manning was my uncle. I used to spend summers in Maine with him as a child, and I read this book while I was there. I had a fascination with sea disasters because of how my father died, and I read the stories over and over again, for some reason inserting my father into every calamity, killing him in fires and explosions and pirate attacks. I suppose it was because his death, and even his very existence, had seemed unreal to me then, so I attempted a kind of magic to make him more substantial somehow. It didn't work, of course; but this has been a very important book in my life, and I hope it will be of some value to you."

Herman could imagine no greater or more thoughtful token of love. He managed to say "thank you" but could muster no other words for a long time. He paged through the volume, wiping away his slowly rolling tears as he read the chapter titles—The Loss of the Hector Frigate; Shipwreck of Madame De Bourk; The Distress and Providential Escape of the Guardian Sloop; Extraordinary Famine in the American Ship Peggy—he felt so loved.

"It's beautiful," he said. When he finally looked up, he was surprised to see that Hawthorne had teared up, as well.

"It is filled with definitions of things one might find at sea," Hawthorne said. He took the book from Herman and found a particular passage. "'The Maelstrom: This dreadful whirlpool is so violent that everything which comes near it, is drawn in and dashed to pieces.' That might also be the definition of Melville." He offered the book back to Herman, and they sat for a long moment staring into one another's eyes.

"If we are to be friends," Herman said, "you must not say such things to me. You know that I love you, and you cannot toy with my affections. I will go mad."

"I'm sorry," said Hawthorne. "You're right." He stood up and walked toward Zenobia, puffing his cigar. Zenobia mooed.

"I don't understand, Hawthorne. I don't understand what you want from me."

"Don't you?"

"You came close to me last summer, and then you wouldn't speak to me or even write a friendly word all autumn, and now you offer me tokens of . . . well, I don't know what. Can't you just say plainly how you feel?"

"I could, if it were plain to me." He turned around to face Herman again. "I know that you are unlike anyone I have ever met. When I am around you, I feel at liberty to express myself completely as I see fit, because I am quite sure you will understand me. It's a freedom I have longed for, but I also know that what you want from me, I cannot give."

"No," Herman said. "That's not true. What I want from you is to know you."

Hawthorne waved his hand dismissively. "Are we speaking plainly or aren't we?"

Herman wilted somewhat and gripped the book of seafaring disasters more tightly. "What I want, given that no other possibility seems available, is to be your friend." He stood up, as well. "I wish there were another name for it, a name that captures the essence of it."

"You wish to be my lover. That's the name for it. But I am a stranger to that form of love."

Herman thought that, by his tone, Hawthorne might have meant that he had simply never acted on his desire for a man and not that he had never *felt* such a desire—but he couldn't be sure. Herman said, "Your heart cannot be so overfilled with love that there is no place in it for me."

"It is not my heart that matters," said Hawthorne. "We are both married men, and you know that Sophia has another baby on the way. Nothing about that has changed."

"But has your heart not changed since last summer? Has something not happened in the meantime, that you feel you want to give me gifts and compare me to a maelstrom that might dash you to pieces?"

A fluttering of wings and bock-bock-bocking signaled a disturbance in the chicken coop, which the rooster quickly put down. A feather floated up into a beam of light and then spun down and landed on Zenobia's head.

"I am not as steady as I may appear," said Hawthorne. "And things do change. Since last summer, I have started and finished writing a new book, and that always alters me. Perhaps I have simply gained a new sympathy for your position, upon long reflection. I have thought of you a great deal. Perhaps," Hawthorne swallowed hard. "Perhaps, I have just missed you more than I thought myself capable, these last few months."

Herman's heart beat wildly, but he managed, like a ship's captain standing steady in a gale, to speak calmly. Nathaniel's openness allowed Herman, for the first time, really, to consider the situation from his friend's point of view. "Admitting a fondness for another man would sully you and mark you, just like Hester Prynne was marked."

"Worse than Hester. I don't know how it is aboard a ship in the

South Seas, but you know as well as I do that they don't merely brand you with a scarlet S for such an offense in New England—they beat you bloody, or tar and feather you, or hang you. You might rather sell yourself into slavery than admit you love another man."

"But you don't have to admit it to anyone but me!"

"Melville, I am not trying to be merely respectable—but to be honorable. Not just for my own sake but for Sophia's, as well—and yours. We have been through this already, have we not? Don't let my sympathy now persuade you that I am any less committed to my wife than I was before. I want to make room in my heart for your friendship, and I believe a friendly affection for you can coexist with an honorable and true love for my wife; but please do not press the issue. Must I recant every honest thing I say because of your insistence on the impossible?"

They heard Una shouting orders outside, directing some sort of game, and the women were laughing along with her. They were having such joyous fun in the snow! Herman felt chagrined: he knew that his work and his moods tormented his sisters and his mother and his wife, and he wished he could find some peace with them, or at least provide some peace *for* them. But he was not convinced, as Hawthorne seemed to be, that happiness in such a life could really exist, either for him or his family.

"Very well," said Herman. "Thank you for the book. And thank you for your loving words. I will treasure them both."

He hesitated for some moments before yielding to the temptation to walk over to Hawthorne and take him in his arms. Nathaniel embraced him warmly, and Herman was careful not to press too firmly against him. He recorded every impression, every feeling, every smell, so that he could return to them later; until, finally, Hawthorne broke their embrace and stepped away.

A knock came at the door. "*Philios*, then," Herman announced. "Friendship." Una pushed the barn door open.

"Come play, Papa, come play!"

They followed Una outside, where the snow-dusted women stood beckoning and calling them. Una dragged her father by the hand until he gave in and ran to join them. Una threw herself into Helen's arms, and Helen lifted the girl up and awkwardly installed her on top of a snowman.

Herman met Lizzie's happy gaze, and her face reminded him of the days when they had first been courting, when she had been vivacious and not yet resigned to eternal days of idle unhappiness. The sadness and regret in Herman's heart burbled up into his throat, and he thought he might cry again. Oh, why can't I be happy? he thought. Lizzie waved to him, inviting him to join in the fun. A look of hope appeared on her face. Herman sprinted out to join them, as well.

After lunch, Hawthorne announced that they were off, back to Lenox. Over Melville's objections, Hawthorne said, "It's but a short tramp into Pittsfield, and we'll catch the evening train home. This much snow will not bother a steam engine."

"I thought you disliked trains," said Herman.

"I promised Sophia that I would not be away long."

The Melvilles expressed their concern for Hawthorne's wife, whose generally sickly condition and particular difficulties with pregnancy Hawthorne had confided to them in surprising detail over lunch. As they parted on the doorstep, Herman clasped Hawthorne's hand between both of his and fixed him with a look as full of meaning and affection as he could make it. "Thank you for the book," he said. "It means the world to me."

"I hope you will enjoy it as much as I have," Hawthorne said warmly.

He and Una walked as briskly as they could through the snow toward Pittsfield. The Melvilles watched them until they were completely out of sight.

"What a lovely man and a delightful little girl," said Herman's mother.

Lizzie put her arm through Herman's and kissed his cheek affectionately, and they all returned to the parlor, which seemed suddenly quite empty. Herman and Lizzie took chairs close to the fireplace, holding hands and staring into the flames.

"Wouldn't it be nice to have a little girl around the house?" said Lizzie dreamily.

"Perhaps it would," Herman conceded.

Spring–Summer 1851

Chapter 15

Hope

By early April, it was clear that Lizzie was pregnant again and had been for several months, a condition that lightened her day-to-day mood considerably, in spite of her morning sickness. One evening, as she and Herman were climbing into bed, Lizzie said, "If it's a girl, I would like to name her Hope."

"After your stepmother."

"Yes, but also because that's how I feel when I think of her. Hopeful."

"A nice idea." He blew out the bedside candle and pulled the blanket around his shoulders. Lizzie snuggled into him.

"Herman, when we were first married, we talked of having a large family. Is that still what you want?"

Herman grunted. "I suppose."

"Meaning that you have reconsidered some part of it?"

"I had not envisioned having my sisters with us for so long." He yawned. "They might live with us indefinitely, so our household . . . "

"But our own family," Lizzie persisted. "I mean, Malcolm, and the new baby."

"Yes?"

The night was unusually warm for April. They heard the chirping of katydids below their window.

"I would still like to have a much larger family," Lizzie said, "but I wonder if it would satisfy you. Honestly, you hardly seem interested in any of us anymore. I sometimes feel that you don't even know Malcolm exists."

"Who could be in our house for an hour and not know Malcolm exists?"

"He should not always be so unhappy. None of us should."

"Please say plainly what you are thinking, Lizzie."

She sat up. When her dark silhouette momentarily blackened the moonlit window, Herman thought of a dolphin arcing out of a silvered sea. "What do you love about Malcolm?" she said.

He considered his son. Malcolm cried constantly and still walked as if he had just taken his first step. He was sickly and lacked curiosity. What does one love about a two-year-old, Herman thought.

"He is my son," he finally said.

His eyes lost focus in the darkness. He became transfixed by the sky behind Lizzie's head, the crystalline looking glass of God that reflected only emptiness.

Lizzie took a deep breath. "Herman, what do you love about *me*?"

This question snapped Herman out of his exhausted reverie, and he sat bolt upright. At first, he saw an army of angry Lizzies behind his wife's eyes, marching toward him, and he scurried behind his battlements. His mind exploded in a volley of blank cannon shots, loud explosions that launched no artillery, for he had no ready answer; but when this first moment of habitual defensiveness passed, he saw that Lizzie was not attacking him but rather seriously asking about the state of their marriage, from a position of practicality and vulnerability, and he pondered the question carefully.

He remembered the early days of their courtship, when they had sat in the Shaw parlor with the whole family, and Lizzie had often asked the most insightful questions and made the most telling remarks; and though she had objected strongly in the beginning to his irreverence, she had ultimately come to accept it as a genuine expression of his desire for the truth. He thought of her long-suffering patience with his mother and her utter dedication to Malcolm during the many nights when he himself could no longer endure his son's crying. He remembered the countless hours she had spent hunched over his manuscripts, copying his impossible script, which she did more out of love than duty. She was an admirable person, he thought, but his feelings did not amount to love in the way she meant it.

He wished that she could be happy with their marriage as a fond social compact; or that he could summon the kind of love she desired; or he wished that they could speak of the differences in their expectations honestly. But how could he honestly tell her that what he truly wanted was a man who wrote dark, quixotic fiction full of allusions to a forbidden inner life that no one else understood?

"You have a superior mind," he finally said. "You are sympathetic, to a fault. You put up with my mother."

"I knew your mother would find a way into it," she said. "Though you are right that my tolerance of her is admirable. What else?"

"You have a fine sense of humor."

"One would have to have a sense of humor to be with you."

"I should have said an ironic one."

Herman lay back again, and Lizzie snuggled in against him. She exerted a little pressure with her pelvis, which forced the growing life in her belly against Herman's side. Herman drifted in and out of sleep, while Lizzie stroked his cheeks and neck.

"You do still love me, don't you?" she asked.

"Of course," he muttered.

"Not of course. Sometimes I can't tell. I would not want to have this baby with a father who didn't love its mother."

"You may rest assured," Herman said, more petulantly than he intended.

"I don't want you to feel only a sense of duty to me. I can always return to my father's house."

He groped for Lizzie's hand under the covers. "Please don't talk nonsense when we're falling asleep. In the day, nonsense is the only kind of sense, but at night it summons demons." He kissed her forehead.

"Why don't you ask me, Herman?"

"Ask you what?"

"Why don't you ask me what I love about you? Or do you take it so much for granted that I do?"

He woke up a little yet again, alarmed. "No. What do you love about me?"

"You are contemptuous and patronizing and ill-mannered, and you think you are better than everyone else."

"I see. You have extremely low standards."

"I have not said all. You are not always entirely honest, especially with yourself. Nor sensible. Nor kind. But you see things about me that no one else sees, when you bother to pay attention, and about the world, which is even more important. I know something about you that you don't know about yourself—that you could never love a single, individual person even if you wanted to, but that somehow you love all of creation in a way that is far beyond what most of us conceive as love, far beyond what they teach us from the pulpit. You are so very far from perfect, but when it comes to the world and to me, you will only accept absolute love, and that's why you always feel unsatisfied, most of all with yourself, because you are incapable of the thing you desire most. That is why it isn't easy to love you, but also why I do."

He had never heard the term absolute love before. Unconditional love, yes—an equally impossible concept—but absolute? He turned it over in his mind: it seemed more aggressive than grace, more demanding than acceptance, the complete opposite of resignation, something austere and grand—even literary. He kissed Lizzie on the cheek and felt a great deal more love for her than he had in a long time, an inkling that, perhaps, he was not quite as alone as he had imagined.

Lizzie said, "You know that we're running out of money again, don't you?"

Herman sighed heavily. "I will handle it."

"How? My father won't lend us anymore."

"I will write to the Harpers and ask them for an advance on *The Whale*."

"The last time you wrote them, they would not give you eight dollars' worth of credit. What makes you think they will advance you money now?"

"The quality of the work itself. I will send them some chapters."

"The Harpers don't care a fig for quality. They will print the most scandalous and indecent books if they think they will sell."

Herman was chagrined that Lizzie had called his bluff, but she was right. The Harpers' first big success, *Maria Monk's Awful Disclosures*, told the supposedly true story of a nun forced to satisfy the sexual needs of priests at a convent hospital in Montreal. The book featured all the hallmarks of a gothic novel, down to secret tunnels and catacombs beneath the convent where the priests committed their unspeakable crimes, and it had sold more copies every year since it had appeared in 1836. Maria Monk had been exposed as a fraud several years after the book had been published—even her pen name was nothing more than a punning satire—and she had recently died in prison in New York City, where she had been jailed for thievery and prostitution; but the Harpers continued to print and sell the book exactly as it had originally been written, with no retractions or explanations. It was just one of many such salacious, wildly popular books in the Harpers' warehouse, and Herman could not imagine that an all-male whaling voyage would inspire Fletcher Harper's confidence of similar success.

In fact, Herman had no clear idea where the money for his household's survival would come from. As Lizzie had said, Judge Shaw would not lend him more. Perhaps Richard Bentley—with whom, after all, Melville had an agreement for the publication of *The Whale* in London and who was the only person in the world really waiting for it—perhaps Bentley might advance him a few hundred pounds, especially if Herman granted him the international copyright he was always agitating for; but then, if word got out that Bentley held the copyright, the American publishers would just steal it and print their own editions, and Herman would never see another penny. He searched his mental archive for friends of his father in New York who might still think fondly of him, and he wondered for the hundredth time if any of his relatives in Lansingburgh might have the funds to see him through to the end of this novel—but soon he would have to stop wondering and actually ask. What will happen, he thought, if there is no money at all? With a horrified shudder, he imagined losing Arrowhead and having to beg Allan to accept his family into Allan's new apartment in Manhattan, after Melville had moved out so ignominiously last summer. Or could they possibly beg the Morewoods for a room at Broad Hall? He wondered momentarily how much Ticknor and Fields had paid Hawthorne for *The House of the Seven Gables*. But to ask for a loan from Hawthorne? It would be worse than death.

"I will find the money," he said. He had spent the day writing and the evening planting beets and radishes in the garden behind the barn, and now he could stave off sleep no longer. "Please, can we talk about this in the morning? And rest assured that I love you. And we can name our child Hope, if it's a girl. Good night."

"Good night," Lizzie said. "Hope is the best name in the world, because it is the best quality of the human mind."

"Is it?"

"For me, it is. It's all I have."

One morning, two magnolia warblers suddenly began singing from the elm tree near Herman's study window; and he noticed that, overnight, tiny buds of green had sprouted from every branch. Melting snow dripped from the buds in great prismatic drops that splintered the pale sunlight into warm rainbows falling to the earth. As Herman stared out his study window, a pair of white loons winged above his fields, looking for the lake they would call their summer home. He put his fingers to the windowpane, which remained frightfully cold; but the world outside had all at once returned to life. For a brief moment, he forgot the seemingly endless battle that was still raging on the pages of his manuscript, and he descended the stairs and walked out the front door to the road. Without even stopping to retrieve his jacket or hat from inside, he wandered, as if in a daze, all the way into town, enjoying the cheerful verdure of leafing shrubs and green grass pushing up through melting snow. Trilling birds filled every budding grove, and his heart sang with them.

Herman cut a bizarre figure on the streets of Pittsfield, disheveled and underdressed, next to the ladies in fox stoles and the gentlemen in light new overcoats, strolling the snow-melted streets in defiance of the lingering chill. Spring! Herman ambled half insensibly into Farley's Dry Goods and was in the process of buying a cigar when he noticed the latest *Harper's* magazine, with a review of Hawthorne's new novel. He snatched it up immediately and walked back along the road to Arrowhead, smoking and reading, not noticing that he was shivering with cold.

The review glowed with admiration, calling Hawthorne a "first-rate romancer" and the novel "as good a book as any produced in this country in the last ten years, including this self-same author's own last novel, *The Scarlet Letter*." It said that *The House of the Seven Gables* was a product of a mind that was "American through and through," though the reviewer went on to claim that some of Hawthorne's characters were "peculiar and marked by puzzling idiosyncrasies" but that "the lugubrious tone and subject matter were redeemed by an ending full of invention."

Herman could not decide whether to be irritated at Hawthorne because he had not even written to let him know that the book was finally available, or to be jealous of such a good review, or to be ever more anxious to finally have his own novel finished so it could trump Hawthorne's, or to be happy for his friend that his book had been so well received. He thought of Captain Ahab storming back and forth across the deck of the *Pequod* and could not imagine any reviewer saying such flattering things about *The Whale*, and he realized that he would have to redouble his efforts in order to outshine Hawthorne's newest work. He walked faster and faster toward home.

"Melville, what the devil are you doing out half naked in the cold?" It was Dr. Holmes, strolling casually up the road toward Pittsfield. "Have you no blood in your veins?" Holmes was dressed for a polar blizzard, in a full-length beaver coat and matching hat with earflaps.

"Hawthorne has a new novel," said Herman.

"Why should that inspire you to leave your house without a coat?"

Herman looked at himself and thought that, for once, Holmes was right: he appeared almost as frightful as if he were at sea, with a dirty, askew shirt and grease spots on his pants. He could only imagine the state of his hair and beard. He handed Holmes the magazine, opened to the review, and the doctor glanced through it.

"Who's this reviewer?" the doctor said. "Never heard of him."

He handed the magazine back to Herman. "I wonder if that gentleman even read the book."

"Why do you say that?"

"Because I've just finished it myself, and this review doesn't even begin to touch its most interesting points."

"You have a copy already?"

"Hawthorne gave it to me a couple of days ago. As I said, I've just finished it."

Now Herman began to shiver in earnest, but not from the cold: how easily Hawthorne could still hurt him, and how quickly his jealousy flared to life! Apparently, he kept in better touch with this flinty blowhard than with Herman himself. "Hawthorne gave you a copy of his book?"

"I just said so. Are you ill, Melville? What is the matter?"

"I am quite all right, Doctor. How did you leave Hawthorne?"

"Hawthorne is well, but his wife is doing poorly. I've never seen anything quite like it. Migraine headaches, sensitivity to light, stabbing pains in her side. Loud noises make her vomit. I suppose it's just childbearing, but the combination of things worries me."

"She used to be an invalid, you know."

"Thank you for mentioning that, Dr. Melville," said Holmes. "Are you sure you're quite well?"

"Did Hawthorne send any message for me?"

Holmes looked at Melville as if he had gone mad. "He was rather preoccupied with his wife." He cleared his throat. "His new book isn't bad, you know. Not as good as this review makes it, but pleasant enough and dark in his usual way. A story about old dead sins laid away in secret drawers of the soul. Very German. Terrible ending. Incidentally, Melville, thank you for breaking off your affair with Jeanie Field."

"I didn't break off my affair. I never had an affair with her, as you surely know."

"Have it your way," Holmes puffed. "I'm just glad it's over."

"Who told you it was over? The same person who told you it existed in the first place?"

"Whatever you're implying, Melville, I don't care. I'm sorry I got mixed up in it."

"Then why did you?"

"To prevent Dudley from shooting you in a duel, as I said at the time. I hate being the holder of secrets or the bearer of gossip—thinking that people are hiding something all the time makes one liable to superstitious fancies, which is bad for the digestion."

"I daresay. Though it would be a man of extraordinary moral fortitude who never had anything to hide."

"If you never do anything dishonorable, you never have anything to hide," said Holmes. "Where is the extraordinary moral fortitude in that?"

"Even God has things to hide, Doctor. Or have you forgotten the Tree of the Knowledge of Good and Evil?"

"Must you always blaspheme, Melville?"

"God's secret knowledge and his refusal to share it with mankind are the reasons we're in this fix."

"What fix?" Holmes rolled his eyes and flapped his arms. "I don't have time to stand here debating Milton and Jeremy Bentham and who-knows-what with you in your underclothes. If I'd wanted to talk nonsense, I would have stayed at Harvard." Holmes set off toward town.

"Always a pleasure to see you, Doctor," said Herman.

The doctor stopped, turned, and stared for a long moment at Melville, and then said, sincerely, "Likewise."

Chapter 16

Dollars Damn Me

April 16, 1851
Arrowhead, Pittsfield

My dear Hawthorne,

I have just finished reading a book you may know, "The House of the Seven Gables: A Romance." The contents of this book do not belie its rich, clustering title. With great enjoyment we spent almost an hour in each abundantly but judiciously furnished gable. There are rich hangings, wherein are braided scenes from tragedies! There is old china with rare devices, set out on the carved buffet; long and indolent lounges to throw yourself upon; an admirable sideboard, plentifully stored with good viands; a smell of old wine in the pantry; and finally, in one corner, a dark little black-letter volume in golden clasps, entitled "Hawthorne: A Problem." It has delighted us; it has robbed us of a day, and made us a present of a whole year of thoughtfulness; it has bred great exhilaration and exultation with the remembrance that the architect of the Gables resides only six miles off, and not three thousand miles away, in England, say. We think the book surpasses the other works of the author. The curtains are more drawn; the sun comes in more; genialities peep out. Clifford is full of an awful truth throughout. He is conceived in the finest, truest spirit. And here we would say that, did circumstances permit, we should like nothing better than to devote an elaborate and careful paper to the full analysis of what so strongly characterizes this author's writings, namely a certain tragic phase of humanity which, in our opinion, was never more powerfully embodied than by Hawthorne. No mind has recorded the intense feeling of the visible truth more deeply than this man's. By visible truth, we mean the apprehension of the absolute condition of present things as they strike the eye of the man who fears them not, though they do their worst to him; the man who, like Russia or the British Empire, declares himself sovereign amid the powers of heaven, hell, and earth. He may perish; but so long as he exists, he insists upon treating with all Powers upon an equal basis. If any of those other Powers choose to withhold certain secrets, let them; that does not impair my own sovereignty in myself. And perhaps, after all, there is no secret. We incline to think that the Problem of the Universe is like the Freemason's mighty secret, so terrible to contemplate until it turns out, at last, to consist in a triangle, a mallet, and an apron—nothing more! Even God cannot explain His own secrets, and He would like a little information upon certain points Himself. We mortals astonish Him as much as He us. But it is this Being of the matter; there lies the knot with which we choke ourselves. As soon as you say God, you jump off your stool and hang from a beam. Yes, that word is the hangman. Take God out of the dictionary, and you would have Him in the street.

    The grand truth about Nathaniel Hawthorne is that he says No! in thunder; but the Devil himself cannot make him say yes. For all men who say yes, lie; and all men who say no—why, they are in the happy condition of unencumbered

*travelers in Europe; they cross the frontiers into Eternity
with nothing but a carpet-bag—that is to say, their own Ego.
Whereas those yes-gentry, they travel with heaps of baggage,
and, damn them! they will never get through the Custom
House. What's the reason, Mr. Hawthorne, that in the last
stages of metaphysics a fellow always falls to swearing so? I
could rip an hour.*

*Walk down one of these mornings and see me. No
nonsense; come. Remember me to Mrs. Hawthorne and the
children.*

H. Melville.

*P.S. The marriage of Phoebe with the Daguerreotypist is
a fine stroke, because of his turning out to be a Maule. If you
pass Hepzibah's cent-shop, buy me a Jim Crow (fresh) and
send it to me by Ned Higgins.*

*May 11, 1851
Arrowhead, Pittsfield*

My dear Hawthorne,

*I should have been rumbling down to you in my pine-
board chariot a long time ago, were it not that, for some weeks
past, I have been more busy than you can well imagine out of
doors, building and patching and tinkering away in all
directions. I had my crops to get in the ground, corn and
potatoes (I hope to show you some famous ones by and by), and
many other things to attend to, all accumulating upon this
one particular season. I work myself hard; and at night my*

bodily sensations are akin to those I have so often felt before, when I was a hired man, doing my day's work from sun to sun. But the true reason I have not been to Lenox is this—the Whale! In a week or so, I go to New York, to bury myself in a third-story room, and work and slave on my Whale while it is driving through the press. That is the only way I can finish it now, I am so pulled hither and thither by circumstances. The calm, the coolness, the silent grass-growing mood in which a man ought always to compose, that, I fear, can seldom be mine. Dollars damn me; and the malicious Devil is forever grinning in upon me, holding the door ajar. A presentiment is on me that I shall at last be worn out and perish, like an old nutmeg-grater, grated to pieces by constant attrition. What I feel most moved to write, that is banned—it will not pay. Yet, altogether, write the other way I cannot. So the product is a final hash, and all my books are botches. But I mean to continue visiting you until you tell me that my visits are supererogatory and superfluous.

I'm rather sore, perhaps, in this letter, but see my hand! Four blisters on this palm, made by hoes and hammers within the last few days. If ever, my dear Hawthorne, in the eternal times that are to come, you and I shall sit down in Paradise, in some little shady corner by ourselves; and if we shall by any means be able to smuggle a basket of champagne there (I won't believe in a Temperance Heaven), and if we shall then cross our celestial legs in the celestial grass that is forever tropical, and strike our glasses and our heads together, till both musically ring in concert—then, O my dear fellow-mortal, how shall we pleasantly discourse of all the things manifold which now so distress us—when all the earth shall be but a reminiscence, yea, its final dissolution an antiquity. Then shall songs be composed as when wars are over; humorous, comic songs, "Oh, when I lived in that queer little hole called the world," or, "Oh, when I toiled and sweated below," or, "Oh, when I knocked and was knocked in the fight." Yes, let us look forward to such things. Let us swear that, though now we sweat, it is that same dry heat which is indispensable to the nourishment of the vine, the vine that will bear the grapes to give us champagne hereafter.

But I was talking about the Whale. As the fishermen say, he is in his flurry. He feels always to be in his flurry and never dies; I'm going to take him by his jaw, however, before long, and finish him up in some fashion or other. What's the use of elaborating what, in its very essence, is so short-lived as a modern book? Though I wrote the Gospels in this century, I should die in the gutter.

Don't trouble yourself about writing; and don't trouble yourself about visiting; and when you do visit, don't trouble yourself about talking. I will do all the writing and visiting and talking myself. By the way, in the last Dollar Magazine, I read your story "The Unpardonable Sin." He was a sad fellow, that Ethan Brand. I have no doubt that you are by this time responsible for many a shake and tremor of the tribe of "general readers." It is a frightful poetical creed that the cultivation of the brain eats out the heart, but it's my opinion that in most cases, in those men who have fine brains and work them well, the heart extends down to the hams. And though you smoke them with the fire of tribulation, yet, like veritable hams, the head only gives the richer and the better flavor. I stand for the heart. To the dogs with the head! I had *rather be a fool with a heart, than Jupiter Olympus with his head. The reason the mass of men fear God, and at bottom dislike Him, is because they rather distrust His heart and fancy Him all brain like a watch. (You perceive I employ a capital initial in the pronoun referring to the Deity; don't you think there is a slight dash of flunkeyism in that usage?) Another thing. I was in New York for four-and-twenty hours the other day, and saw a portrait of N.H. And I have seen and heard many flattering allusions to the* Seven Gables. *So upon the whole, I say to myself, this N.H. is in the ascendant. What reputation H.M. has is horrible. Think of it! To go down to posterity is bad enough, any way; but to go down as a "man who lived among the cannibals!" When I speak of posterity, in reference to myself, I only mean the babies who will probably be born in the moment immediately ensuing upon my giving up the ghost. I shall go down to some of them, in all likelihood.* Typee *will be given to them, perhaps, with their gingerbread. I have come to regard this matter of Fame as the most transparent of all vanities. I read Solomon more and more, and every time see deeper and deeper and unspeakable meanings in him. I did not think of Fame, a year ago, as I do now.*

My development has been all within a few years past. I am like one of those seeds taken out of the Egyptian Pyramids, which, after being three thousand years a seed and nothing but a seed, being planted in English soil, it developed itself, grew to greenness, and then fell to mould. So I. Until I was twenty-five, I had no development at all. From my twenty-fifth year I date my life. Three weeks have scarcely passed, at any time between then and now, that I have not unfolded

*within myself. But I feel that I am now come to the inmost leaf
of the bulb, and that shortly the flower must fall to the mould.
It seems to me now that Solomon was the truest man who ever
spoke, and yet that he managed the truth with a view to
popular conservatism; or else there have been many
corruptions and interpolations of the text. In reading some of
Goethe's sayings, so worshipped by his votaries, I came across
this, "Live in the all." That is to say, your separate identity is
but a wretched one—good! But get out of yourself, spread and
expand yourself, and bring to yourself the tinglings of life that
are felt in the flowers and the woods, that are felt in the
planets Saturn and Venus, and the Fixed Stars. What
nonsense! Here is a fellow with a raging toothache. "My dear
boy," Goethe says to him, "you are sorely afflicted with that
tooth; but you must live in the all, and then you will be
happy!" As with all great genius, there is an immense deal of
flummery in Goethe, and in proportion to my own contact
with him, a monstrous deal of it in me.*

H. Melville.

*P.S. "Amen!" saith Hawthorne. This "all" feeling,
though, there is some truth in it. You must often have felt it,
lying on the grass on a warm summer's day. Your legs seem to
send out shoots into the earth. Your hair feels like leaves upon
your head. This is the all feeling. But what plays the mischief
with the truth is that men will insist upon the universal
application of such a temporary feeling or opinion.*

*P.S.S. You must not fail to admire my discretion in
paying the postage on this letter.*

June 29, 1851
Arrowhead, Pittsfield

My dear Hawthorne,

The clear air and open window invite me to write to you.
For some time past, I have been so busy with a thousand
things that I have almost forgotten when I wrote you last, and
whether or not I received an answer, though in truth I suspect
I have not heard one peep from you in many weeks—no doubt
because you are being feted in all the capitals of our small
Republic.

This most persuasive season has now for weeks recalled me
from certain crotchety and over-doleful chimeras, the like of
which men like you and me must be content to encounter now
and then, and fight them the best way we can. But come they
will—for, in the boundless, trackless, but still glorious wild
wilderness through which these outposts run, the Indians do
sorely abound, as well as the insignificant but still stinging
mosquitoes. Since you have been here to visit me, I have been
building some shanties of sheds and outbuildings (connected
with the old one) and likewise some shanties of chapters and
essays. I have been plowing and sowing and raising and
painting and printing and praying—and now begin to come
out upon a less bustling time, and to enjoy the calm prospect of
things from a fair piazza at the north of the old farm house here.
Not entirely yet, though. The Whale is only half through
the press; for, wearied with the long delay of the printers, and
disgusted with the heat and dust of the Babylonish brick-kiln
of New York, I came back to the country to feel the grass— and
end the book reclining on it, if I may. I am sure you will
pardon this speaking all about myself; be sure all the rest of

*the world are thinking about themselves ten times as much.
Let us speak, although we show all our faults and
weaknesses—for it is a sign of strength to be weak, to know it,
and out with it—not in a set way and ostentatiously, though,
but incidentally and without premeditation. But I am falling
into my old foible—preaching.*

*I am busy, but shall not be very long. Come and spend a
day here, if you can and want to; if not, stay in Lenox, and
God give you long life. When I am quite free of my present
engagements, I am going to treat myself to a ride and a visit
to you. Have ready a bottle of brandy, because I always feel
like enjoying that heroic drink when we talk ontological
heroics together. This is rather a crazy letter in some respects,
I apprehend. If so, ascribe it to the intoxicating effects of the
latter end of June operating upon a very susceptible and
peradventure feeble temperament.*

*Shall I send you a fin of the Whale by way of a specimen
mouthful? The tail is not yet cooked—though the hell-fire in
which the whole book is broiled might not unreasonably have
cooked it all ere this. This is the book's motto (the secret one)—*
Ego non baptizo te in nomine patris, sed in nomine diaboli!
H.M.

*July 21, 1851
Lenox*

My dear Melville,

*I think the face of nature can never look more beautiful
than now. The sunshine fills the airy woods with fresh green
light; Monument Mountain and its brethren are all clothed in*

green, and the lightness of the tint takes away something from their massiveness and ponderosity, and they respond with lively effect to the shine and shade of the sky. Each tree now within sight stands out with its own individual hue. This is a very windy day, and the lights shift with magical alternation. In a walk to the lake, just now, with the children, we found abundance of flowers—wild geraniums, violets of all families, red columbines, and many others, known and unknown, besides innumerable wild strawberries. The housatonias quite overspread some pastures. Not merely the flowers, but the various shrubs one sees, when one is seated for instance on the decayed trunk of a tree, are well worth looking at, such a variety and such enjoyment they seem to have of themselves and their growth. Amid these creations, we see the remains of others that have already run their course—the hoary periwigs, I mean, of dandelions long since gone to seed. And water weeds, on the edge of the lake, whose roots seem to have nothing to do with earth but only water.

Quoth I to Julian, "Are you a good little boy?" "Yes," said he. "What are you good for?" asked I. "Because I love all people," answered he. A heavenly infant, powerless to do anything but diffuse the richness of his pure love throughout the moral atmosphere, to make all mankind happier and better. Or perhaps he understood the question to be for what reason he was good—and meant to reply, that good deeds gushed forth from his heart of love as from a fountain. I am raising up a new Fourier, I fear, or a Pangloss. You must not fail to remind me some day to tell you of my sojourn at Brook Farm, which I fear has influenced Julian covertly, nevermind that it happened before he was born—that is, after all, just how such things happen.

Sophia's sister Elizabeth is here now, helping to care for our new little Rose, but at the end of this week, she and Sophia and Una and Rose will all travel to Boston to make the rounds of the family, leaving just Julian and me to our devices in our little cottage. They will be away for three weeks, and if you came during this time, we might have opportunity to speak of eternity and things of this world and the next, and books and publishers, and all possible and impossible matters, at our leisure.

yours,
Nath. Hawthorne

Chapter 17

Happy Birthday, Herman

At midday on his thirty-second birthday—August 1, 1851—as he finished baling the last of the season's hay, Herman stood in his field and exhaled the longest breath of his life, as if filtering all the air in the heavens. After a long summer of toil and sweat, he had finally caught up with the farmwork; and, by coincidence, that very morning, the carpenters had finally finished building his northern porch, facing Mount Greylock, so that, from now on, he could take his evening brandy sitting in a rocking chair and gazing in awe at that breaching whale of a mountain, seemingly placed there by Providence for him to look upon. He did not even regret his extravagance in spending money to have it built—not yet, at least—because, unbeknownst to his family (even to Lizzie) and underlying all the other more prosaic reasons for his relief and contentment, he had finally finished writing the narrative of *The Whale*.

In this perfect moment, with all of his work finished—the book, the field work, some renovations to the house—he splashed water in his face from the little rivulet below his hay field and drank deeply of its cool water and then walked, still covered in hay dust and dirt and sweat, to his new porch. He stomped on the pine boards and knocked at the solid posts and took in the panorama of mown fields and deep green groves and glorious mountains. He breathed deeply the sweet honey of switchgrass and hay mixing with the pungent funk of his own body, and he heard the whirring of a grasshopper's wings, which stopped abruptly with a thump as the little creature landed on the porch—and he felt happy.

His mind raced; he was still taut as a wire from the monumental effort of finishing the book, on top of everything else he had still been required to do around the farm, but it was done, all done, and all the evidence he saw before him favored his own personal definitions and nomenclatures—the universe was exactly as he defined it. *The Whale* was swimming through typesetting machines in New York to become the plates of a book, and he knew that the small drop of new cash in his bank account, courtesy of a secret loan from an old family friend in Albany, would soon turn into a roaring river spilling into an ocean of money from the book's success.

He still had not secured an American publishing contract, but he had no doubt that he could do so, so much confidence did he have in the quality of the writing and the profundity of his themes. He wondered only half whimsically if President Fillmore would invite him to the White House after he had read it, so clearly did it portray such a vital piece of the American economy, and he imagined his lecture tours of the colleges, speaking on everything from whaling to the cultures of the South Seas to American expansionism to slavery to the nature of God Himself, all matters he felt he had explained satisfactorily in his book. In a few weeks, he would return to New York to proof the typeset pages and make final changes to the tumultuous ending, but for now it was out of his hands.

He had completed the concluding chapters in such a fever—of writing and building and mowing and caring for Lizzie with her pregnancy and her hay fevers and traveling back and forth to New York with the pages—that he was no longer quite sure even of the order of events at the very end, except in their broad outline and the fate of Ahab; but he felt he had delivered on the promise of the original idea and brought out the underlying themes that had drifted so lazily in the undercurrents of his imagination until Hawthorne had fished them out. He believed that he had even out-Hawthorned Hawthorne in the breadth and depth of his central allegory—and he could not wait for the older author to read it! He reveled in a feeling of divinity, that he was as much a part of eternal consciousness at that moment as it was possible for any mortal to be.

Everything suddenly seemed simple. His mind raced across vast cosmic distances in an instant, and he saw the whole long reach of philosophy and history and aesthetics plainly, as if all the ideas that had come before had been laid on a buffet for him to select or reject; and he felt, looking back on the sweep of his novel, that he could write another book better than *The Whale* starting tomorrow and it might take only tomorrow to do it.

His peace on his birthday unfortunately had not rippled into the rest of the Melville household. Lizzie was lying abed with a nose stuffed up so badly that she could hardly breathe, and her whole face had turned the bright rosy red of the stripes of the American flag; and Malcolm was suffering from another of his mysterious snot-filled ailments, which usually accompanied his mother's illnesses. But Herman did not wish to think of Lizzie's pregnancy or Malcolm's illness: he simply wished to be left alone with his feelings of peace and triumph, which he felt he had achieved in spite of his family and not because of them.

Everything was in such perfect order in his mind that he had only one real birthday wish, one final piece of blue sky that would make his puzzle complete—to ramble down to Lenox to see Hawthorne, to take Nathaniel up on his invitation to visit without the ever-watchful presence of Sophia to circumscribe their conversation. He was eager to tell Hawthorne that *The Whale* was finished— it would have been Herman's preference simply to present the book to him, already published, to give the first copy of the first edition to the man to whom it would be dedicated—but it would be some time yet before the book would come out, and it was finished now. It was done! He had written "The End," and he wanted Hawthorne to be the first to know.

He bathed himself and changed clothes, donning a floppy green hat that he had won from a Spaniard in a card game on board his first whaling ship. Then he saddled his horse and set off down the road toward Lenox.

The day became stiflingly hot and humid as the afternoon progressed, and he quickly soaked his fresh clothes with sweat; but not even the bottle flies feeding on his horse's neck and the bees that landed on his own skin could bother Herman today. He rode down the white dirt road, through meadows sprinkled with turtlehead blossoms and yellow celandines and loppyheaded bluebells, and he felt like laughing.

He passed a great deal of traffic, and he decided that he would greet everyone he met in Spanish, to match his Spanish hat. He said a hearty "*buenos días*" to the passengers of several farm wagons, two stately carriages, and a barouche, and to a few Shakers on foot he said "*¡Qué hermoso cielo!*" He was rewarded with puzzled looks, which delighted him; but, in one instance, a gentleman returned his greeting and asked a rather long question in Spanish, which Melville did not understand, so he replied, "*E aha ta'oe i pe'au mai?*"— one of the few phrases in Marquesan that he still remembered, which meant, "What did you say?" The gentleman and he stared at one another for a moment and then silently resumed their trips in opposite directions.

About half a mile outside of Lenox, Herman spied a man stretched out in the shade of a tree along the road, reading a newspaper. As he drew close, he discerned that it was none other than

Hawthorne himself! He pulled the brim of his hat down low, rode up near him, and said in a hammy, gruff voice, *"Buenos días, señor."*

Hawthorne looked up. "Yes. Hello." He flicked his wrist, waving the horseman on.

"El cielo está hermoso esta tarde."

A little tango of bemusement danced across Hawthorne's features. *"Sí,"* he said, and he flicked his wrist again.

"I am afraid I am at the end of my Spanish, Hawthorne, unless you would like me to name parts of a ship. *Velamen. Mástil."*

"What the devil? Melville!" Hawthorne folded his newspaper and stood up. "I mistook you for a conquistador."

"Señor, it was no mistake." He dismounted. They shook hands with gusto. Herman indicated the paper, now under Hawthorne's arm. "What news?"

"They are still finding pieces of Fort Des Moines in New Orleans. How swims *The Whale*?"

"He's fin up," said Herman proudly. "The manuscript is done. Nothing left but to proof it and deliver it to Bentley."

"Congratulations," said Hawthorne. "And when shall I have a copy?"

"You know how these things are," Herman shrugged. "Weeks, I hope, rather than months."

"I look forward to it. Shall we walk? Julian is in a blackberry patch up the road." Herman led his horse, and the two authors walked side by side. "I am coming out with a book for children later in the year, only a few hundred pages, but it's mostly done. A simplified retelling of Greek and Roman myths, in an American setting."

Herman was astonished. "You act like a man of leisure but come out with a book every three months."

"It was Sophia's confinement that did it this time. We have entertained practically no visitors for months, and my days have been filled with nothing but reading, writing, and fetching things for Sophia—or, more recently, for the new baby. And, as I have told you before, I knew that you were hard at work over in the next hamlet, and I have been inspired to accelerate my usual dawdling pace as a result. I will write whole Bibles in the Berkshires, at this rate."

"I suppose I must get back to work immediately, if I am to keep pace. What will this one be called?"

"*A Wonder Book*. Wonder frees your mind from necessity so that you can marvel at possibilities. And yours? Have you settled definitely on *The Whale*?"

"Bentley is convinced that that's the right title for the English edition, but I am inclined to call it *Moby Dick* for the American."

"*Moby Dick*? After the whale that sank the *Essex*?"

"His name was Mocha Dick, if you'll recall."

"Do sailors call all whales Dick, then?"

"All whales, and some other things, besides."

A loud ruckus of snapping twigs and rustling brush signaled Julian's appearance from beneath a berry bramble. He came running across a grassy field toward the road, shouting merrily, his face smeared purple with juice. "Herman Melville, Herman Melville," he yelled. He collided roughly with Herman's legs and threw his arms around them.

"And how are you for a horseman, Master Julian?"

"Capital!"

"Then up you go." Herman hoisted Julian up by the armpits, onto his horse. When he was steady in the saddle, Melville let him go and said, "*Salve Rey Julian*."

Julian was bright with glee. "What's his name?" He rubbed the horse's neck and tugged his mane.

"Anonymous."

"Animus," Julian tried. "That's a funny name."

"Anonymous," Herman said again.

"Anomalous." Julian made a sour face and flopped his legs against the saddle. "I'm going to call him Herman."

Hawthorne said, "The boy is wise beyond his years. Animus Anomalous Herman: he has you pegged in every particular."

Herman took off his hat and placed it on Julian's head. It swallowed up his entire face. Hawthorne took the hat off his son and put it back on Melville's head with a friendly pat on the crown. Herman thought he would die of happiness.

They walked at a leisurely pace to Hawthorne's cottage, chatting amiably about Lizzie's pregnancy, and about the newest Hawthorne child and Sophia's extraordinary recovery. Once Rose had been born, Sophia's migraines had returned to their normal frequency and intensity, finally falling into the background of her everyday life, and the mysterious stabbing pains in her side had vanished, and so they chalked the whole episode up to a difficult pregnancy rather than a lapse back to the frailty of her youth. In fact, Hawthorne said, Sophia had recently been out for long walks around the lake and had even taken the children berrying just before she had left for Boston, and he was greatly encouraged. Herman told Hawthorne of Lizzie's hay fevers and summer colds, and they discussed how worrisome it was to care for someone who is ill and whose condition was liable, at any moment, to take a turn for the worse.

Having brought each other up to date about their books and their wives, they walked the rest of the way in contented silence, Julian beaming delightedly all the while and occasionally offering up an earnest non sequitur, such as "My mother is one hundred years old," and "When I am grown up, everyone must mind me." When they arrived at the cottage, Hawthorne said, "Shall we see if any string beans are ready?" He led the way around the side of his house to the garden.

"How is *Seven Gables* doing?" Herman asked, as he unsaddled his horse and Hawthorne inspected the beans, and asparagus, and heads of lettuce sticking up out of the carefully weeded black loam. Julian began digging for worms.

"I think I have reached that stage where I do not care, essentially, for anybody's opinion." Hawthorne crouched and handled several heads of lettuce before picking the one he wanted. "I have heard and seen such diversity of judgment that I'd be a bewildered man if I attempted to strike a balance among them—so I take nobody's opinion to heart, unless it happens to agree with my own. I think this book was more characteristic of my mind and more proper and natural for me to write than *The Scarlet Letter.*"

"I was asking about sales."

"Oh—of course. It has sold better than *The Scarlet Letter* and, I think, is more sure of holding its ground for the long run. I understand that it's popular in England, as well, but I don't have copyright for it there yet, so the pounds flow into someone else's pockets for the moment—you know how tiresome that is, with the rights all in dispute." He tossed the lettuce to Herman and then picked string beans until both his hands were full. "Would you like to tell me anything about the final shape of *The Whale*, or would you prefer that I simply read it?"

For an instant, Herman was tempted to reveal that he planned to dedicate the work to Hawthorne, but thought better of it. "I will say only this: that, among other things, *The Whale* is still white. And frightful."

Herman followed Hawthorne into his parlor, where they placed the vegetables on the table. Hawthorne opened a box of Havana cigars and offered it up for Herman's selection. They each took one and walked outside again.

"Insofar as I think about such things as I write," said Hawthorne,

"I try to exemplify in fiction those spaces in human society where the actual and the imaginary may meet, and each imbue itself with the nature of the other, whether those pairings be religious or aesthetic or what have you. To me, that is the whole purpose of fiction, to provide us occasions of meditation in which we may find the intersection of the timeless with time. The idea of original sin, for instance, is useful not because it may literally be true but because it provides an occasion for discourse about the mysteries that lie beyond the power of the human mind to encompass."

"You do love original sin, don't you?"

"Original sin is not merely a moral conundrum but includes the idea of origination itself; or, I should say, it allows us a way to discuss the question: what is society's proper relationship to that which came before it and lies beyond it?"

Hawthorne lit their cigars, and they stood in the shade of the oak tree beside the cottage and puffed contentedly for a while. Julian walked up, holding, in his cupped hands, an earthworm, vivisected into three pieces, each of which writhed unpleasantly in search of the others. Julian offered this prize as a mute question.

"Do you know the story of Jonah, Master Julian?" asked Herman. Julian shook his head no. "It is from the Bible, and in it, a man is swallowed by a whale; but your worm reminds me of it, because a worm also appears in that story."

"What *doesn't* remind you of whales, Melville?"

Herman ignored Hawthorne's ribbing and began telling Julian about Jonah—how God had commanded him to go preach against the city of Nineveh, but Jonah didn't want to go and instead fled to Joppa, where he got on a boat headed for Tarshish; but God caused a terrible storm to threaten the boat, and the crew discovered that God was angry at Jonah, and they threw him overboard, where he was swallowed by a whale.

Hawthorne clapped Herman on the shoulder. "But where is the worm in Jonah's tale?"

"After the whale vomits up Jonah, he goes to Nineveh and preaches as God had commanded, but everyone ignores him," said Herman. "So he leaves the city and curses God and finds some plants out in the desert to shelter him, and God sends a worm to eat the plants."

First one, then another of the pieces of the worm in Julian's hands stopped struggling, until only one third seemed at all alive. He flung the pieces as far as he could, scattering them in the grass. "God hates worms and so do I," he said.

"I am not sure that that is the moral of the story," said Hawthorne.

"I want a whale," his son shouted.

Hawthorne ushered his son inside and told him to clean his hands and face; then he returned to Herman out in the meadow, and they strolled aimlessly around the cottage, circling back and crossing and crisscrossing the paths that they made through the grasses, smoking and chatting. Impudently, Herman slipped his arm through Hawthorne's as they strolled, and Hawthorne, instead of protesting or resisting, walked closer to Herman.

Herman wished he could exchange all the tomorrows that would ever come for this instant, for this closeness, for this knowingness and being known—but wish though he might, they did not pass into eternity. The breeze fluttered the leaves overhead and bent the goldenrods, and the low white clouds shuttled fleeting shadows across the face of the earth, and voices from the faraway sea murmured indecipherable secrets in Herman's ears.

After their cigars, they went inside to find Julian playing with a lively little snow-white bunny, which Hawthorne explained had come to them rather recently and had become Julian's captive playmate. Julian introduced him as Hindlegs, and the little rabbit went hopping up to meet Herman. True to his name, the bunny stood up on his hind legs and twitched his pink nose.

"He wants food," said Julian.

Hawthorne said, "He eats constantly but turns up his nose at any leaves or grass that aren't entirely fresh." Julian grabbed a jackknife from the corner table and ran outside, while Herman patted the bunny. "When he first came to us," Hawthorne went on, "he seemed to pass his life switching rapidly between torpid slumber and quick apprehensiveness and no state in between. Something about how easily startled he was, and how lifeless he seemed most of the time, made me want to eat him. Now, there is the influence of the Evil One! But he has grown quite familiar to us now and hops to meet us whenever we come in and likes to inspect our clothing for the smells we bring home. He gnaws at Julian's shoes when we are sitting quietly— I believe it is his way of drawing attention to himself—and always contrives to hop into Julian's lap. It is odd to speculate what he thinks of human company and how he manages to quell his fear of us, since we must be so peculiar to him—so big and frightening and yet so amiable and always bringing him food."

Julian returned with fresh-cut pigweed and lettuce and swept a few crumbs of bread off the dining table into his hand, all of which the bunny devoured greedily. He kept up a running conversation with Hindlegs, mainly about local dragons and the location of their lairs and the times of day when they came out. When Hindlegs had consumed all the greens, he hopped under the table, and Julian immediately forgot about him and demanded to have his hair curled.

To Herman's surprise, Hawthorne handed Julian a basin and told him to go outside and fill it with water from the pump. Herman followed Hawthorne out in the opposite direction, up the hill in front of the cottage, and they gathered sticks of various thicknesses and brought them back into the parlor. Herman sat by and watched while

Hawthorne washed and rinsed his son's hair and then screwed lockets of it around the sticks rather poorly, catching it constantly and nearly pulling the hair out of the boy's head. Julian squealed and laughed all the while. Herman would never have thought to carry on in such a supplicating way with Malcolm, and he thought of Lizzie's question again: what did he love about Malcolm? He considered asking Hawthorne what he loved about Julian—he suspected he would receive a fuller answer than Herman could provide about his own son. Julian babbled on and on; and though Hawthorne seemed to tire of the lad's prattle, Herman believed that he, in fact, was enjoying himself as much as his son was. It had never occurred to Herman that a father and son might enjoy each other as people, beyond their family roles. His own father had taken little interest in him beyond telling him constantly what to do and how poorly he was doing it, and Herman recognized with a start that he had always been just as indifferent toward Malcolm as his own father had been toward him. The bunny withdrew into the darkest corner beneath a chair on the opposite side of the parlor and huddled into itself, seemingly fearfully, reminding Herman disturbingly of Malcolm; and the whiteness of the rabbit conferred, in Herman's imagination, a special poignance on the scene, lending it the power of milky Jove himself.

They passed the afternoon with Hawthorne at Julian's beck and call and the three of them exchanging nonsense at Julian's lead, until dinner. Melville thought they could almost have been a family, the three of them, and to blazes with tradition and even biology. Perhaps, he thought, even Malcolm could be happy in their impossible family, and they would all flourish in the care of Hawthorne's fatherly love.

Dinner consisted of lettuce, boiled string beans and asparagus, raw tomatoes, and a cucumber, accompanied by slices of black bread with butter. The bunny partook of most of the dishes and seemed to relish them more than anyone. Herman was rather astonished at this fare: his own evening meals nearly always featured meat and a great deal of wine.

"Do you always eat like this?" he asked.

"We would normally not have cucumber *and* asparagus in the same meal, but your presence here makes it a special occasion," said Hawthorne.

After dinner, as the sun dipped below the horizon, Hawthorne lit a lamp and Julian corralled Hindlegs and carried him upstairs. Hawthorne washed the dinner dishes in a basin and then rinsed and refilled the basin outside at the pump. Father and son met again at the foot of the stairs, Julian dressed now in a loose white bedshirt; and Julian kissed his father on the cheek and threw his arms around Herman's legs, after which he ran upstairs without looking back, calling "good night good night good night" all the way into his room, until his door shut with a dry wooden snap.

"He wakes up talking and falls asleep in midsentence," said Hawthorne. "But he occasionally says things that are accidentally wise."

"Or perhaps not accidentally."

"Spend a few days here, and you will see that almost everything with Julian is accidental," Hawthorne said, with affection.

Because Herman was a very different sort of father than Hawthorne, and because Julian seemed so much happier than Malcolm, Herman found that this gentle, fatherly talk opened his heart to Nathaniel even more than everything else that had come before. Herman's own childhood had been filled with incomprehension, high expectations, secret failure, and seething anger, and he wondered how his life might have turned out differently had he been raised in such an atmosphere of tolerance and good humor.

In Herman's mind, his life had buckled and collapsed like bricks scattered from an earthshaken wall, each brick a separate and unconnected aspect of himself—sailor, author, success, failure, father, brother, husband, debtor, blasphemer, adulterer, liar, son. The wall had fallen, the bricks strewn and heaped chaotically without structure or meaning; but now it all finally made sense, and he relabeled every brick in his self "Hawthorne" and rebuilt the wall, so that between him and the rest of the world was a barricade of Hawthorne, with only Nathaniel himself enclosed beside him.

"I assume you still have a taste for brandy," said Hawthorne, motioning for Herman to follow him into the study. Hawthorne threw open the windows, and the cool night breeze seemed like the very breath of Hebe, goddess of youth, on Herman's brow. Hawthorne opened the lower drawer of the cabinet next to his desk and withdrew a clear bottle with a caramel-colored liquid inside, and red wax sealing the mouth. "My friend Pierce sent it to me during the first success of *Seven Gables*—Pierre Chabanneau Cognac, 1811. Do you know it? Means nothing to me, but I thought it might appeal to a connoisseur like yourself."

Herman took the bottle and weighed it in his hands appreciatively. "It is eight years older than I am," he said.

"Pierce made a special point of mentioning that it was bottled under the Great Comet that passed that year. Pierce is always searching for magic and signs."

Hawthorne tore the wax off the top and unstoppered the cork underneath. He set the bottle on his desk and excused himself to get glasses. Herman breathed in the scent of the cognac: a green, herbaceous odor, mixed with citrusy sweetness, which lingered thickly at the back of his throat, like fat. Nathaniel returned and poured. They held their glasses up to the light, appreciating how the brandy became a tawny copper color in small volumes. Hawthorne toasted "the angels in the dark corners of our hearts," and Herman drank and let the concoction linger on his tongue and in his nose, the sweet taste and perfume of oranges giving way to the woody smoke of lavender and finally an acridness like coriander, the whole blending finally into something deliriously soft and faraway, the distant magnolias of childhood memories.

Hawthorne offered him another cigar, and they took their epicurean delights back into the parlor, where they opened all the windows and sat in the armchairs. "Sophia does not permit smoking indoors," he said, lighting their Havanas. Herman contentedly puffed and sipped. He watched their smoke drift languidly around the room and then outside, where fireflies winked yellow polka dots into the dark fabric of the night. He found himself wondering if Adam had smoked in the Garden of Eden, and if Eve had made him take his cigars out among the cattle and sheep—but he could not remember if God had already given them fire before the serpent had appeared. The devil certainly had fire, he thought. Perhaps the devil had taught man to smoke. He followed this daisy chain of fanciful thoughts for a while until it led to "Rappaccini's Daughter," Hawthorne's own story of Eden corrupted, and he remembered a notion he had long wished to discuss with him.

"I am toying with an idea," said Herman. "A prophetic theory, or a cautionary tale, if you like. Namely: if America is the New Eden, the White Man has come to destroy it, in an act of revenge for our expulsion from the original Eden. Our entire enterprise as a nation is a violent revenge against God for tempting us into sin and heaving us out of paradise. Thus, we found a new paradise, the New World, and are destroying it, as an affront to God."

"You are obsessed with violence, Melville."

"No more than you are obsessed with sin, and this theory has the appeal of combining the two. So-called original sin—which is really just God's way of sabotaging man's innocence by making knowledge inherently corrupt—sets the stage for the revenge of knowledge on paradise; or, to put it another way, the destruction of nature through technology is our way of proving that we are more powerful than God and did not need him or his magic Tree of Knowledge to acquire his secrets for ourselves. We must avenge ourselves on God by destroying what is his."

Hawthorne said, "But the revenge will not be against God, since God does not have to reside in the New Eden. If your theory is correct, even if we destroyed the New Eden, God would remain uninjured and we ourselves would be destroyed, thus proving God's original position that we should not have been entrusted with such knowledge to begin with. And I have read nowhere that the intent of the Mayflower colonists or any of their descendants was destruction. No one wishes to destroy this paradise, if paradise it be—except you! They wish to tame it and prosper from its conquest."

"But in taming it, we do destroy it. Civilization is the name we give to the destruction of nature."

"Would you have us all become savages, Melville?"

"Were Adam and Eve savages?"

"I believe you may be taking the story of Eden a little more literally than it was intended."

"We were raised in different churches, you and I."

Hawthorne poured them each another glass of fine cognac. Herman could not remember a better birthday.

"I would like to tell you a story, Melville, of a scene I saw once in a circus in New York. Nothing much interested me in the circus except a sick monkey, a very large and elderly one, it seemed to me. His keeper brought him some pieces of apple, and some water and some tea. The keeper said that the monkey had quite lost his appetite and refused all ordinary diet, but he came eagerly when he smelled the apple, and the keeper exhorted him to eat it. But the poor monkey shook his head, with the most pitiable expression I ever saw, at the same time extending his hand to take the keeper's hand, as if claiming his friendship. But the keeper, who was rather a surly fellow, refused his hand; and by and by, he essayed harsher measures and insisted that the monkey should eat; and thereupon ensued a struggle and the tea was overturned upon the straw of the monkey's bed and the slices of apple scattered. Then the keeper scolded the monkey and seized him by one arm and dragged him out of the little cage of his bedroom into the larger surrounding pen, upon which the monkey began a loud, harsh, reproachful chatter. Observing us spectators in front of the pen, the monkey seemed to appeal to us directly and stretched out his lean arm and black hand between the bars, as if trying to claim the grasp of any friend he might have in the whole world. He was pliable, however; for when the keeper called him in a gentler tone, he hobbled back toward him with a stiff and rusty movement, and in the end they affectionately hugged one another. To me, this analogy might be more apt than your New Eden. God has created a circus, with us monkeys as the attraction and his angels as the audience, to whom we must appeal. But ultimately, no matter how we are mistreated, we must return to the embrace of the Creator, for he is our only source of sustenance, even though he be a surly fellow."

"And what role does the devil play in your circus?"

"Perhaps the devil plays the crank organ that mocks everyone." Hawthorne took a healthy drink of brandy. "I am analogizing on the fly, Melville, and the details may need some work. What role does the devil play in your New Eden of America?"

Herman squinted through the smoke. "The devil created everything in the first place."

"But that merely makes you a Zoroastrian, and we know how

unfashionable that is, these days. You should try something more Hindoo, perhaps."

"Or cannibalistic."

"Sometimes, Melville, I think you truly aren't a Christian at all."

Their conversation continued in this vein for some time, becoming more playful and less coherent as the brandy and cigars took effect. By the time Herman had officially subscribed to Zoroastrianism and Hawthorne had become a Coptic, the cognac was three quarters gone, and they had each smoked yet another Havana; and finally, Herman looked at his empty glass and at Hawthorne, wondering if they should finish the bottle; and Hawthorne said that he ought to try to get some sleep, since he had promised to take Julian to the Highwood estate across the lake the next morning to play.

They stood up simultaneously. Hawthorne, who was less used to drinking such large quantities of alcohol, lurched awkwardly into Herman, who caught him and encompassed him in an awkward hug. Hawthorne regained his balance by pushing heavily into Melville's body, and they both stood up straighter, Herman embracing Hawthorne quite strongly now.

The two men stood literally nose to nose, their smoky, brandied breath filling each other's nostrils, the heat of their embrace warming their bodies. Herman realized with heart-stopping joy that he needed but turn his head slightly to kiss Hawthorne. Now! he thought, Let eternity begin now!—and Hawthorne became very still, standing with his body pressed into Herman's but seeming to withdraw spiritually into a shadow inside himself. Herman tried to read the look in Nathaniel's eyes, but he was too close, and Hawthorne's features swam formlessly before him. Herman pushed his pelvis gently into Hawthorne's, with ever so carefully increasing pressure, and he felt Hawthorne respond. He almost couldn't believe it was true, so he rubbed his hip a little against him—but it was true! Herman turned his head and kissed Nathaniel full on the mouth. Hawthorne did not pull away. Herman kissed him again, a lingering, wet kiss.

For the first time in his life, Herman truly believed in the soul, for he felt his own soul as a phantom rising up inside him, as if it had journeyed from below the earth itself on its way to the heavens. It filled his entire body, until he nearly burst with the strength and energy of the divine within: he was a column of soul connecting the earth and sky through Nathaniel's kiss.

Hawthorne turned his head aside, and a thrill of terror shot through Herman's whole body—he clutched at Hawthorne, who convulsed and gasped, and this shuddering continued wordlessly for a few moments. The room seemed veiled in supernatural shadows. Finally, Hawthorne took a single step backward, so that Herman saw the shock of disbelief in his eyes.

Nathaniel now bent at the waist in a most unnatural way and hung his head, so that his gaze fell to the floor. Herman did not know quite how to address him, and he felt a complicated mixture of elation and disappointment.

Hawthorne's breathing gradually returned to normal, but he continued to stare fixedly at Herman's feet, the mystic shadows in the room deepening. Herman wanted to reach out to him, to take him in his arms, to say some words of love or understanding; but Nathaniel seemed possessed by something deep within himself, as if an abyss had opened before his eyes and he could not look away from it to the solid forms around him. He could only guess at the thoughts struggling against one another in Hawthorne's mind: he tried to think back to the first time he had kissed a man in such a way, tried to remember all the confusing emotions it had inspired.

"Nathaniel," he breathed.

Hawthorne held his hand up for silence, and then took another step back, awkwardly, as if one of his legs had become wooden.

"Nathaniel, I know how you must feel." Melville immediately regretted his pleading tone.

"I do not believe you do."

"Then tell me. Tell me how you feel." Herman took a step forward, and Hawthorne retreated, until his back collided with the door frame. "Tell me, Nathaniel. Believe me, I will understand."

Hawthorne glanced furtively over his shoulder up the stairs, but no one was there. "Please be gone, Melville," he said.

"Nathaniel, let me into your confidence."

"What is there to say? What would I say to Sophia, if she came in now?"

"But she will not come in now. Please."

Hawthorne straightened up to his full height, and his forced dignity made Herman sad. "The situation could not be more grave," said Hawthorne. He lifted his left arm straight out, his index finger pointing toward the front door. "Go."

"I cannot," Herman said. "I cannot go. Please talk to me."

"Begone!" He peered up the stairs toward his son's room.

Herman no longer recognized the person behind Hawthorne's empty, enraged, haunted eyes. This was the New Eden—slightly different from the way he had foretold it—and now he was being expelled. His body felt as heavy as a sperm whale's. He moved gracelessly toward the door.

He placed his hand on the knob and stood for an interminably bleak moment; he wanted to turn around, but he did not want the memory of Nathaniel's face, as it must look now, carved forever into the marbled fissures of his mind; so he opened the door and stepped out into the night without looking back. The moment he crossed the threshold, he heard Hawthorne's quick steps, and the door slammed with finality behind him.

He walked toward his horse; in his mind's eye, he became the sick, elderly monkey in the story that Hawthorne had told him, the dying, scolded, speechless beast holding out his hand for love but getting, in return, only anger. He saddled up his horse in the moonlight, mounted, and turned toward home—the home that was no home; the home that was the whole homeless world.

Chapter 18

Madness Maddened

A rain shower had been falling all day and persisted now, sometime after nine o'clock at night. Herman stood in a boggy puddle outside Hawthorne's cottage, beard astraggle, his clothes soaked through, his pant legs soiled. Days had passed—maybe weeks—he had lost track of the rising and setting suns, the number of letters he had written that Hawthorne had not answered, the sleepless nights buffeted by Nathaniel's brutal silence.

A gust of wind swayed the trees overhead. Lamplight shone through the windows of the parlor. Inside, Sophia and Nathaniel were hosting a middle-aged woman, with whom they sat talking intensely over cups of tea. Melville knew the woman—he had seen her lecture in Manhattan—Fredrika Bremer, a Swedish novelist and abolitionist. She sat now where Herman had sat enjoying Hawthorne's brandy and cigars: would that moment still exist, Herman wondered, if Hawthorne denied it?

Herman felt all of his hairs stand on end and then lightning sizzled directly above him; in the momentary brilliance, Fredrika Bremer turned her face toward the window and met Herman's gaze directly. They both gasped and then the darkness swallowed Herman again, as thunder shook him from the inside out. He could see her gesturing for the Hawthornes to look out the window, pointing directly at him, and he froze. He could not be caught lurking outside Hawthorne's parlor in the rain. He had to flee or go to the door and knock: however untoward his appearance there, at such an hour, it would be better to announce himself candidly than be discovered; and yet, what would he say? He willed himself to run but his feet remained glued to the spot. He saw Hawthorne inside opening a box on his mantel and striding purposefully to the front door—he was coming out alone! Herman withdrew a few feet under the boughs of an elm tree.

The door flew open and Hawthorne walked out. He was holding a knife. "Hello!" he said. "Is anyone there?"

Herman answered in a deep bass whisper, which he had learned at sea, a kind of low grunt that cut through the wind and the rain. "Hawthorne, I must speak with you."

Hawthorne walked cautiously a few feet farther. Herman waved his arms until Nathaniel saw him.

"Melville! Are you mad? You cannot just appear at my window in the middle of the night wagging your beard. Sophia is at home, and we have a guest."

"Your silence is cruel and pitiless. I demand that we resolve the matter between us."

"And what matter lies between us?"

"What matter?" Herman cried in despair. Lightning flashed, showing Herman's ginger beard silvered with raindrops. Strands of Hawthorne's wet hair snaked across his face. Thunder clapped, and Herman saw Sophia silhouetted in the doorway. Melville lowered his voice to an urgent hiss.

"I did not come here to argue, or condemn, or judge," Herman said. "I only wish that you could admit the true nature of the love lying in your heart and thereby attain the highest possible happiness. In your own heart is the strength you need to accept the love you feel."

Sophia yelled from the doorway, "Nathaniel? Do you need assistance?"

"Hawthorne, do you know your true nature and yet lie to me, or have you misled us both?"

"True nature? That has no meaning here," said Hawthorne. "The only matter under discussion tonight is whether or not I am an adulterer. And I am not."

Sophia called again from the doorway. She took a hesitant step out into the rain.

"A moment," Hawthorne yelled back. He lowered his voice again and said to Herman, "We will settle this another day."

"I will not be put off to suffer your silence again. You have misused my heart too often in the past."

Sophia said, "Who is that with you?"

"I beg of you, Melville, go!"

Herman turned toward the cottage and yelled hoarsely, "Sophia!" He strode past Hawthorne, kicking up water and mud with his heavy boots. "Pardon this intrusion, and the lateness of the hour. I had been berrying, and my horse wandered out of sight, and in my fruitless searching I found myself suddenly near your door."

From the parlor, Fredrika Bremer exclaimed, "Berrying? At night? And in this weather?"

"Come in, Herman," Sophia said, taking him by the arm and escorting him inside. "Dry yourself a little and have a cup of tea. You can take up the search again when the rain has passed."

Hawthorne followed Herman inside in great agitation. Sophia brought them each towels, with which they dried their hair and faces, Herman staring all the while at Hawthorne, Hawthorne keeping his eyes on his boots. Melville was drenched through, and he continued to drip even after his towel was saturated, so that he felt unable to take the seat Sophia offered him. A puddle formed around him. Sophia poured four fresh cups of tea, and then said, "I have completely forgotten myself on such a strange night! Allow me to introduce Mr. Herman Melville. Herman, this is Fredrika Bremer."

He took her hand. "I have met you once before, madam." He felt as if he were in a dream. "You spoke at an antislavery rally I attended in New York."

He remained standing in front of the other three, who all sat down with teacups and saucers. It was as if they were waiting for a show, or at least a better explanation of his presence. Herman suppressed the impulse to perform, to clown and joke his way out of trouble. He had caused this untenable situation: he had raised the stakes by charging into the house, yet now that he was here, he understood that Hawthorne's parlor held no solace, no solution. He saw a riot of fear and anger erupting behind Hawthorne's eyes.

Finally, Fredrika said, "I have read your book, Mr. Melville."

"Which one?"

"The one where you speak out against the cruelty of the missionaries toward the South Sea Islanders."

"*Typee*. Or *Omoo*."

"Yes, *Omoo*. Do you find that your work has made a difference?"

"No."

Fredrika sipped her tea and looked away. Herman continued to stand in front of them, dripping, without knowing how to end the charade.

Sophia said, "When does your next book come out, Herman?"

"Soon. They are proofreading it in London."

"And is your new book another call for social change?" Fredrika asked doggedly.

A fine question, Herman thought. What *is* my new book about? He fixed his gaze on Hawthorne, and even took a step in Nathaniel's direction. "It is a book of hatred," he said. "Of vengeance, of the longing for something denied, which, even if we grasp it in our hands, is taken from us by the machinations of fate and the misunderstanding of others and the indifferent disregard of nature, which binds our spirits to the gross mortal world, unto death. It is a book about the limits of human suffering, and will, and loneliness."

"Funny," Hawthorne said coldly. "The draft I read seemed mainly about blubber."

Herman stared at Nathaniel in horror. His hands began to shake, rattling his cup and saucer. He looked to Sophia for help but found only bewilderment. He looked to Fredrika Bremer, who was exactly as puzzled as she had been before. When his gaze met Hawthorne's again, Herman's eyes welled with tears. Hawthorne stood, his face flushed red.

"Melville," Hawthorne said. Herman set his teacup down, turned, and left the house.

The moment the wind and rain hit his face, he began to run, and he did not stop till he had reached the top of the hill overlooking the cottage. No one chased after him; no voices followed him into the night. At the hillcrest, he turned, panting, hands on his knees, staring back at the warm yellow light shining from the parlor, and wept.

Autumn 1851

Chapter 19

Hopeless

Jeanie Field walked purposefully along Pearl Street in Manhattan, searching the doorways and windows for the Harper & Brothers sign. The high, cool October sun shone pleasantly between red-brick buildings, and she enjoyed the rustling bustle of her petticoats beneath her new scarlet-and-black striped dress—but she had already passed the block to which she had been directed. She stopped momentarily to gaze up and down the street, at the passing horses and carriages and the brusque, bewhiskered gentlemen rushing by on errands of commerce. It was a dreary part of town, devoted to business. She walked on.

Beyond the curve at Wall Street, near the East River wharf, she spied a bearded, redheaded man holding a sheaf of papers before him, reading intently as he walked. His floppy, wide-brimmed hat partially obscured his face, but he had the unmistakable rolling gait of a sailor. Jeanie stole up behind and poked him in both sides with her index fingers. "Herman!"

Melville took a tremendous hopping step. He lost his papers for an instant, clutching them against his chest at the last possible moment before they scattered away. He unleashed a blue streak that caused even grown men around him to protest.

"I knew it was you!"

"Miss Field," he said dismissively, then immediately turned and strode away, shuffling his papers back into order.

Jeanie rushed to catch up. "And a very great pleasure it is to see you, as well." She put her arm through his and slowed him down. "Your brother Allan said I might find you here."

"And what business did you have to call on him?"

"There's no need to be surly. I'm sorry I startled you."

"No, you aren't. You intended to."

"Selling your grand whaling adventure, then?"

"On the contrary, I have sold a pair of English copyrights for a crust of bread."

"Whatever do you mean?"

Herman steered them east on Gouverneur Lane, toward the water. He waved the papers at Jeanie, but their fluttering permitted no close inspection. "*Typee. Omoo*," he said.

"Yes?"

"I have assigned their English copyrights to John Murray in London."

Jeanie puzzled over this. "I'm afraid I don't understand."

"They have been pirated so many times in England that I have seen neither pound nor penny from them in five years, so I have sold the English copyright to Murray. Since the Harper brothers are famous pirates themselves, I thought they would like to know that I have joined Murray on the side of the law, so I have delivered a copy of the agreements to them—a kind of shot across the bow."

"But even Dudley says that no one pays any attention to copyrights. They have no value whatsoever."

"They have no value *because* no one pays attention to them."

Jeanie yanked Herman to a stop. "Are you saying that you don't own the rights to your own works anymore? Are you sure this Murray is not just taking advantage of you?"

Herman took a deep breath. "Miss Field, how do my copyrights concern you?"

"I love your books, Herman. It matters to me what happens to them."

Herman looked into her speckled gray eyes and appraised her open, pretty young face. She does love my books, he thought. As nettlesome as her attentions had been, Herman saw that her admiration truly sprang from his writing; and he suddenly recognized that, for a girl who could not escape New England herself, his early books might seem like a passage to freedom. "I am afraid you do not understand the problem," he said, softening. "By giving Murray the copyright, I am allowing him standing in the English courts to sue on my behalf. He is enjoining George Routledge—who has sold thousands of copies of *Typee* and *Omoo* without paying me—to stop selling my books illegally. And if Murray sells some in the future himself, legally, he will at least send me a penny or two."

"A penny or two does not seem enough to feed a new baby."

"Thank you for pointing that out." Herman pulled his arm away and walked on toward the water. "Who told you?"

"Mrs. Morewood. It's no secret that Mrs. Melville has given you another son, and congratulations! What is the matter with you?"

"You seem to know all the best sources for gossip. Does Mrs. Morewood also believe that you and I are having an affair?"

"On the contrary, I have invented one for you and Mrs. Morewood. Don't be surprised if Dr. Holmes pays you another visit and insists that you stop seeing her."

Melville stared at her in disbelief. "You would make a good sea captain, Miss Field. Your whims are incomprehensible, you set sail in whatever direction you please no matter the weather, and it is impossible to disobey you."

"You do, at every turn. But let us talk about something serious for a moment."

"I will not move to New Lebanon with you."

"No, really serious: how does this copyright situation affect your whaling adventure? I saw Mr. Duyckinck last week and he said your new novel would be in stores any day now."

"So it will, and who knows what will happen, in terms of the copyright. The first three months after its release will be critical—that's about how long it takes for publishing houses to begin printing illegal versions—but no one will bother to pirate the book if the legitimate editions fail to sell."

"I know it will be a success, Herman. I can't wait to read it myself, and all of my friends are excited to have it."

"How many friends do you have?"

They arrived at the wharf and turned north. The water of the East River was steel gray, and the wind blew it into choppy little waves. Ahead, on a pier enclosed by a white wooden fence, men were rolling barrels off a ship.

"You might at least be a little kind to me," said Jeanie. "Surely you know how unpleasant it feels to try to impress someone you love and yet still suffer his disapprobation."

Herman looked heavenward. In his mind's eye, he saw Hawthorne's angry face. "Yes, you're right. I apologize, Miss Field."

She smiled and playfully caressed Herman's cheek. "Thank you."

He led Jeanie down the pier, and they half sat against the wooden crossbeams of the fence. They listened to the chatter of the dockworkers and the scraping and thumping of wood against wood as the men transferred cargo to land; and they stared across the harbor at the ugly river, and beyond, at the low white clouds streaking the sky over Brooklyn.

"What have you named your son?" Jeanie asked.

"We have not yet decided. Lizzie believed that the child would be a girl, which she wanted to call Hope. Now that it's a boy . . . well, Hope is hardly a proper name for a boy."

"Hopeless might do, though, and seems appropriate. Hopeless Melville. It has a masculine ring to it." Herman could have thrown her into the river. "Tell me, truthfully," she said, "what darkens my dear Herman's brow? Debt only? Or something truly troublesome?"

He wondered how it had come to pass that his only confidant on earth was an impudent girl. "The problem is Hawthorne, of course. Something has happened. A disaster. I wonder now if he will even read my book."

Jeanie leaned into him and put her hand on his back. "Are you going to Catharine Sedgwick's party?"

"What party is that?"

"Hawthorne's going-away party."

The look on Herman's face told Jeanie all she needed to know about the state of affairs between Hawthorne and Melville.

"Where is Hawthorne going?"

"He is moving to West Newton. He is breaking his lease with the Tappans."

Herman swooned. "Why?" He nearly let the contracts he was holding fly to the wind.

"I have heard several reasons. Eliza Fields says there was a dispute with the Tappans about fruit picking, but James says it was because their friend Mrs. Kemble is letting them stay at her house in West Newton for almost nothing. My brother says it's because the cottage in Lenox is too small, now that they have a third child. Dr. Holmes says it was because Hawthorne hates the weather in the Berkshires, and the climate has made his wife more sickly. In fact, there seem to be a thousand reasons."

Yes, Herman thought, a thousand conjectured reasons and not

one of them true, except the one that Hawthorne couldn't tell. "When is he leaving?"

"I don't know. The party is on a Tuesday, oddly enough—Tuesday after next. Why don't you go, and you can ask him yourself?"

He felt as if he would vomit into the river. Hawthorne leaving, and without a word to him? Had he done something so unforgivable? It was too much to bear; and yet, what choice did he have but to bear it? Could he risk further disaster by going to Miss Sedgwick's party and trying to force Hawthorne to speak to him? To what end?

He looked up and down the river at the ships on the wharf and wondered if he could just sail away, as he had done before—sign aboard a whaler and disappear for four years, or forever. Jump ship on the Marquesas Islands again. Find a job as a postal clerk in Honolulu. Build a house in Melbourne and never come back.

"How long will you be in Manhattan?" Jeanie asked.

"I'm leaving for Pittsfield on the afternoon train."

"May I call on you there? I will be splitting time between Dudley's house in Stockbridge and the Fourier phalanx in New Lebanon for two weeks starting tomorrow, so I will have many occasions to pass through Pittsfield."

"If you call on me, please do so properly. Announce your visit and come with an escort. Don't just show up in the middle of the night."

"Perhaps you could escort me to Mr. Hawthorne's farewell party."

Herman scoffed. "I believe you are the only person alive with less sense of propriety than I have. No, you may not call on me." And he stalked off down the river.

Chapter 20

Bonne Chance, Nathaniel

Catharine Sedgwick's grand manor house lorded over Lenox from a hill at a little remove from the village. It could have materialized directly from *The House of the Seven Gables*, so imposing did it seem compared with the houses below it. It lacked only the time-eaten decay of Hawthorne's moldering imagination: its three stories were freshly painted a fetching bright coral with black trim; diamond-shaped white lattices beautified the ledges and window frames. Quaint figures of angels—stamped in glittering plaster—ornamented its whole visible exterior; and copies of Renaissance sculptures beckoned visitors up the gravel path from the street. To the rear of the house, a white, vine-entangled gazebo commanded a view of twenty miles of valley, all the way to the Taghkanic Mountains.

In addition to being an outspoken abolitionist and suffragist, Catharine Sedgwick was the most accomplished American writer living in the Berkshires, having published ten well-received novels, whose sentimental plots captured readers' imaginations and whose sympathetic portrayals of women stirred debate in parlors and lecture halls. Despite having had many suitors, she remained unmarried at age sixty-one and advocated that no woman should marry if she were not inclined to—a controversial position. She shared her home with her brother, Charles, who was a lawyer, and their elderly mother.

Sophia Hawthorne had read all of Catharine's novels and occasionally took tea with Miss Sedgwick and her brother; but Nathaniel had always found reasons to miss these friendly get-togethers. In fact, all of Miss Sedgwick's attempts to draw Hawthorne out of the cocoon of his lakeside cottage—church outings, picnics, ice cream socials, and the like—had met with polite denials and evasions. However, even a recluse like Hawthorne could not, with any propriety, resist tonight's invitation to her house: in addition to honoring Hawthorne himself with a "*bon voyage* and *bonne chance*" on the occasion of his departure from the Berkshires, Miss Sedgwick's party would also introduce the prolific English novelist G.P.R. James and his wife to local society. James had recently moved from London to Stockbridge, but his prodigious literary output had preceded him to America by decades—he had published over one hundred historical novels and romances—and his reputation immediately cast a long shadow over Berkshire literary society. It would be a grand party, and despite the chill in the air, Catharine and Charles waited on their front porch to welcome each of their guests personally.

The Melvilles were first to arrive. Their wagon rattled up to the Sedgwicks' walk, banging and bumping—Herman, as usual, drove helter-skelter, and he yanked the horses to a halt so abruptly that Maria, Augusta, and Helen—bundled into beaver muffs in the back of the wagon—toppled forward into a pile. They disentangled themselves and climbed out of the wagon, grumbling and scolding Herman, who paid no attention. They walked up the front path, rubbing their arms and necks, while Herman hung back to give the horses oat bags and tie their reins.

Since Herman's stormy visit to Hawthorne's cottage, he had left the ordinary world behind; he wandered through dreadful emotional labyrinths of such awful complexity that he could no longer picture a way out, and his bloodshot eyes communicated perpetual shock and horror to everyone around him, no matter how banal the subjects of his conversation. Hieronymus Bosch grotesques populated his imagination. His heart thumped wildly day and night. His bowels churned.

His sleep was so near waking that he was no longer sure where reality ended and dreams began. In this heightened state, he walked up the path to the Sedgwicks' front porch, wearing the disguise of his own body and acting the part of Herman Melville. His mother and sisters had already disappeared into the house.

Catharine Sedgwick wore a full-length blue cape and peacock-feather hat. Charles wore an expensive but nondescript tan suit. "Miss Sedgwick," said Herman, gallantly taking Catharine's white-gloved hand and kissing it, as Herman Melville might do. It worked! Despite his hollow madness, Miss Sedgwick took him for Herman Melville and introduced him to her brother as such. "Welcome, Mr. Melville," Charles said. Herman shook Charles's hand and made a proper half bow. Charles then explained that their mother did not always recognize everyone by sight any longer and might greet him with incomprehension, so he should not take it amiss if she introduced herself as if for the first time. "She is very old and also nearly deaf, Mr. Melville, so please speak loudly, so that she hears what you are saying."

"Not to worry." Herman winked. "In my family, we are used to compensating for debilitating infirmities of all kinds." He passed with affected jauntiness into the parlor, where he found his mother and sisters shouting into the ear trumpet of old Mrs. Sedgwick, a frail, stooped woman so small and bent—and dressed in such abundant red, green, and white lace—that she could have been an end table decorated for Christmas. When it was Herman's turn to introduce himself, he shouted, "Call me Ishmael."

"What? Ishmael?"

"Mother," Charles ran in to intervene, with a censuring look at Herman. "This is Mr. Herman Melville."

"Oh, yes," Mrs. Sedgwick cackled. "I've heard of you. You are the Man Who Lived Among the Cannibals."

Herman wanted to spit into the old woman's trumpet. He yelled, "Does one ever stop living among cannibals, Mrs. Sedgwick?"

"Why, yes," she answered. "But tell me, Mr. Melville, have you eaten people yourself?"

Charles began a stammering apology and tried to step between them, but Herman shouted, "Yes. Quite."

"I have been wanting to know: what do people taste like?"

"Oyster pudding."

Charles was aghast. Mrs. Sedgwick pondered Herman's answer for a moment before thrusting her finger into the air and shouting, "I knew it!" Then she teetered to the credenza and shakily poured herself a glass of port.

With a chary look, Charles said, "Is that really true, Mr. Melville?"

"Of course not."

"Then why did you say so?"

"To please your mother. Shall we serve ourselves?"

Charles scowled; but he rang a bell, and soon a servant came in and poured glasses of port all around.

Herman's mother took Charles by the arm and apologized—in a confidential tone that was still loud enough for everyone but old Mrs. Sedgwick to hear—for the fact that Lizzie could not come this evening. "My daughter-in-law's absence is no reflection on her feelings toward you or your family," said Maria, implying by her tone that it somehow was. "She is still suffering from the effects of her recent childbirth."

"I'm sorry to hear that," said Charles, implying by his tone that he was not. He excused himself to the front porch, leaving the Melvilles alone with Mrs. Sedgwick, among the parlor's vast, puffy, salmon-colored sofas. They stood saying nothing for quite some time, until Mrs. Sedgwick sat down, and they all followed suit. Mrs. Sedgwick noisily tongued her port.

Herman looked at the massive crystal chandelier overhead, the crystal port glasses, the étagères crowded with expensive ceramic figurines, the bookshelves stuffed with leather volumes—all demonstrating clearly to him how abject his own home was. No amount of renovating or decorating could make Arrowhead's parlor truly grand, like this one—it would always strike its guests as a hodgepodge, a miscellany, a failure. He drank down his port.

A gang of chipper neighbors arrived, swinging mantles, doffing coats, and kissing the Sedgwicks on both cheeks. Catharine and Charles rounded the parlor introducing the new guests; and more servants appeared, bearing silver trays of wine, hard and soft cheeses, and bite-sized pâté sandwiches. Herman immediately tired of the affable who-what-where that ensued, though he took the opportunity to drink another glass of port and gobble half a round of Camembert; and he brooded, ever more apprehensively, on the prospect of Hawthorne's appearance.

Herman thought Hawthorne might simply refuse to speak to him; or, even worse, offer him meaningless small talk; or he might turn and flee. Whatever was about to happen, Herman feared it; and so he counted it something of a relief when Ellery Channing, the transcendentalist poet, arrived, wearing a fringed buckskin tunic, as if he were Davy Crockett.

Channing's black hair was pomaded up to a ridge at the top of his skull, from which a single heavily waxed lock curlicued down to his forehead. Herman detested Channing's poetry. He stood up and went to meet him by the credenza that held the liquor.

"Melville," Channing said, shaking Herman's hand as if it were a competition. "I hear you have a new book coming out. Good work!"

"I will gladly sell you a copy," said Herman. "Have you produced any poetry lately?"

"I thought you'd never ask." Channing bounded over to the

fireplace, stepped up onto a hearthstone and shouted everyone into silence. "Ladies and gentlemen, I would fain interrupt your merriment, but Mr. Melville has asked me to recite my most recent poem, which I have just completed." The guests applauded without enthusiasm. "I call this *The Restless Mind*." He cleared his throat and recited with flamboyant gestures toward the packed balcony that appeared in his imagination.

> By the bleak wild hill,
> Or the deep lake still,
> In the silent grain
> On the upland plain,
> I would that the unsparing Storm might rage,
> And blot with gloom the fair day's sunny page.

The poem continued in this vein for three more stanzas, after which Channing made a deep bow, and the guests again clapped politely and immediately resumed their conversations. The poet rejoined Herman by the liquor. "What did you think, Melville?"

Herman said:

> That bottle's wine
> Will soon be mine,
> The poet's verse
> To blot and curse,
> I've had my fill of doggerel—
> Give me the rhymes of cask and still.

He took a deep bow, and then, to authenticate his satire, he poured himself another glass of port, which he drank immediately. Unconcerned, Channing held out an empty glass, which Herman grudgingly filled.

"They're printing it in next month's *Graham's*," said Channing, "along with a daguerreotype of my face. Perhaps we'll see your name in a magazine again soon, Melville."

James and Eliza Fields entered with Oliver Wendell Holmes, and Holmes quickly detached himself and joined Melville and Channing. Herman poured himself another glass of port.

"Go easy, Melville," said Holmes. "Your cheeks are already flushed, and your eyes are bloodshot."

"It's not from the wine, Doctor. Channing here has just recited a new poem, and, as you can see," he waved his hand at the parlor, where everyone was chatting courteously in little groups, "the effect has been wildly stimulating. Have you any new rhymes today?"

Holmes cleared his throat and said, "I prithee by the soul of her that bore thee, pour me a ruby port and I'll adore thee." Herman poured the doctor some port, and they clinked glasses. Channing left to try his luck with Eliza Fields.

Holmes held his glass up above his head and gazed at the chandelier through the wine. "Have you met this G.P.R. James fellow yet? The English scribbler?"

"He hasn't arrived."

"I've just finished his *Castle of Ehrenstein*. Leaves me only a hundred books short of reading his entire list, and he has two new novels going through the presses in London as we speak. He'll be pushing ours right off the shelves."

"He also has too many initials and too few names. What is this G.P.R. about?"

"Perhaps his parents were shy of vowels when he was born. Has Hawthorne arrived?"

At the mention of Hawthorne, Herman drank down his wine. He began to feel strangely taut instead of drunk. "Not yet. Both guests of honor are tardy."

"Just like Hawthorne to be late for his own farewell party. Though, if there's one person who doesn't need a special farewell, it's Hawthorne."

"Why do you say that?"

"Outside of hermits and convicts, he's the least sociable person I ever met. Every time you see him, it's a farewell party, since there's no guarantee you'll ever set eyes on the man again."

John and Sarah Morewood arrived, hallooing and offering up a magnum of champagne, which old Mrs. Sedgwick insisted be popped immediately. As the cork flew across the room, Dudley and Jeanie Field walked in, and Jeanie snatched it neatly out of the air. She accepted the ovation of the guests with a puckish bow; then she held the cork up in one gloved hand and passed her other hand in front of it, making it vanish. Everyone applauded again and continued applauding as she made the cork reappear from her brother's left ear. Dudley flushed with embarrassment.

After procuring a glass of champagne, Jeanie made her way to Herman. "Mr. Melville," she said. "Dr. Holmes. Have you left your wives at home this evening?"

Holmes grunted noncommittally. Herman said, "Mrs. Melville is ill."

"How intriguing!" Jeanie put her hand on Herman's arm. Holmes tsk-tsked and shook his head no.

"No, Miss Field," said Herman. "Mrs. Melville is *really* ill. She is still having a difficult time after the arrival of the baby."

"Of course, of course, I'm so sorry to hear it."

Holmes looked around the room for more suitable companions.

"Tell me," Jeanie said, "have you decided on a name for the child yet?"

"Stanwix."

Jeanie frowned. "Is that plural?"

Maria Melville, who had been eavesdropping from a nearby sofa, stood up and joined them. "It's a name of great honor, Miss Field," she said. "Stanwix is the name of the fort that my father, Peter Gansevoort, saved from the British during the Revolutionary War. If not for my father, our side might have lost control of the Hudson River, to say nothing of the war itself!"

"Fort Stanwix," Jeanie repeated. "I don't believe we covered that battle at my school."

"You may have forgotten it," said Maria, "but you are an American because of it."

"I suppose it's a courageous name, then, Mrs. Melville. Of course, it's nothing like Hope."

Maria narrowed her eyes. As far as she knew, the prospect of naming Lizzie's baby Hope had never been mentioned outside the family, so now she was certain that Herman was dallying with this impertinent young girl and telling her all their secrets. "It's better than hope, Miss Field—it's victory!"

Dudley sauntered up. "What hope do we have of victory?" he asked.

"None that I can tell," said Herman. He excused himself with an abrupt bow and walked to the table where Mrs. Sedgwick was guarding the army of crystal champagne coupes. He toasted the dowager matron and drank a glass; and at last he did begin to feel drunk, which was one more thing he had to worry about when Hawthorne arrived.

The front door opened, and Catharine came in again, escorting an extremely well-dressed middle-aged lady, who was smiling rather artificially. Her long yellow scarf coiled around and around her neck so many times that her head seemed to emerge directly from it, with no connection whatsoever to the rest of her body; and so many feathers festooned her hat that it seemed her head might take flight.

Catharine struck a spoon several times against a wine glass to call for quiet. "Dear friends," she said, "may I present our new neighbor, Mrs. Theodora James."

The guests clapped. Mrs. James began speaking before the applause had ceased, in a clear voice with a highborn English accent. "Ladies and gentlemen, I am honored to be in your company. I have been given a message to deliver from my husband. He says that he deeply regrets missing this opportunity to make your acquaintance, but he has, this very afternoon, begun writing a new novel, and he simply cannot be torn away from it for anything in the world; but he greatly looks forward to making your acquaintance on another day, and he knows that the writers among you will understand. Thank you." Mrs. James took a glass of champagne and raised it; and, without awaiting return salutations, sipped and nodded at Mrs. Sedgwick. The room had gone completely silent, and everyone gawped as she bustled across the parlor. She sat down between Augusta Melville and Eliza Fields, as coolly as if she were at home. Mrs. James turned to Augusta and said, "Who is the best silversmith in this area, would you say?"

The other guests went back to chatting in their groups; though now every one of them talked in hushed, excited voices about the extraordinary cheek of Mr. and Mrs. G.P.R. James.

Holmes joined Herman at the champagne, and said, "This James fellow can't stop scribbling long enough to have a glass of wine. Gives writing a bad name."

Melville heard Holmes's words without comprehending their meaning, so lost was he in his own despairing thoughts. Oh, why could he not control himself the least little bit? What was this mutiny in his heart? His love for Hawthorne had become the most horrible thing he could imagine. He could not even enjoy the triumph and expectation of having his new book in print, since he feared that its only true audience might refuse to read it. In fact, his sole object this evening was to delay Hawthorne's departure from the Berkshires long enough so that he could present him a copy of *Moby Dick* in person.

He took another glass of champagne and wandered toward the hearth. Herman had the impression that someone was saying something to him, but he zeroed in on the fire, with unwavering steps, taking a place next to Ellery Channing and James Fields, who were arguing about some new Indian war that had broken out in California. Herman pretended to listen to them, and he achieved a momentary numbness, with the jabber of the entire party combining with the crackle of the fire to form a meditative hiss and babble in his ears.

A blast of cold air swirled across the room and a welcoming chorus ended his transitory calm. He felt it even before he turned around: Hawthorne! As with Mrs. James before him, Catharine quieted the crowd by tinkling a glass and welcoming Mr. Hawthorne—who, unlike Mrs. James, seemed mortified to be the center of attention.

"Thank you for inviting me," he said quietly. "My wife regrets that she could not be here, but she wished that I would assure you of how much she has enjoyed the company of everyone in Lenox during our sojourn here—as I have—and how warmly she will remember our time among you—as I will."

This speech met with "Hear! Hear!" and raised glasses. A group gathered around Hawthorne, who stood still only with the greatest effort, judging by the panic in his eyes. Someone handed him a glass of champagne, and he held it up almost defensively.

Where, Herman thought, is that easy, funny, brilliant Hawthorne that I have known in private? How can two such opposed people exist in one man's breast—the gregarious, genial man of letters, and the petrified wallflower disdainful of all company? He walked slowly toward Hawthorne. Who is this man who can display such warm, loving feelings one moment and such glacial disregard the next? What is your secret, Hawthorne? Do I know it already?

Herman gulped down his champagne and deposited his glass on the table at his mother's elbow, utterly ignoring something his mother was saying. He slipped around the cluster of bodies encircling Hawthorne. Dr. Holmes was delivering a benediction when Herman caught Hawthorne's eye and held it.

Holmes was saying, ". . . and I anticipate seeing you five times as often, after you've established your new home. Boston is spitting distance from West Newton, and I expect you to spit on Boston as often as I do." He raised his glass, and the group followed, with the lone exception being Hawthorne himself, who seemed transfixed by Herman's stare.

Jeanie stepped into the silence after Holmes's toast and said, "Mr. Hawthorne, I wonder if I could ask you something that has been puzzling me about your latest romance."

"Of course," said the flustered Hawthorne.

"It's rather an idiotic question." She fluttered her eyelashes coquettishly. "I would be embarrassed. Might I steal you for just a moment alone?"

Hawthorne uncomprehendingly allowed Jeanie to take his arm, and she led him a few paces away to the piano. She made a little nod of her head to Herman, and then she positioned herself between Hawthorne and the rest of the party.

Herman approached. He felt all the alcohol he had drunk come rushing into his tongue, which slithered along the insides of his teeth.

"Hawthorne, I must sincerely apologize to you. Please—"

"No," Hawthorne said, with passion. "It is I who owe you the apology, Melville. It was I—" He stopped abruptly and looked at Jeanie. "What question did you mean to ask me, Miss Field?"

"You have answered it. Thank you, Mr. Hawthorne." Jeanie turned her back and withdrew a step.

Hawthorne continued in a whisper, "I know I led you to believe things that were not true. Or that I wished not to admit." Perspiration appeared on his forehead. "That is to say, I have behaved horribly, Melville. You must forgive me! I have handled everything so badly—with you, with everyone."

Herman could not believe what he was hearing; yet, he did not quite understand it, either. He tried to console himself and Hawthorne at the same time by saying, "It isn't easy to know what to do."

"I have been the source of much torment for you, and I'm sorry."

"But if you feel this way, why are you moving to West Newton? What has happened?"

Jeanie was loudly asking Charles Sedgwick about a certain kind of cheese and shuffling back toward Herman, signaling with her hand behind her back that their moment to talk privately was coming to an end. Herman moved closer to Hawthorne and whispered with great urgency.

"Please delay your move until I can come to Lenox and give you a copy of *Moby Dick*. It would mean the world to me to give it to you personally."

"When?"

"Bentley has shipped copies from London, and the Harpers are printing the American edition right now. I don't know which will come first, but perhaps a week. Ten days at the latest."

Hawthorne considered. "All right." This concession, combined with Hawthorne's miraculous apology, lifted Herman's spirits so much that he almost felt human again, and even oddly sober.

Sarah Morewood broke into their tête-à-tête. "Mr. Hawthorne, my brother says that you have a new children's book coming out."

Herman withdrew and practically floated back to the fireside. He did not notice that he stepped on his sister Helen's foot, or that he bumped Channing's arm, causing him to spill champagne, or that he knocked over the fireplace tools when he leaned against the mantel. He became aware of himself again only when Jeanie snapped her fingers in front of his nose and handed him yet another glass of champagne.

"You're welcome," she said.

Catharine persuaded Melville to favor them with a sea shanty. He asked Jeanie to accompany him on the piano, and they huddled near the instrument for a brief discussion of possible tunes, while the rest of the guests whispered privately among themselves and with a great deal of delight about the affair that Herman and Miss Field were so obviously having and how scandalous it was, with Melville's baby still barely arrived in the world and Lizzie home sick. Herman's mother thought she would die. Jeanie sat down at the piano and played quickly through the chords of a song, then nodded.

"Sea shanties work best," Herman announced, "as call-and-response songs." He barely knew what he was saying. "Work songs. So we are going to put you all to work." Everyone groaned. "Come now. We'll never make it around the Cape of Good Hope with that sort of attitude!" He taught them the melody to "Haul Away, Joe," and talked them through a verse and a refrain for practice, instructing them when to sing their "haul away, Joes." He did so with such warmth and enthusiasm, and the group so enjoyed disapproving of his scandalous behavior that they actually managed a rousing chorus.

Jeanie pounded out the chords in earnest. Melville sang as if he truly were leading a shipboard work detail.

> Louis was the king of France
> Before the revolution

Away, haul away, we'll haul away, Joe!
But then he got his head chopped off
Which spoiled his constitution
Away, haul away, we'll haul away, Joe!
Once I was in Ireland
Digging turf and pratties
Away, haul away, we'll haul away, Joe!
And now I'm on a Yankee ship
Hauling sheets and natties
Away, haul away, we'll haul away, Joe!
To me, way, haul away
We'll heave and hang together
Away, haul away, we'll haul away Joe!"

The song had dozens of standard verses, and a nearly infinite number of possibilities for someone like Herman, who could rhyme couplets off the top of his head; and he led the singing for some minutes, remembering verses haphazardly and improvising when his memory failed, until he sensed that their enthusiasm was flagging. He nodded to Jeanie, who built loudly toward a finish, which he improvised as a final farewell for Hawthorne:

Hawthorne was a famous man
Lived in a Berkshire village
Away, haul away, we'll haul away, Joe!
With his ink and with his pen
He plundered and he pillaged!
Away, haul away, we'll haul away, Joe!
To me, way, haul away
We'll heave and hang together
Away, haul away, we'll haul away Joe!

With the final chord, everyone cheered and held up their glasses and searched the room for the famous plundering and pillaging author. Only Herman had noticed, early on in the song—during the first flush of everyone's pleasure—that Hawthorne had slipped quietly away, into the night.

Chapter 21

In Token of My Admiration for His Genius

Ten days later, Herman sat in a cold, drafty passenger car with three other travelers on the Hudson and Berkshire Railway, clattering toward Lenox. His soul felt like a torpedoed man-of-war, blasted and timbered. As Herman had requested, the moment the first shipment of *The Whale* had arrived from London, Evert Duyckinck had sent a messenger boy with half a dozen copies by train from New York to Pittsfield, at no small expense. Coincidentally, on the very same day, the Harper and Brothers American edition of *Moby Dick* had come out, and Herman had commandeered presentation copies of the Harper's version, as well; so now the box of books that sat beside him as he journeyed toward Lenox and his meeting with Hawthorne contained six fresh-off-the-boat copies of *The Whale*, the English version, and six fresh-off-the-press copies of *Moby Dick*. These two editions were supposed to be identical in every way except for their titles; however, upon closer inspection, Melville had found a number of pages missing from the English edition, including the very last page—the epilogue—which made sense of the rest of the novel. Without that final page, without the survival of the main character, Ishmael, no narrator would exist to tell the tale, and the conceit of the narrative would collapse. Herman had nearly torn his beard out when he'd discovered the error, stamping and swearing and cursing Bentley, as if Captain Ahab had taken control of his body. Finally, he had calmed down enough to compose a letter to Bentley explaining the mistake and begging him to withdraw the copies he had already sent out to reviewers, but he feared it was too late. Could the English magazines be alerted before their reviews appeared? How quickly could the bungled copies be replaced, and at how much expense, and who would ultimately pay for it? A printing error that sabotaged the entire work! It was difficult to believe and even harder to swallow.

He sat on the train brooding over this disaster, his mind blank with despair. He would simply have to hope that the mistake could be corrected before reviews of the misbegotten version destroyed its prospects utterly. Harper's, at least, had produced a faithful version of his manuscript, so American reviewers would have the chance to evaluate *Moby Dick* as Herman had intended it. Perhaps that would be enough, since the American market would matter more in the long run; but Herman felt as if he had been rammed by this misshapen and hideous *Whale*, and now his soul lay shivered, hull up in the waters of eternity, waiting to sink.

If nothing else, Herman told himself by way of consolation, I will at least be able to give Hawthorne the correct version. He held the copy of *Moby Dick* that he had selected for Nathaniel, the best example of the lot, with crisp, uncut pages, a flawless cover, and that true last page. Oh, how could they have left off the last page? he thought. It was a trick so cruel that only God or the devil could have contrived it, and Herman entertained the possibility that heaven and hell had called an armistice just long enough to collaborate against him.

By the time the train approached Lenox, the afternoon had turned ashen gray, and the day seemed to share Herman's exhaustion. His love for Hawthorne and the energy he had squandered on it for so long, day and night, had worn him down to a state of nervous fatigue, which seemed permanent to him now. He felt Captain Ahab charging madly through the pages of *Moby Dick*, raving and ripping, a howling caricature of pain—his love turned inside out. Had it been worth it? Oh, Hawthorne, why could you not have talked to me more, and more openly, instead of damning me alone to my pages?

Though Hawthorne was moving only the relatively short distance to West Newton, he might as well have been going to the moon. Herman only ever traveled to the Boston area these days to visit the Shaws, and he could imagine no excuse that might take him to the suburbs during a stay with his in-laws. And Hawthorne had demonstrated with painful clarity, again and again, that he would be making no special efforts to visit Herman or even communicate with him. This was farewell, and as a parting concession from the Fates, Melville would be allowed to present Hawthorne with all of his love and obsession and despair bound in leather. Hawthorne would carry away Herman's soul, set in type, and Herman would be left out in the Berkshires, loveless, with his botched English copies of *The Whale*. Under the circumstances, Herman almost did not want to see Hawthorne again, but this meeting was now the only thing he had left.

The train pulled into the Lenox station and huffed to a stop. Herman left his box of books with the Lenox stationmaster, taking with him only the *Moby Dick* he would give to Hawthorne, and walked up Main Street toward the Curtis Hotel. He tipped his hat to the few people he met on the street. The town seemed so different now from the sunnier aspect it wore in summer, when happy vacationers overwhelmed the locals; today, the breeze was frigid, and low clouds threatened rain, or snow; and Herman met only gray old-timers shuffling along, huddled into their coats.

Herman had sent a messenger to precede him into Lenox—it was a luxury he could not really afford just now, but he needed the peace of mind that came with this expedience more than he needed the money—a messenger who had arranged for Hawthorne to meet him at the Curtis. Herman could not face another visit to Hawthorne's cottage with Sophia and their children, and he could think of nowhere better for a rendezvous than the grandest hotel in the center of town. It would be mostly empty now, with the holiday season over, and no Lenoxite with a home of his own would eat dinner at a hotel. He hoped they would have some solitude, right out in the open.

He arrived and stood outside for a moment, looking up at the hotel's three stories of rough, red clay bricks. Shiny black shutters framed every window. He wondered if Hawthorne was already inside—but this prospect caused him no palpitations of the heart now, no sweating of the palms, no nervous tics. He was exhausted; and he dared not allow himself to hope for anything from their meeting, to wonder what Hawthorne had meant by apologizing so heatedly at Catharine Sedgwick's party. He was grateful simply to have the opportunity to present his book to Nathaniel, and that's all he expected from this afternoon—if, indeed, Hawthorne appeared at all. He reminded himself that Hawthorne had disappointed him many times in the past, and Hawthorne's hypervigilant conscience could conceivably keep him at home with Sophia again today; or, for all Herman knew, he might have silently recanted his vow to wait for *Moby Dick* and already moved to West Newton. No, Herman could not afford to hope. He walked up the stone steps and a valet opened the door and escorted him to the dining room.

Melville ordered a coffee with whiskey and settled into a table near a window with a view of downtown. The table linens were real linen, the coffee cup, when it arrived, was actual china, the silverware was genuine silver, and the coffee and whiskey were both first-rate. The ghoulish specter of the cost of all this finery emerged from the steam of his drink, but he exorcised it immediately by saying out loud, "Who steals my purse steals trash," and he took out his wallet and placed it on the table. If anything merited a trip to the poorhouse, this occasion did. He sipped his expensive coffee and watched the sun set.

Half a dozen diners had wandered in and taken tables by the time Hawthorne arrived, just after dark; and despite his earlier despair and exhaustion, Herman felt a jolt of energy just from seeing Nathaniel's tall, elegant figure in his black double-breasted frock coat striding across the dining room. Hawthorne slung his satchel off his shoulder and threaded hastily between tables, upsetting an empty chair so that it teetered. His cheeks were red from the cold, and he seemed somewhat out of breath, as if he had been hurrying, which pleased Herman. His wavy brown hair fanned out like a lion's mane, windblown and lustrous. Herman stood to greet him, and Nathaniel shook his hand warmly and swept into his seat. The waiter came immediately, and Hawthorne asked for "whatever my friend is having," and the last of Herman's weariness lifted. Hawthorne seemed entirely present: he seemed almost the same as when they had first met, eyes twinkling and cheery, and Herman cautioned himself to take some care with his own heart, even as he fell helplessly once again into those luminous brown eyes.

"Do you know," Hawthorne said, "I have lived here for nearly two years and never dined in this hotel? It's quite splendid, isn't it?"

"It is now," Herman said. He could not help himself. He blushed and looked down into his empty cup.

"If I had known about this place," said Hawthorne, "I might have come here often and sent myself to the almshouse. Perhaps it's better if this memory is the only one I take from it."

Herman wished he could ask about that night they had spent drinking in Hawthorne's cottage, about how it had ended, about his feelings now, but he dared not. Hawthorne's reaction was clear—he was moving away—but his presence across the table indicated that the matter remained far from simple. Oh, Nathaniel, he thought, would I love you less if you spoke more openly?

He held out the copy of *Moby Dick*—as far as he knew, the first American copy available—and Hawthorne took it, passing his hand sensuously several times over the front cover, caressing the spine with his fingertips.

"New books feel special," said Hawthorne. "They're like babies born into the skin of old men." He turned it over and hefted it several times and then reached into his satchel and withdrew a copy of his *Wonder Book*, a slender tome that had also just been published, which he handed to Herman. "I don't pretend it can compete with your whale," he said, "but I thought it would please you." Herman took the book, and Hawthorne opened it even while it lay in Herman's hands, so their fingers touched. Hawthorne flipped the pages until he found a particular passage. "Here," he said, and he pointed to a line a couple of hundred pages in. "A little tribute."

Herman read aloud: "On the hither side of Pittsfield sits Herman Melville, shaping out the gigantic conception of his 'White Whale,' while the gigantic shape of Greylock looms upon him from his study window." Herman had to read the sentence three more times, silently to himself, before he could believe it; and even then, he turned the book over and read the spine and the cover, trying to convince himself that it was real. He felt his eyes welling: Hawthorne had mentioned him in a book! He set *A Wonder Book* aside and opened *Moby Dick* in Hawthorne's hands. He used a butter knife to cut the opening pages apart and pointed to the dedication.

Now Hawthorne read aloud: "In token of my admiration for his genius, this book is inscribed to Nathaniel Hawthorne." Hawthorne fell back into his seat; and now it was Hawthorne's turn to read the sentence several times and reheft the volume in his hands. "After all

I made you endure!" The tear in Hawthorne's eye did not quite crest onto his cheek before he wiped it away.

Herman was acutely aware that the other diners were now staring at them, surreptitiously, gawking over their menus and cups and talking behind their hands—two men crying over books! He caught the amused eye of one of the waiters, who must have recognized Hawthorne as a local resident; and for once Herman felt protective of Nathaniel's reputation, even while two big happy teardrops rolled down his cheeks. But if Hawthorne noticed the effect they were having on those around them, he seemed not to care. The waiter came while they were both wiping their eyes, and Hawthorne ordered a bottle of their best champagne.

"Had it not been for you," said Herman, "I could never have written this book. Not as it is. It is your book as much as mine."

"Be careful—I may ask for a share of the royalties." Hawthorne busily cut the pages and opened randomly to chapters here and there, scanning paragraphs and nodding appreciatively. "Don't worry," said Hawthorne. "I will also read it in order."

The waiter came back with champagne, and the uncorking of it caused even more of a stir among the other diners. Hawthorne and Melville made a pact with their eyes to ignore everyone, and they ordered a luxurious meal of roasted beef, potatoes with gravy, carrots, and biscuits, and a bottle of Bordeaux to follow the champagne.

"Have you had any reviews yet?" asked Hawthorne. Herman said that he had not but feared the worst because of the mistake in the English edition, which he explained morosely. Hawthorne said, "The American reviews will be out before anyone here reads the English magazines. The mistake will become known, and it will reflect badly on Bentley, when all is said and done, not on *Moby Dick*."

"I wish I could be as optimistic. But I feel almost as if the spirit of Moby Dick himself is rising up to sabotage me. Have you heard about the sinking of the *Ann Alexander*?" Duyckinck had sent Herman the newspaper article about it, and now Herman related the story of the ship, stove and sunk in the South Pacific by an enraged sperm whale. "The incident happened on the very day in August that I sent my final pages to New York to be typeset," said Herman. "And the first news of it appeared in the papers four days before my book was published in England. The crew survived but the whale escaped with two harpoons in its head. It is a powerful coincidence."

"So you think your novel conjured this ferocious living whale?"

Herman felt genuinely superstitious about the incident. "Whales destroy whaleboats all the time—whaleboats being the tiny rowboats that the crew lower from the ship to give chase to their prey—but rarely does a whale attack an entire ship, much less sink it."

"Like the *Essex*."

"And like my *Pequod*, the account of which you hold in your hand—which, though fictional, has anticipated the real-life attack on the *Ann Alexander*. It is a story that should not have been told, perhaps—in the same way that the Hebrew name of God should never be uttered, lest it unleash an irresistible fury."

"You are more constantly in thrall of divine augurs than any religious person I know, my dear Melville. One might mistake you for devout, if one were not paying close attention."

"The *Ann Alexander* lies at the bottom of the sea, stove by a whale—an event which, in all the annals of seafaring, has happened only three times. The book you now possess was being typeset at the very moment that ship went down. Draw your own conclusions." He lifted his glass. "To the crew of the *Ann Alexander*." They drank and poured out more champagne.

"And to whales," said Hawthorne. "And to *Moby Dick*!"

Their platters of roast beef arrived, and their waiter brought new glasses for their Bordeaux and poured it. Hawthorne asked for a candle, and they soon were dining by candlelight.

"A sperm candle," Herman noted. "See how cleanly it burns, without dripping. The spermaceti is the only part of the whale not tried out aboard ship."

Herman launched into a detailed explanation of spermaceti, blubber, whale oil in general, ambergris, the tryworks, and the shipboard processing of materials harvested from butchered whales. He did so mainly because he could not bring himself to ask Hawthorne about his feelings, yet he could also not keep quiet; and something in him still believed that, if he could reduce the world by enumerating and explaining the concrete properties of it, he could still make it real to his own mind—which it was not quite, somehow.

When Herman had finished his disquisition, Hawthorne said, "It seems you have, at least, convinced yourself of the reality of whaling," and Herman felt completely understood.

"In truth," Herman said, "I remain unconvinced about reality in general, because the most real thing, the human soul, violates every principle of the known world. What is more real than the soul—the internal experience we have of ourselves—yet what is less substantial and less subject to proofs? Inquiring after the soul leads only to fairy dust and moonshine. It is real only according to our experience of it, and nothing else; but this one unprovable thing is so real that it makes me question the reality of everything else."

"My dear Melville, the very method of such inquiry destroys its object. One must begin with different questions, as I have said all along. The world itself is the soul of God, and that is the truth so clumsily expressed in the parable of Adam and Eve: it is the alienation wrought by inquiry without heart that causes man to suffer. That is the unpardonable original sin."

"You mean pride? Pride divorces us from the very nature of reality?"

"Yes. Your inquiry itself is the source of your alienation."

"And what should I do, instead? Pretend that these questions never occurred to me?"

"No. Just accept the mystery. Explain the whale until there is nothing left to explain and express your soul until there is nothing left to express, and know that both remain mysterious."

Herman nodded at his book. "But I have already done that."

"Then be happy." Hawthorne held up his glass and toasted.

"You are least credible when you speak of happiness, Nathaniel."

As their dinners disappeared—and, more to the point, their second bottle of wine—their metaphysics became more circular and their toasting more frequent, and their waiters stood in the kitchen doorway laughing at them. A few guests came and went, dining in much more purposeful ways than the two authors, and by the time Hawthorne ordered blackberry cobbler and Herman asked for apple pie, they were alone in the grand dining room. They finished their desserts over a heated but friendly disagreement about Thomas Aquinas and then ordered brandy.

Herman asked if they might smoke cigars in the dining room. The waiter assented, and Herman produced two cigars from his coat. They lit them at the spermaceti candle and smoked in silence until the waiter returned with their brandy and an ashtray.

"It is all very well to talk of whales and Thomas Aquinas," said Herman, "but I have a rather particular question about our meeting at Catharine Sedgwick's party. What did you mean when you said that you had led me to believe things that were not true or that you did not wish to admit? I have puzzled over these words without coming to the bottom of them."

"I apologize for that, Melville. I was speaking in haste, and I did not choose my words well."

"You may take your time now."

Hawthorne stuck his nose into his brandy snifter and took a long drink. Afterward, he did not quite lower the glass, so that, when he spoke, his words reverberated off the inside of the glass before they found their way to Herman's ears, resounding like a statement and an echo at the same time. This doubling effect—as much as the words themselves—would remain with Herman for the rest of his life, becoming more and more ghostly as the years passed.

"If I told you I loved you, Herman, it would change nothing."

The words rebounded around Melville's brain like a prayer said in Latin, its meaning almost comprehended but its words foreign and magical. It was a declaration without an assertion, a misdirection without true bearings: had Hawthorne just declared his love? They were alone, yet still he would not speak plainly.

"If you told me you loved me, Nathaniel, it would change everything."

"No. Nothing would change. I would still be leaving for West Newton with my family. And you would still be staying in Pittsfield with yours."

"Everything would change *for me*." Herman leaned in. "Surely, you of all people must know that a change of heart means more than any change of circumstance or anything society holds valuable. Isn't that ultimately the moral of *The Scarlet Letter*? Be true? Love is not a material change—*it is a change of heart*—and feeling love at all, especially the mutual and expressed love of one true heart for another, changes everything forever—for those hearts, even if not for the rest of the world."

"But it is the feeling itself that changes it. Not the telling of the feeling."

"No. 'In the beginning was the Word, and the Word was with God, and the Word was God.' The feeling and its expression are not separate." Herman pounded his fist on the table. "Why will you not say what you feel?"

The waiter returned to the table, with a disapproving frown for Melville. "Will there be anything else, gentlemen?"

Hawthorne said, "No, that will be all." The waiter left the check, and Herman looked at it as if it were written in Aramaic. "Come, let us be on our way," said Hawthorne.

Herman refused Hawthorne's proffered cash and laid his own money on the table. The waiter came back immediately and watched them gather their things and put on their coats.

Hawthorne led the way through the lobby and into the icy night, Herman unsure quite what to do next, beyond following him. Their breath materialized like spirits wispily fleeing their bodies. Down the steps of the hotel, left on Main Street in the direction of Hawthorne's cottage—they walked slowly, Hawthorne half a step ahead, Herman staring at him in a confusion of alcohol and tobacco and love and exasperation. The street was empty. They were utterly alone now. And still Hawthorne would not speak.

They came to the country lane that led out of town, down into the dell, toward Lake Mahkeenac. Herman stopped.

"I cannot follow you any further tonight," he said. "I must catch the last train to Pittsfield."

Hawthorne stopped, several paces away from Herman, a little down the hill. "Of course. Thank you for the book. And for dedicating it to me. I will read it at once."

Herman shivered. Hawthorne took a few more steps down the hill and away. Herman called his name. Hawthorne stopped and faced him again. Herman could not believe that they were parting like this, with so much between them still unsaid and undiscovered. Time had somehow turned backward—Omega before Alpha.

Herman said, "Will you not say it, even once?"

"Say what?"

A sudden gust whipped their hair and fluttered their coattails. Herman's eyes watered from the cold. Hawthorne waited till the breeze died down to speak, and when he finally did, his words came out in a whisper.

"I love you, Herman."

Melville thought his whole body might unwind like a yarn puppet. "I love you, too, Nathaniel."

Hawthorne nodded, turned away, and walked down the path into the dell, into the darkness. He did not look back.

Chapter 22

A Pantheistic Feeling

November 16, 1851
Lenox

My dear Melville,

What a book you have written! It gives me an idea of much greater power than your previous ones, and you should not think that, because I have read it so quickly, I have treated it in any way superficially. Since my belongings have been packed in crates for days, I have had little to do but anticipate your book; so I fell to it immediately and have done nothing but swim in its deep waters ever since.

Where to begin in responding to a work with so many facets catching so much light? The mystical descriptions of the seas! I felt I could see through the placid waters to the nursing baby whales in the Grand Armada, and feel the wind howling through the hawsers off the Java coast, and feel the commotion of the massacre of the sharks. Truly, I have been on a voyage around the world, peering across the bulwarks of my armchair. And the rhapsodies of Captain Ahab! You capture a madness that argues for the supreme sanity of the author, for what lunatic could deliver such mania so sympathetically and with such clarity? It is a grand feat that we commiserate with Ahab's outrageous quest and find therein our own search for meaning, because the Captain himself cavorts so recklessly and destroys all around him so ruthlessly—we find in his actions no parallel to our own yet understand him to be a seeker after the same truth. He cooks his brains, and we savor the dish. And you have, withal, invented a new form of writing—not a romance nor an adventure nor a philosophy nor a natural history, but all rolled into one. Your disdain for form quite arrests my imagination—first Ishmael tells the story, then we stand at the elbow of Professor Melville for some research into whales, then we are on a vast stage where the actors perform dialogue that Shakespeare himself might have written, and then we are inside the mind of Ahab himself. I would fain attempt such acrobatics in a novel myself. One wonders that there is no chapter from the point of view of the White Whale itself, but perhaps the entire work might be considered to emanate from the perspective of that one particular creature, since it is his story as much as anyone's; but I fear that my appreciation may take a chaotic form similar to your book itself, but with less coherence or depth, merely grazing over those qualities of the novel that struck me most forcefully, and so I may miss the deeper profundities where your leviathan swims; so I will begin again.

I see that, in cataloging the known and concrete facts about whales and placing them alongside Ahab's impassioned quest, you are trying to give shape and form to the human desire to—well, to what? Comprehend the world as it is? Tame and civilize the wilderness? Find fellow-feeling among men through all the ages by means of learning and philosophy? Yes, all of that. And in the friendship of Ishmael and Queequeg, you show that a fraternal regard and even love may exist in like-minded souls where nothing but differences exist on the surface—yes, that, too. And yet, for all of your classifying and sorting and explaining, for all of the fellow-feeling of Ishmael and Queequeg, for all of Ahab's raging, for all of the violence and lyricism and breathtaking chases, the most important thing in the novel is something that you have left out, which yet permeates the book, and no sensitive reader could fail to comprehend it—the heart of Captain Ahab.

It appears at first that Ahab is enraged because Moby Dick has removed his leg—but, not so, as you illustrate clearly when the Pequod *of Nantucket meets the* Samuel Enderby *of London and Captain Ahab speaks with Captain Boomer of that latter ship. Boomer has had his arm removed by Moby Dick, yet he is good-humored and sensible, while Ahab has had his leg removed and is ferocious and fanatical. What, then, is the difference? Will a man lose an arm with equanimity but recoil at the removal of a lower limb? No. Because it is not only the lower limb that Ahab is missing— Moby Dick has taken something infinitely more valuable: his heart. Yes, Ahab is heartless, but he does not see that his heart cannot be recovered by conquering Moby Dick. He does not even see that he has lost his heart, so blinded is he by his more obvious loss; but it is veritably his heart and with it his soul that he has given up to the whale; or, in other words, to the iniquities of the world. His quest were better turned inward to that bottomless sea inside of him, which somewhere hides his missing humanity.*

You say that the secret motto of the book is the one that Ahab gives when he baptizes his harpoon with blood—"I baptize you not in the name of the father, but in the name of the devil"—but I say that this is not the true motto, after all.

*Your book is steeped in allusions to the Old Testament, but
you have not quoted the most important verse: "The pride of
thine heart hath deceived thee." Ahab's pride of heart is the
problem that he cannot solve, and so his tragic maiming goes
unavenged—because he seeks vengeance for the wrong loss.*

*I am deeply moved by the dedication of this book, my dear
Melville. It is a work of fury and pain and strength and
beauty, and it honors me that my name is attached to it—
through no merit of mine own.*

> *yours,*
> *Nath. Hawthorne*

> *November 17, 1851*
> *Arrowhead, Pittsfield*

My dear Hawthorne,

*People think that if a man has undergone any hardship,
he should have a reward; but for my part, if I have done the
hardest possible day's work, and then come to sit down in a
corner and eat my supper comfortably—why, then I don't
think I deserve any reward for my hard day's work—for am I
not now at peace? Is not my supper good? My peace and my
supper are my reward, my dear Hawthorne. So your joy-
giving and exultation-breeding letter is not my reward for my
ditcher's work with that book, but is the good goddess's bonus
over and above what was stipulated—for not one man in five
cycles, who is wise, will expect appreciative recognition from
his fellows, or any one of them. Appreciation! Recognition! Is
love appreciated? Why, ever since Adam, who has got to the*

meaning of this great allegory—the world? Then we pygmies
must be content to have our paper allegories but ill
comprehended. I say your appreciation is my glorious
gratuity. In my proud, humble way—a shepherd-king—I was
lord of a little vale in the solitary Crimea; but you have now
given me the crown of India. But on trying it on my head, I
found it fell down on my ears, notwithstanding their asinine
length—for it's only such ears that sustain such crowns.

Your letter was handed to me last night on the road going
to Mr. Morewood's, and I read it there. Had I been at home, I
would have sat down at once and answered it. In me divine
magnanimities are spontaneous and instantaneous—catch
them while you can. The world goes round, and the other side
comes up. So now I can't write what I felt. But I felt
pantheistic then—your heart beat in my ribs and mine in
yours, and both in God's. A sense of unspeakable security is in
me this moment, on account of your having understood the
book. I have written a wicked book, and feel spotless as the
lamb. Ineffable socialities are in me. I would sit down and
dine with you and all the gods in old Rome's Pantheon. It is a
strange feeling—no hopefulness is in it, no despair.
Content—that is it; and irresponsibility; but without
licentious inclination. I speak now of my profoundest sense of
being, not of an incidental feeling.

Whence come you, Hawthorne? By what right do you
drink from my flagon of life? And when I put it to my lips—lo,
they are yours and not mine. I feel that the Godhead is broken
up like the bread at the Supper, and that we are the pieces.
Hence this infinite fraternity of feeling. Now, sympathizing
with the paper, my angel turns over another page. You did

not care a penny for the book. But, now and then as you read, you understood the pervading thought that impelled the book—and that you praised. Was it not so? You were archangel enough to despise the imperfect body, and embrace the soul. Once you hugged the ugly Socrates because you saw the flame in the mouth, and heard the rushing of the demon— the familiar—and recognized the sound; for you have heard it in your own solitudes.

My dear Hawthorne, the atmospheric skepticisms steal into me now, and make me doubtful of my sanity in writing you thus. But, believe me, I am not mad, most noble Festus! But truth is ever incoherent, and when the big hearts strike together, the concussion is a little stunning. Farewell. Don't write a word about the book in the magazines. That would be robbing me of my miserly delight. I am heartily sorry I ever wrote anything about you there—it was paltry. Lord, when shall we be done growing? As long as we have anything more to do, we have done nothing. So, now, let us add Moby Dick *to our blessing, and step from that. Leviathan is not the biggest fish—I have heard of Krakens.*

This is a long letter, but you are not at all bound to answer it. Possibly, if you do answer it, and direct it to Herman Melville, you will missend it—for the very fingers that now guide this pen are not precisely the same that just took it up and put it on this paper. Lord, when shall we be done changing? Ah! it's a long stage, and no inn in sight, and night coming, and the body cold. But with you for a passenger, I am content and can be happy. I shall leave the world, I feel, with more satisfaction for having come to know you. Knowing you persuades me more than the Bible of our immortality.

What a pity, that, for your plain, bluff letter, you should get such gibberish! Mention me to Mrs. Hawthorne and to the children, and so, goodbye to you, with my blessing.

Herman

P.S. I can't stop yet. If the world was entirely made up of Magians, I'll tell you what I should do. I should have a paper-mill established at one end of the house, and so have an endless riband of foolscap rolling in upon my desk; and upon that endless riband I should write a thousand—a million—billion thoughts, all under the form of a letter to you. The divine magnet is on you, and my magnet responds. Which is the biggest? A foolish question—they are One.

P.P.S. Don't think that by writing me a letter, you shall always be bored with an immediate reply to it—and so keep both of us delving over a writing-desk eternally. No such thing! I shan't always answer your letters, and you may do just as you please.

After *The Whale*

AN EPILOGUE AND A NOTE ON SOURCES

After Hawthorne left Lenox, he and Melville corresponded very little, and they saw each other only three more times—once in Concord, Massachusetts, in November 1852; and twice in Liverpool, England, in the winter of 1856–57. During the period between their visits in Concord and Liverpool, Melville's fortunes went from bad to worse.

Moby Dick was a critical and commercial failure, selling fewer copies than any of Melville's five previous books. His next novel, *Pierre, or the Ambiguities* (1852), was an even bigger disaster, universally condemned by critics. He failed to find a publisher for his subsequent effort, a novel called *Isle of the Cross* (now lost), and he published only shorter works in magazines for the next few years. The last novel Melville published in his lifetime, *The Confidence Man* (1857), was yet another commercial failure, after which he stopped writing prose for thirty years.

The period of Hawthorne's close association with Melville was the most productive of Hawthorne's life. During that time, he published a new edition of an older story collection, *Twice-Told Tales* (1851), and he wrote *The House of the Seven Gables* (1851), *A Wonder Book for Boys and Girls* (1851), *The Blithedale Romance* (1852), and *The Snow Image* (a new short story collection, 1852). After 1852, Hawthorne began five more novels but completed only one—*The Marble Faun* (1860).

The Blithedale Romance, the novel that Hawthorne wrote immediately after leaving Lenox, prominently features a character named
Hollingsworth, a charismatic, handsome, gruff social reformer who
has the physical characteristics of Melville. Hollingsworth has a relationship with the book's narrator, Coverdale, who resembles Hawthorne in his self-restraint and reserve. The correlations between the
fictional relationship of Coverdale and Hollingsworth and the actual
relationship of Hawthorne and Melville are striking: in each case, the
two men develop a close friendship based on an intellectual rapport
with strong sexual undercurrents, and in each case, a crisis of intimacy causes them to separate. At the end of chapter XV (titled "A
Crisis"), Hollingsworth declares his love for Coverdale and asks Coverdale to run away with him to form a Utopian colony. "Coverdale,"
Hollingsworth says, "there is not the man in this wide world whom I
can love as I could you. Do not forsake me!" A little later in the same
highly charged scene, Hollingsworth says to Coverdale, "Will you
devote yourself, and sacrifice all to this great end, and be my friend of
friends, forever?" The moment ends when Coverdale rejects Hollingsworth, reporting that, in doing so, his "heart-pang was not merely fig-
urative, but an absolute torture of the breast."

In March 1852, soon after leaving Lenox, Hawthorne purchased
a home from Louisa May Alcott's family in Concord, where he twice
invited Melville to visit him. Melville declined the first invitation, in
July 1852, but accepted one in November of that year. The visit was
cordial, and the two talked about a true story that Melville had
heard, which he tried to convince Hawthorne to write as a novel.
The story concerned a woman who married a sailor she had found
on a beach after a shipwreck, and Melville thought Hawthorne's approach to fiction would suit the subject matter better than his own;
but Hawthorne was not interested. They wrote several letters back

and forth about it, making it the most sustained topic of their whole correspondence, but neither ultimately used the material.

Their final meetings occurred in Liverpool. Hawthorne's college friend Franklin Pierce had become president of the United States in 1853, and he had appointed Hawthorne the U.S. Consul in Liverpool. Because Melville had fallen on such hard times, Hawthorne attempted to get him a consulship post, as well, but could not; and when Hawthorne left for England to assume his own post, the two fell out of touch. By late 1856, Melville's family feared so much for his sanity that his father-in-law, Judge Lemuel Shaw, financed a trip for Melville to Jerusalem, and on his way, Melville made a side trip to see Hawthorne. Hawthorne recorded the visit in his notebook, in an entry dated November 20, 1856:

> A week ago last Monday, Herman Melville came to see me at the Consulate, looking much as he used to do (a little paler, and perhaps a little sadder), in a rough outside coat, and with his characteristic gravity and reserve of manner.... We soon found ourselves on pretty much our former terms of sociability and confidence. Melville has not been well, of late; he has been affected with neuralgic complaints in his head and limbs, and no doubt has suffered from too constant literary occupation, pursued without much success, latterly; and his writings, for a long while past, have indicated a morbid state of mind.... I do not wonder that he found it necessary to take an airing through the world, after so many years of toilsome pen-labor and domestic life, following upon so wild and adventurous a youth as his was.... He is a person of very gentlemanly instincts in every respect, save that he is a little heterodox in the matter of clean linen.... Melville, as he always does, began to reason of Providence and futurity, and of everything that lies beyond human

ken, and informed me that he had "pretty much made up his
mind to be annihilated"; but still he does not seem to rest in that
anticipation; and, I think, will never rest until he gets hold of a
definite belief. . . . He can neither believe, nor be comfortable in
his unbelief; and he is too honest and courageous not to try to
do one or the other. If he were a religious man, he would be one
of the most truly religious and reverential; he has a very high
and noble nature, and better worth immortality than most of us.

Melville stopped in Liverpool again on his way back from Jerusalem, in order to retrieve a trunk he had left at the U.S. Consulate,
but he saw Hawthorne only in passing.

After his trip, Melville tried but failed to support himself by lec-
turing, and he continued to spiral into debt. In 1863, he was forced to
sell Arrowhead to his brother Allan, after which he moved his family
to Manhattan, ultimately finding work as an inspector at the New
York Customs House, where he worked until he retired in 1885.
During this long period, he wrote constantly, composing poems that
were published in small editions financed by Melville's father-in-law
or paid for with money from Lizzie's inheritances. When critics
bothered to notice his poetry at all, they reviewed it unfavorably.
One such poem, an epic called *Clarel*, is the longest poem in American letters at nearly eighteen thousand lines, and it features a character based on Hawthorne, called Vine. *Clarel* is a meditation on the
interrelationship of erotic and metaphysical longing and contains allusions to Melville's own yearning for Hawthorne.

Melville was shocked to hear the news of Hawthorne's death, in
May 1864. After Hawthorne's funeral, which Melville did not attend, Ralph Waldo Emerson wrote, "I thought there was a tragic
element in the event . . . in the painful solitude of the man, which, I
suppose, could no longer be endured, & he died of it."

Melville's poem "Monody" commemorates his feelings about Hawthorne's death. The two stanzas of the poem were written at different times, the first most likely just after Hawthorne died and the second probably after Melville visited Hawthorne's grave in Sleepy Hollow Cemetery, Concord:

> To have known him, to have loved him
> After loneness long;
> And then to be estranged in life,
> And neither in the wrong;
> And now for death to set his seal—
> Ease me, a little ease, my song!
>
> By wintry hills his hermit-mound
> The sheeted snow-drifts drape,
> And houseless there the snow-bird flits
> Beneath the fir-trees' crape:
> Glazed now with ice the cloistral vine
> That hid the shyest grape.

Sources for *The Whale* include biographies of Melville and Hawthorne, critical interpretations of their work, and the surviving letters and journals of many of Melville's family and associates during the time of the writing of *Moby Dick*, especially Melville's sister Augusta, the publisher Evert Duyckinck, and Nathaniel and Sophia Hawthorne. Archivists at the Berkshire Historical Society (headquartered at Melville's old home of Arrowhead) and the Berkshire Athenaeum (Pittsfield's public library, which holds a Melville collection)

generously provided research assistance. An invaluable resource for tracking the movements of Melville and people associated with him is Jay Leyda's two-volume *Melville Log*, a day-by-day account of Melville's life composed of references to and quotations from primary documentary sources. I have been as faithful to primary sources and historical reality as possible. In referring to *Moby Dick*, I have followed Melville's own practice of writing it without the now-familiar hyphen, which was added to the first American edition because Melville's brother Allan mistakenly hyphenated it in a letter to the Harper brothers, and they unwittingly used the mistake. Hyphens were common in book titles in the nineteenth century—Melville's own previous novel was called *White-Jacket*—and subsequent editors adopted Allan's punctuation, as well. I have also tried my best to represent the opinions of every historical person in this novel as accurately as possible, based on their own surviving writings and the letters and journals of people in their circles.

Jeanie Field's character is the exception to this commitment to strict verisimilitude, though her character still corresponds in most ways with her historical reality. In real life, as in this novel, Jeanne Lucinda Field was the younger sister of the lawyer Dudley Field and the daughter of David Dudley Field II, a legal reformer and abolitionist. We know that she was at the picnic where Hawthorne and Melville first met because Hawthorne identifies her by name in his journal entry about the event, and we know that she socialized with Melville and Hawthorne and their acquaintances and that she traveled between her family's homes in Stockbridge and New York City. However, there is no historical evidence to indicate that she played the role of mediator between Hawthorne and Melville.

All of Hawthorne's actual letters to Melville have been lost or destroyed, save one, a brief note from Hawthorne asking if Melville would check on a package that Hawthorne had been expecting at the Pittsfield station and requesting that Melville buy a clock in a Pittsfield shop for $1.50. In the present novel, I used this real note as the basis for the note of August 21, 1850. All of Hawthorne's other letters to Melville are inventions, in some cases created as likely responses to surviving Melville letters and in others borrowed from Hawthorne's private journal entries or adapted from letters Hawthorne actually wrote to other people regarding Melville. In all cases regarding Hawthorne's invented letters, Hawthorne's surviving writing was used as a guide.

Melville's letters to Hawthorne in *The Whale* are real, with the following exceptions: first, the pair of letters concerning Hawthorne's recommendations for revision of *Moby Dick* (beginning on page 85); second, the letter that uses chowder as an allegory (page 120), the concept for which is borrowed from an early chapter of *Moby Dick*; and third, the letter describing Melville's Thanksgiving celebration at Arrowhead (page 127), which was adapted from a letter from Augusta Melville to her sister Helen describing that same Thanksgiving celebration.

In one case, a mundane matter was edited out of one of Melville's letters, since it held little significance for the emotional development of Melville's and Hawthorne's relationship. Expressions of feeling have not been added to any of Melville's actual letters, nor have any been edited to heighten their emotional effect: the letters contain Melville's actual sentiments, and one can read them in whole or part in myriad books and online at melville.org/corresp.htm.

Acknowledgments

Thank you:

Joel Snyder, Rita Porfiris, Mark Votapek, Diana Kerr, and Michael Havens, for reading early drafts and offering invaluable criticism and comments.

Louisa Lebwohl, for the time at Arrowhead.

Stuart Bernstein, for believing in the soundness of this ship when no one else did, launching it into open waters, and guiding it through all kinds of weather.

Carole DeSanti and Christopher Russell, for finding so many ways to deepen and enrich this story.

Jane Cavolina, for your meticulous, insightful copyediting.

Everyone at Viking, for your kindness, imagination, and generosity. *Merci mille fois à la Reine des Bois.*

Miguel Espinoza, for your big heart and the space to read and write.

Maha Almannai, for your faith and commitment to beauty.

Cynthia Gin, for reading between the lines.

Margaret O'Neill, for all the stories (and the coat hanger whale).

Raquel Stecher, for your unwavering enthusiasm and friendship.

Rose Todaro, for believing that our life together was a journey worth taking, and taking it.

Jeff Barnet: words cannot express my gratitude. But thanks.